Outstanding praise for the sexy a̶...
Joan Elizabeth L...

CLUB FANTASY

"This novel combines a well-written plot with sexually charged erotic scenes that are both tasteful and titillating. Readers will enjoy their trip to *Club Fantasy*."

—*Romantic Times*

NEVER ENOUGH

"Lloyd's steamy scenarios and passionate interludes will keep readers engrossed."

—*Booklist*

"Kept me engrossed to the very end."

—*Rendezvous*

"Be sure you have a fan handy, some of the scenes will have you experiencing hot flashes."

—*Old Book Barn Gazette*

THE PRICE OF PLEASURE

"I devoured every page of this enthralling tale . . . the secondary characters were magnetizing and add their own special charm to this evocative yet heartwarming story of love and friendship. The passion absolutely sizzles and the sex scenes are vivid but tastefully written."

—*Rendezvous*

"From the first page, fans of erotic romance will delight in Joan Elizabeth Lloyd's sizzling signature fantasies. Her engaging characters come alive with dreams, hopes, disappointments and love. Although the romance is secondary to the story, readers will love following Erika's page-turning tale from beginning to end."

—*Romantic Times*

Books by Joan Elizabeth Lloyd

THE PRICE OF PLEASURE

NEVER ENOUGH

CLUB FANTASY

NIGHT AFTER NIGHT

THE SECRET LIVES OF HOUSEWIVES

Published by Kensington Publishing Coporation

The *Secret* Lives of Housewives

JOAN ELIZABETH LLOYD

KENSINGTON BOOKS
http://www.kensingtonbooks.com

KENSINGTON BOOKS are published by

Kensington Publishing Corp.
850 Third Avenue
New York, NY 10022

All Kensington titles, imprints and distributed lines are available at special quantity discounts for bulk purchases for sales promotions, premiums, fund-raising, educational or institutional use.

Special book excerpts or customized printings can also be created to fit specific needs. For details, write or phone the office of the Kensington Special Sales Manager: Kensington Publishing Corp., 850 Third Avenue, New York, NY 10022. Attn. Special Sales Department. Phone: 1-800-221-2647.

ISBN 0-7582-1275-5

First Kensington Trade Paperback Printing: March 2006
10 9 8 7 6 5 4 3 2 1

Printed in the United States of America

The *Secret* Lives of Housewives

Chapter

1

"It's pouring," a statuesque redhead with great cheekbones and an atypical, peaches and cream complexion moaned as she and the rest of the yoga class walked to the front door of the East Hudson Community Cultural Center, the 3Cs.

Housed in an old elementary school, the 3Cs was used for various activities. One side was devoted to a thriving senior citizens' center which held activities such as craft sessions and art classes and also served hot lunches for those who needed them. Another set of classrooms was set aside for a small local museum. For the general population it housed free art and pottery classes, an amateur theatrical group that put on quite professional performances in the old auditorium, and the yoga class Monica Beaumont had found mentioned in the local Pennysaver. "Where the heck did that rain come from?" the redhead continued. Everyone knew that the weather at the end of July in New York was notoriously unpredictable but the sky had been hazy blue when she'd arrived an hour earlier.

"The weatherman said only scattered showers," Angie Cariri, the woman who led the class said, staring at the fat drops covering the parking lot with a thick layer of rainwater. She'd introduced herself to Monica before the class and ascertained that Monica had done yoga previously, although not for many years. "I guess we're in one of the scatters. Damn. I've got to get to the supermarket and then home to the kids."

"I watched it roll in as the class ended," Monica said, brandishing her oversized, blue and white paneled umbrella in long, carefully manicured fingers, "and I'm glad now that I thought to bring this thing. We won't melt anyway. It's just warm summer rain. I'll lead. I think we can all fit under." She had to get home. Lots of work to do: schedules to check, proposals to be meticulously edited, costs to be estimated.

Several men and women shook their heads at the offer of the umbrella, and pulling the hoods of jackets or scarves over their heads, dashed out into the torrents until only a few stragglers, including Monica, Angie, the redhead, and one other woman, a plain-looking brunette, remained behind the old wooden door. "Thanks for the offer but I think I'll just wait a few minutes until it slows down," the fourth woman said, pulling her lightweight windbreaker around her shoulders and settling her rimless glasses more firmly on the bridge of her nose.

"Anyone want to share my umbrella?" Monica said. When the three others shook their heads yet again, Monica paused, her hand on the doorknob, ready to run to her car.

A few days earlier she'd had a bit of a scare, chest pains and a bit of difficulty breathing. She'd gone to her doctor, a stick-thin, middle-aged man whom she hadn't seen in much too long.

"Monica," he'd said, "you'd better slow down or you'll have a coronary before you're forty."

"This wasn't a heart attack?" Monica had said, relieved. Coronary was such a scary word.

"Not this time, but your blood pressure is much too high." He finished writing orders for blood tests and a prescription for a hypertension medication, then leaned back in his chair. "Women have heart attacks, just like men. It's less common but not unheard of, and you're heading there at breakneck speed. You've got to slow down. You've told me you work hundred-hour weeks. You can't do that and not have your body protest. You don't get enough rest or enough exercise and as a result you're killing yourself."

"Come on, doc, I can't take time off. I've worked my ass off to get where I am and I like it here." Monica was senior account executive for a large Madison Avenue advertising agency. The term senior wasn't awarded for length of service but for the annual gross dollar billing of the business she brought in. That meant that to keep it, she had to not only keep her existing clients happy but pitch new business, as well.

"It's your body and I know you'll do as you please so I can only offer you advice. Slow down. Take time off, at least on weekends. Work only eighty hours a week, not a hundred. Make friends. See your family. Learn to meditate. Take a yoga class. Go to a concert. Learn to relax!"

Gazing at the rain Monica remembered that voice and hesitated, then took a deep breath. She had a lot to do that afternoon but she kept hearing the word *coronary*. With another deep breath she turned to the other woman. "I'm Monica Beaumont, by the way."

"Thanks for the offer, Monica," Angie said, "but I think I'll give it a few minutes, too. If you're still here, I might take you up on your umbrella then." Monica dropped her hand and reread the slogan on the front of Angie's T-shirt: "The Hurrieder I Go, The Behinder I Get." She'd caught snippets of conversation before class and learned that the woman had ten-month-old twins. She bet that Angie, a small, late twenties, slightly frowsy woman with a fly-away, mousey brown ponytail got very "behinder." *Heaven save me from that.*

As the door closed behind a good-looking man in a deep blue baseball jacket and gray sweatpants, Monica licked her lips with an exaggerated motion. "God, that's really quite a hunk. He's the best thing about the class. Just watching his crane position is worth the price of admission." *Probably has the brains of a flounder and the ego of a rock star. Comes into a class of mostly women, does yoga, but in reality poses in his tight tank and butt-hugging shorts for an hour, pulls on his sweatpants, and exits without a word to anyone.*

"Yeah, he's really gorgeous," the redheaded woman said, tucking a strand of hair that looked like a shampoo commercial behind one ear. *God, she's really a knockout,* Monica thought. "Those tight T-shirts show him off at his best," the woman continued. "I'm Cait Johnson, by the way." She reached out a smooth hand with perfectly shaped nails polished a pale mauve. Taller than Monica's five-foot-seven, Cait was probably in her mid-thirties, a classy-looking knockout, with a model's figure and carefully styled, jaw-length, Titian hair. She wore a diamond solitaire on her left hand the size of a small cube of sugar and the studs in her ears had to be at least two carats each. Monica couldn't help but wonder how Cait, who obviously did yoga frequently and sweated like everyone else, ended up looking like an ad for cosmetics.

Monica took the proffered hand and grasped it firmly. "Nice to meet you." She turned to the sad-looking woman whose eyes always seemed to be on the floor.

Hesitantly, the woman said, "I'm Eve. Eve DeMilo. Like the Venus." The average-looking, slightly plump woman tentatively extended her hand, and Cait, then Monica, took it and squeezed. *Eve, huh?* Monica thought. *Well, if the original Eve had been as aggressive as this one, Adam would have remained celibate.* Eve had come into class a few minutes late, but although there was plenty of room, she'd laid her mat out in the back corner of the room. Monica thought that Eve could be anywhere from twenty-eight to forty, of average height, with hair that her mother would have called dirty blond, and hazel eyes covered by her glasses. Eve was attractive enough, but she could have been the poster child for "Shyness is Next to Godliness."

"Listen, Angie," Cait said, "I've been meaning to tell you

how much I enjoy your class. It's really made a difference for me. I feel more limber and I use your breathing techniques when I'm stressed. Really. You're a great teacher."

Angie lowered her chin and her cheeks reddened. "Thanks, but they aren't my techniques."

"Don't be embarrassed," Monica said, realizing she was having a pleasant non-business conversation, something she had few of in recent months. Maybe this was what Dr. Spitzer was talking about. "Cait's right. You're really good at this stuff. Although this is my first day, I can tell. You made me feel right at home."

"Well, I've been doing yoga most of my life," Angie admitted, tucking an errant strand of hair behind her ear.

"I have to tell you, those babies of yours are just adorable," Cait said.

Angie beamed. "They're the best."

"You should see them, Monica," Cait said. "Twins. How old are they now?"

"They're almost ten months." She turned to Monica. "I bring them every now and then when Tony—that's my husband—can't watch them."

"Which side do the twins come from, yours or Tony's?"

"Neither. Brandon and MaryLee are the first multiples on either side."

"I'll bet it's been tough, having twins and all," Eve said, her look envious. "I always wanted kids."

"You don't have any?" Angie asked.

There was a heartbeat's pause, then she said, "No." She turned and studied the curtains of rain still falling outside the converted school.

"I love other people's kids," Monica said. "I have several nieces and nephews and I spoil them all mercilessly. My sisters have almost drummed me out of the auntie brigade." She hadn't seen any of them in more than a month. Maybe, if she finished the proposal quickly this afternoon . . .

"None of your own?"

"I'm not married," Monica admitted. "Not interested."

"In men?" Cait said, looking aghast.

"That's not what I meant," Monica said with a chuckle. "I'm a pure heterosexual. It's just that men are great for decoration and for fucking, but not for permanent relationships." Men. Not a one of them was worth his salt. Well, maybe a few, but not many.

"That's an amazing attitude," Cait responded.

"The rain seems to be letting up," Monica said, changing the subject and staring out the window that filled the upper half of the school's massive front door. *Coronary. Relax. Make friends who have nothing to do with work.* Maybe this was the moment to give his advice a try. "Anyone up for a cup of coffee across the street?" Monica indicated the Hudsonview Diner. She had work to do, but she'd let it wait. It would be good for her.

"I wish I could," Eve said, sounding genuinely disappointed, "but I can't today." Her voice got still softer. "Maybe next week after class?"

"Yeah. That sounds great," Monica said, turning to the other two women. She had no idea what they would have to talk about but it was worth a half an hour's investment. "What about you guys?"

"I can't today either," Angie said. "Tony is home with the babies and he's totally helpless if they wake up. I have to stop at the supermarket on the way home, too. I'm going to dash." She pulled the hood of her sweatshirt over her head.

"Next week then, Angie," Monica said, not allowing the sentence to end with a question. Among the three of them they should be able to find some common ground. "Tell Tony that he can watch the babies for an extra half hour and let's have coffee. All of us."

"I don't know," Angie said. "I'll see what I can do."

"Cait?" This pampered princess wouldn't be her choice to complete a foursome, but who knew?

"Logan usually plays tennis on Saturday morning so I can probably join you next week. I'll let him know beforehand so he won't worry, that's all. He's very protective."

Monica grinned. Friends. What a concept. "We could be like those girls on *Sex and the City*. We can be Sex in the Suburbs."

"Sure," Angie said. "I really like that show and I still watch it in reruns." She giggled. "Actually, I usually watch it through my eyelids. I can't seem to stay awake past eight these days. I guess I'm Charlotte. Married. Wanting a quiet life with a husband and kids. Cait, who are you?"

"Since they all work, and I don't, I guess I'm not any one of them."

"You don't work. Kids?"

There was a flash of something haunted in Cait's expression but it vanished quickly before Monica was sure it was really there. "Nope. Logan doesn't want me to work and we don't have kids."

"What do you do all day?" Eve asked. "I think I'd go crazy if I didn't work."

"I'm on about a dozen charity committees, I shop, play bridge, and do aerobics three times a week. And this, of course. It's amazing how much I do."

As abruptly as the rain had started, it stopped, and a few shafts of weak sunshine lit the parking lot. "Well, ladies, whoever we are, I've got to run," Angie said with a twinkle. "I guess my parting question is, who's Samantha, the sex fiend? She's the one I want to meet."

"Who indeed?" Monica said. *Little do they know that I probably have sex more often than any of them, just not inside of any permanent relationship.*

"I'm out of here, too," Cait said. "Oh, and my name's Cait, short for Caitlin, not Kathryn. C-A-I-T. Just clearing that up."

Figures, Monica thought. *Even a pretentious name.*

"Okay. See you all in class next week," Eve said, opening the heavy main door. "Maybe afterwards, too?" It came out as a question as she headed out toward the parking lot.

"Maybe. I'm out of here." Angie said. "See ya."

As Monica crossed the parking lot toward her Lexus, she watched Angie climb into an older model sedan, Cait into a current-model-year Honda, and Eve into a Toyota that looked like it had seen better days—lots of them. "Interesting group," she muttered to herself. "Samantha? Maybe that's exactly who I am."

Chapter

2

Cait turned the key to her Accord V6 and waited for the GPS system to boot. Although she certainly knew the route home, she liked to watch the map out of the corner of her eye as she drove. Finally the screen activated and she pressed OK, then thumbed the voice button on the steering wheel and said, "XM Channel 10." The feminine voice echoed back at her, then after a slight pause contemporary country music poured from the speakers and filled the car. They were playing Loretta Lynn's "You're Lookin' at Country," and she tapped her fingers on the steering wheel in time to the cheery tune. She turned the thermostat to sixty-six, knowing that the climate control system would almost immediately kick in and fill the car with cool air, and flicked the wipers twice to squeegee the rain from the windshield.

As she pulled out of the parking space, she waved in the direction of the other women. *Decent sorts*, she thought. That Monica was a bit pushy but okay. Coffee after next week's class? Only if Logan was planning to be home. If he was planning to be out she'd have better things to do with her time than sip coffee with a bunch of suburban housewives.

She turned onto Willow Brook and headed for Sheraton. As

she was growing up, this was the neighborhood she'd always dreamed of living in: four-acre zoning, no house under seven figures, long driveways and large sloping lawns with gardeners and landscapers to tend them. Wooded areas separated the houses. She knew that on a parallel street there were two large horse farms with riding stables and fenced areas for jumping. She took in a deep breath and smiled. Imagine. Caitlin Gaffney, from a run-down section of Omaha, living here.

She remembered when she'd first arrived in East Hudson. Ms. O'Leary, her new fourth grade teacher, had introduced her to the class. "This is another Caitlin," she'd said. *Another Caitlin?* The teacher had held her shoulder and indicated a ponytailed girl in the second row. "This is Caitlin Hanley. We call her Caitlin. And this," she'd said, pointing to a blonde with carefully styled hair toward the back of the room, "is Caitlin Oakes. We call her Cat. What about you? What would you like to be called?"

"Caitlin," she said, her voice small and trembling. That was her name and she liked it. Caitlin Gaffney.

"I'm sure you can see how confusing *that* would be." Ms. O'Leary's voice sounded kind, but there was an edge to it and her teeth showed bright white as she smiled a bit too widely. "When I call on Caitlin to answer a question, how would you know whether it was you or Caitlin Hanley? How about we call you Cait?" It sounded like Kate. "We could spell it C-A-I-T. That would make everyone feel better. We'd have a Caitlin, a Cat, and a Cait. Isn't that a great solution?"

Not for me, she thought. *I want to be Caitlin.* But even at nine she understood that rank had its privileges, so she'd nodded and became Cait.

As she drove down Sheraton Road, now singing along with Dolly Parton's rendition of "Here I Come Again," she noticed several lawn maintenance trucks parked along the roadside, and heard the sounds of Hispanic men pushing double-wide mowers. If she opened the windows, she knew she'd smell the wonderful odor of newly cut grass, but she kept them closed and enjoyed the cool air now pouring from the vents.

She arrived at the large colonial on 214 Sheraton Road and turned the car into the long, upwardly sloping driveway, shaded by massive maples that turned the most fabulous colors in October each year. She pressed the button above her head and watched the garage door slowly rise. Then she played her usual game. She'd learned exactly when to take her foot off the accelerator so the car arrived inside the three-car garage just as it slowed to a complete stop. If she had to touch the brake pedal, she lost the game. Pressing the control to lower the door again, she saw that Logan's sports car wasn't in its spot beside their van. *Great*, she thought. *I've got some time.*

She walked into the large house, and in the spotless kitchen she saw the light blinking on the answering machine. Pressing PLAY, she heard, "Cait, it's Logan." He always referred to himself in the third person. Who did he think it would be? Cait scoffed. "Parker Clay invited me to join him in a doubles match so I'll be home about three. Don't wait lunch for me, I'll just grab something with the guys here." She glanced at her watch. Twelve-fifteen. Plenty of time. "Oh, and don't forget that we've got dinner with the Prescotts. Why don't you wear that new green dress that looks so good on you with the gold shoes I like, the ones with the sexy high heels? See you."

The call ended and the machine said, "Ten-forty-seven, Saturday." She pressed the ERASE button.

Cait rushed upstairs and quickly pulled off her designer leotard and underwear and dropped it all into the hamper in the bathroom. She turned on the water in the stall shower, adjusted the controls so the nozzles on three sides shot out a soft, warm spray, and climbed in.

The bathroom was a microcosm of the whole house, starkly

modern, with primarily white tile and black fixtures. Inlaid, hand-painted, Mexican-style tiles added the only color. Once she'd bought several handmade Mexican pots and filled them with greenery to soften the atmosphere. Logan hadn't particularly liked the plants, so when they died from lack of proper care, she put the pots on a shelf in the garage.

When she finished her quick shower, she wrapped herself in a huge white bath towel and hurried into the bedroom. She ran a quick comb through her auburn hair, glad that it was easy enough to care for so that the blow dryer could stay in the closet, to be used only on special occasions. The bedroom was luxurious. The drapes, quilt, and pillow coverings were white, as was the deep pile carpeting. Fortunately Clara came three times a week, and after vacuuming, used stain remover on any small imperfections. The dressers, head and foot boards of the bed, and her dressing table were Chinese, black enamel, with brass fittings. The spread was squares of black and white satin, accented with lipstick-red throw pillows and red ginger jar lamps on the black enamel end tables.

Still wrapped in her towel, Cait strode into the den, where Logan kept his computer, booted it up, and watched the familiar Windows logo appear. She pulled off her engagement and wedding rings and put them on the desk beside the keyboard. She dropped into the ergonomic chair Logan had insisted on and pressed the familiar series of keys. The "Paul's Place" logo appeared at the top of the screen and the window to the chat room opened. She read down the "who's here" list. Hotguy344. They'd chatted before, with delicious results. She saw her screen name appear on the list, Loverlady214.

Hotguy344: Hi, Loverlady. How's tricks?
Loverlady214: Great. Wanna get private?
Hotguy344:Your place or mine =>> evil grin

Loverlady214:You set it up and I'm there =>> panting with expectation.

There was a moment's pause.

Hotguy344: Ready, Loverlady. I can't wait.

She knew that when she clicked the correct keys she and Hotguy344 would be alone in cyberspace. She felt herself getting wet in anticipation. Her nipples were already tight, sticking out from her white flesh.

Hotguy344: I was hoping you'd show up this morning.

Cait's hands shook as she typed.

Loverlady214: I just finished my yoga class.
Hotguy344: Did you shower? I like to picture you in the shower.
Loverlady214: Yes.
Hotguy344: Are you naked?
Loverlady214: I'm wrapped in a towel.
Hotguy344: Umm, I like that picture even more. Would you take the towel off for me?

Cait found herself looking down. When she and Hotguy344 had chatted before, he'd described himself: twenty-eight, muscular, with shaggy brown hair and deep blue eyes. Was that what he truly looked like? Probably not, but she didn't care. After all, she'd taken ten years off and told him she was twenty-five with long, ebony hair. She'd always wanted to be a brunette so she'd described herself that way. On the 'Net, she could be anyone she wanted to be. As she typed she pictured

Hotguy as he'd described himself. Who cared who he really was?

Loverlady214: Sure baby. I'm taking the towel off now.

Cait stood and removed the towel. Her well-toned body trembled with expectation. She resisted the temptation to touch herself. She'd let it all wait. After all, anticipation was the best part.

Hotguy344: Did you get the camera? You know how much I want to see you, in person, while you take pleasure.

Last time they had chatted, Hotguy344 had suggested that she get a digital camera and attach it to her computer so they could see each other as they played. Hot chatting with a camera on each person would make it so much better. At first she'd worried about him recognizing her somehow, but the odds that Hotguy or anyone else came from this little Hudson River town built around a train station were minimal. And wouldn't the risk make it sweeter?

She hadn't yet figured out a good story to tell Logan about getting a camera. Why would she need one? Maybe to talk to her parents and his. Yeah, that might work. He'd always wanted her to get closer to his folks, and since they lived in the city, that hook might just work.

She'd have to tell Hotguy344 what she really looked like before he saw her, of course, but he'd understand. Anyway, she'd keep the camera pointed at her torso, with her head in shadows.

Loverlady214: Soon I hope.
Hotguy344: I can't wait. I want to be able to see you and watch what you do while we're talking.

Loverlady214: Me too.

Hotguy344: Thinking about me watching you is getting you hot, isn't it?

Loverlady214: Yes.

Hotguy344: Tell me how hot.

Loverlady214: My pussy is dripping.

Hotguy344: And your nipples?

Loverlady214: So tight. What about you? Are you naked?

Hotguy344: Of course.

Loverlady214: Hot?

Hotguy344: My cock started to swell when I saw your name appear in the room.

Loverlady214: Are you touching it?

Hotguy344: Not yet. I want to do it with you.

Loverlady214: Okay ==> sliding my palm over my nipples.

Hotguy344: ==>Holding my cock and sliding my hand up and down.

Loverlady214: Make it wet.

Hotguy344: ==>filling my hand with slippery stuff, typing onehanded.

Loverlady214: ==>touching my pussy. Its really wet. Feels gooddd.

Hotguy344: Push your fingers inside.

Cait rubbed her slippery fingers over her clit, then pushed two inside her channel. She too was typing one-handed, so the conversation got much slower. She was used to that and it increased both her excitement and her anticipation.

Loverlady214: So hot.

Hotguy344: Me too, getting closer.

Cait laughed. He was so easy. He usually came before she did but today she was ready really quickly. It was amazing to

her. After she refused to continue trying to conceive, sex with
Logan had quickly dwindled until it became nonexistent, and
she had been getting more and more frustrated. At first, the
idea of hot chatting on the Internet at all seemed silly to her,
but she'd been so desperately bored one afternoon that, with
no idea how to find an erotic chat room, she'd clicked over
from a truly tedious recipe site to the chat room area. She'd
done what someone had called lurking, just watching the conversations, and had been bored silly. TV shows and movies, diets
and lawn care. She'd bounced from one to another. Then, in a
Let's Talk About Texas room, one person had asked another to
click over to Paul's Place. Curious and hopeful, she'd clicked
over, too. She knew better than to use her own name so she selected the screen name Sheraton35 after her street and her age.

It had been deliciously embarrassing. The people were talking openly about sex. Positions, lubes, sex toys. Using words
like pussy, cock, snatch, and fucking. Over and over, couples—
at least she assumed they were couples—disappeared to private rooms. The idea of being "alone" in cyberspace with
some guy was surprisingly exciting. Anonymous sex. Then a
guy named SuperStud333 had sent her a message.

SuperStud333: Sheraton35. M/F?
Sheraton35: I'm afraid I don't know what you're asking.
SuperStud333: You must be new at this. Male or female? I
    can't tell from your screen name.
Sheraton35: Female

That was how it had begun. She'd selected a new screen
name that said she was female and that she was interested.
Loverlady. When she couldn't have that one because someone
else was already using it, she added her house number, 214,
and that name was accepted by the system. Then she began to
sign on more and more often.

Reading Hotguy344's messages, Cait was breathing as if she'd run a mile and her pulse was pounding in her ears. She rubbed her pussy, feeling her clit get more and more prominent.

> Loverlady214: getting closer you
> Hotguy344: yeah
> Hotguy344: yeah
> Hotguy344: going to come

Cait realized that she was close also and just typed:

> Loverlady214: Yes Yes Yes

She came, as she usually did, hard and fast. She heard her moans as her body spasmed over and over. When she could think again, she typed:

> Loverlady214: Came . . . very good
> Hotguy344: Now!!!!!!!!!!!!!!!!

She'd helped him come and it was a gas. She got almost as much enjoyment from the fact that she'd been partly responsible for Hotguy344's orgasm. She wasn't a total loser the way she felt she was with Logan.

> Loverlady214: Great feeling good gonna run now.
> Hotguy344: Okay. Next time, camera, and stay longer.

She quickly signed off and took another shower. Then she found the green dress Logan wanted her to wear and spread it out on the bed. "Okay," she said aloud, tucking a strand of hair behind one ear. "Now I'm ready for anything."

Chapter
3

Nice women, Angie thought as she climbed into her five-year-old Ford and thought, for the hundredth time, how much she and Tony needed a larger car. She'd been watching ads on TV and, knowing that the babies' two car seats took up the entire back, almost drooled at the seven-passenger vans. Of course, with only two children, she and Tony could manage but if there were more, well . . . She'd always wanted lots of kids, and when she got pregnant, she'd dreamed of three or four, spaced a convenient two or three years apart. Now, with the twins, she wasn't so sure she ever wanted to see another diaper, but they were so adorable. She knew she was a good mother and she loved the job. In a year or two they might be ready for more kids, one at a time. But even with only the twins a bigger car would certainly help.

When she'd discussed a new car with Tony, he'd told her flatly that, with the extra expenses of two babies, the chances of affording even a late-model used car, much less an expensive new van, were slim to none. "Angie, baby, you know I can't do it on my salary, even with my second job." Tony taught English in a high school in New York City, and during the summer and on weekends during the rest of the year, he worked with his brothers doing electrical contracting. He wanted to get some time to work during the week but his commute to the Bronx got him home too late to get in any meaningful amount of time. "We'll just have to keep the Ford running and make do with less room." When Angie looked totally defeated, he'd added, "Maybe we can ask our folks for help. Eventually."

Angie sighed, put the car in gear, and, waving to the women she'd just left, drove slowly out of the community center's parking lot. *What nice women*, she thought again. Coffee at the diner next week. God, it would be so great to have someone to talk to who didn't focus on kids. She talked to her folks and Tony's frequently, but they seldom even asked how she was. "How are my babies?" her mom would ask. *My babies*. Like they were hers. Maybe she could come over sometime and actually help take care of them instead of sipping coffee and talking baby talk to them. *Stop it*, she told herself. *Mom is what she is. Be a good sport and take her as she is.*

"Are the twins still taking two naps a day?" Mary Cariri, Tony's mother, would ask. Although Tony's folks had moved to North Carolina, Mary called almost every day for an update. Often she called at the worst minute, but Angie tried to talk to her at some length anyway, while juggling the babies, bottles, and dirty laundry. "Tell me about them. Any sign of them walking?"

When did I stop being a person, too? Angie wondered. *Even for Tony.*

She flipped on the car radio and tried to relax as soft music filled the passenger compartment. She used her yoga breathing and focused on the tall oaks and pines that lined the quiet streets of East Hudson. Summer flowers were in full bloom in front of well-maintained houses. Now that the clouds had passed and the sun shone brightly, she knew that all the neighborhood children would be outside playing in their yards: toddlers with balls and brightly colored plastic toys, digging in sandboxes or splashing around in small inflatable wading pools, older children on bikes or skateboards or shooting baskets, parents sitting together and sipping iced tea. *God, I can't wait until the twins don't need me every waking moment.* Maybe she could make some friends, too, like those women she'd been with briefly after class that morning.

She turned onto Judy Lane, a typical suburban street with paved sidewalks and impossibly green lawns. Her split level was halfway down the street, and as she approached, she thought about Tony, waiting for her. She let her mind drift into her favorite fantasy. He'd be at the door to greet her. She could see it.

"I'm so glad you're home," he'd say. "I missed you so much." His kiss would be warm and deep, his hands stroking her back, wandering down to her cheeks.

"I missed you, too," she'd say as she came up for air. His kisses always made her breathless.

"The babies are still asleep," he'd whisper. "Come into the bedroom with me."

He'd draw her into their room, where the sun shone through windows open to the soft summer breeze. He'd slowly remove her clothes and stroke each part of her body as it was revealed. His soft hands on her shoulders, his lips on her neck would heat her blood and increase her heart rate. Then his mouth would find her breast and he'd bite lightly on her already erect nipple. Shards of pleasure would arrow to her groin, making her swell and moisten.

Soon his fingers would slide between her thighs and stroke her hungry body. God, how she loved the feel of him opening her, penetrating her. He'd tell her how she aroused him, how he wanted her and only her.

They'd be on the bed now, naked, his large cock sliding into her soaked body, filling her, then teasing her by pulling out. In and out, until she was writhing beneath him. They'd climax together, then doze.

She returned to reality as she pulled into the driveway of

their small, three-bedroom house and turned off the engine. She remembered when the Ford had fit into the small garage, but now the space was filled with baby stuff: a second high chair—they'd have to find room for it in the house somewhere now that the twins were feeding themselves—a twin stroller, two toddler tricycles and two wagons, portable cribs for trips to who-knew-where, boxes of hand-me-down clothes from caring neighbors, and enough other stuff that she'd actually lost track of what was in some of the cartons.

Angie climbed out of the car and walked past the few straggling salvia and zinnias left from her flurry to put growing things around the house one afternoon several months ago. She'd spent two hours with the baby monitor beside her while the twins were sleeping and it had looked really good for quite a while. Now, however, with her lack of time for care or water, most of the plants had wilted in the summer heat. Maybe this morning's rain would perk them up.

She opened the front door and walked into the small entryway. "I'm home," she said softly, hoping the twins were still asleep. She reached down and picked up Gizmo, their six-year-old chocolate brown miniature poodle, so he wouldn't bark and wake the babies. Reflexively, she scratched him behind his ears as he wriggled joyfully in her arms.

The living room was its usual shambles, filled with baby toys, books, blankets, a pile of clothing from the wash she hadn't had time to fold yet. A pile of diapers and a box of baby wipes lay on the coffee table on top of a pile of art books she'd bought to add color to the room. The babies' bottles from their pre-nap feeding still sat on one end table. Beneath it all was the comfortable, contemporary furniture she and Tony had bought when they were first married, when they had two incomes and could afford to buy pretty much what they wanted. They'd actually decorated, poring over magazines and haunting furniture stores, local art shows, and craft fairs. She breathed in the standard smell of baby lotion, formula, and just a hint of baby poop.

She glanced into the kitchen, at the sink filled with dishes that needed to be stuffed into the dishwasher and several bowls on the tray of the twins' single high chair. Again she realized that they needed to find room for the second one. Where could it go? she mused. The kitchen was too small for two high chairs and the dining area carpet was still in pretty good condition. For the moment she was feeding one baby in her arms, while the other sat in the chair, but that wouldn't work for long. Maybe they could put a throw rug down in the dining area or just use a sheet of plastic.

"Hi, hon," Tony mumbled, not looking up from the computer game he was playing. "MaryLee fussed a bit about an hour ago but then went right back to sleep. Brandon, as always, is out like a rock."

Tony. She loved him, she really did. He was warm and caring with long, slightly shaggy dark hair and soft brown eyes. He wasn't exactly gorgeous but even now, when her libido was almost nonexistent, his sexy body, sensual face, bedroom eyes, and tight, jeans-encased butt still stirred her.

"That's great," Angie said, sighing as she thought about the ordeal when they woke: changing diapers then feeding a pair of hungry babies. Fortunately they were exceptionally good children, seldom cranky even at mealtimes.

"Did you get the beer?" Tony asked, still using his controller to shoot at enemies. As explosions flashed on the screen Angie was pleased that he had at least turned the sound off.

"Oh, baby, I'm sorry," Angie said. "I completely forgot to stop at the store. I got to talking to a few of the women from the class and it just slipped my mind." She turned and started toward the door.

"Don't bother," Tony said, pushing the pause button. "I'll go."

"Why don't you wait until we're through with the babies and then I'll go? Or we can put the kids in the car and both go. I've got the list right here." She fumbled in her pocketbook and found the scrap of paper she'd scrawled on.

"That's okay. Don't trouble yourself. I'll do it." He grabbed the car keys from Angie's hand.

Right. You'll find any way you can to get out of baby duty. Can't you just once volunteer to take the babies off my hands? But she sighed and said, "Okay, babe. I'll see you in a few minutes."

"Actually this works out really well. Jordanna bought a new sound system and I told her I'd help install and wire it up for her. I'll just stop there on my way home."

Jordanna. Tony's ex-wife, who couldn't seem to stay totally ex. On one hand, Angie was glad they had a good relationship. So many divorced couples were so hateful to each other. But why did they have to be *so* friendly? Gorgeous Jordanna with her corporate job and high five-figure income. Never-had-a-kid Jordanna with no stretch marks and perky breasts. Clever Jordanna with her sneaky ways to keep Tony close. Jordanna, who'd be there to pick up the pieces should things go wrong with Tony's marriage to poor little Angie.

Angie bit back an angry reply. It really was good that they got along. Wasn't it? Damn them both. Tony would spend a few hours with the lovely, needy Jordanna and by the time he arrived home, the babies would be changed and fed and he'd be relaxed with his ego bursting. She took a deep breath. *Get along. Be a good sport. Don't make problems where you don't have to.* "Whatever. Say hello to Jordanna for me," she said. *And feed her a cyanide cocktail for me, too.*

She heard the front door close behind her husband and chastised herself for her negative thinking. She wandered into the kitchen, spread a thick layer of peanut butter on a slice of bread, and folded it over. Chewing, she poured baby cereal into a bowl and pulled a jar of strained apricots out of the closet. Empty baby bottles covered the back of the kitchen counter and she scooped powdered formula into two of them. *Brandon gets the lap this time*, she remembered, *and MaryLee gets the high chair.* At least they weren't breast-feeding any more. What a relief it would be when they held their own bottles. She'd read that ten-month-olds should be doing that, but hers seemed to be conspiring to give her extra work.

Stuffing the last bite of her sandwich into her mouth, Angie heard the first slight rustle through the baby monitor. If the twins woke slowly, as they usually did, she'd have about ten minutes to change out of her sweaty clothes and then it would be "Twins Time!"

Chapter

4

With a small prayer, Eve started her 1996 Toyota and heaved a deep sigh when the engine caught. She really had to get it over to the mechanic today but she didn't want to take the time. She needed to get home, just in case.

She drove through the center of town, down Main Street with its collection of stores, gas stations, and restaurants. Villa Moretti's. Yeah. She hadn't been there in quite a while and a plate of linguini with meat sauce would taste really good. She had long since stopped minding sitting by herself, reading a good romance novel, and filling her stomach. She'd go there later—if she felt like going out.

For now she turned onto Pinetree. East Hudson was such a nice, ordinary little town, she thought. Ordinary streets with ordinary people doing ordinary things. A ball field and kiddy park. An elementary school on the next block. That was fine with her. She was basically an ordinary person with ordinary needs.

This particular section of town was filled with apartments and inexpensive condos, near enough to the railroad tracks for some commuters to make the long walk to the station and for her to hear the train whistles. Others thought the sound of the long, low wails was lonely, but to her it was a dreamy sound, particularly on a hot summer evening when all her windows were open.

It made her think of the movie *Picnic*. She loved old films and that was one of her favorites. William Holden and Kim Novak making love beside the railroad tracks. You never saw anything that wasn't G-rated, but it was obvious that they did it that night.

She must have seen that film at least two dozen times, and each time she played it she worried that eventually her videotape might just wear through. If it did, she'd buy another. William Holden would be much too old now for her thirty-one years but in that film he was everything she wanted.

She considered what she wanted and realized that Mike might be calling right now. She resisted the temptation to speed but she had to get home. She knew he wouldn't leave a message, no tangible evidence. Maybe his wife would go out for lunch or take the kids somewhere and he'd be able to call and talk for a few minutes. It seemed like forever since she'd seen him. Of course, it had been only yesterday at the office but that wasn't the same as really seeing him. She pushed her glasses further up on the bridge of her nose and deliberately slowed down to twenty.

They'd been able to get a funch, as he called it—fuck for lunch—the previous Tuesday. God, those were good. Grab a hot dog, separately, of course, from the vendor on the corner or bring in sandwiches from the deli on the next block, then hurry to a small nearby hotel where no one asked any questions. Okay, when she really thought about it, it did seem a bit furtive, but it was always worth it. Mike was wonderful in bed.

Frustrated, she arrived at the Garden Grove Apartments, parked her car in its assigned space, grabbed her purse, and dashed up the walk. She'd had to drive through the complex really slowly since the street was filled with children. Bikes and balls filled the sidewalks and spilled over onto the roadway. Elementary school girls covered the walkways with colored chalk designs and drawings while the teens and preteens talked in small groups.

Her unit, number 206, was up one flight in the back, very private. She had dreams of Mike being able to get an evening to spend with her. As she headed for her building she allowed herself just a moment to fantasize.

He'd come to her apartment. No one would see. His hair would be a bit mussed and she'd smooth it away from his face. His wonderful face. It wasn't handsome exactly, with its heavy nose, chiseled chin, and heavy, black-framed glasses. But his eyes. God, his eyes. Almost black and so seductive. When he looked at her, even in the office, she'd melt. His mouth was full and so sexy that it took all her willpower not to rush over and kiss it.

"This is heaven," he'd say, looking around her modest apartment, and she'd watch his lips form the words. She'd be able to look at him to her heart's content. No need to be circumspect. They'd share a glass of wine and talk about romantic movies, novels, or television shows, anything but the office. He'd put his feet up on the coffee table, lean his head back onto the sofa cushions, and relax.

Then he'd turn to her, cup his hand on the back of her head and pull her close—close enough for a long, searing kiss. She'd touch him, stroke him, undress him slowly, and he'd do the same for her.

Then they'd walk, hand in hand, to the bedroom and stretch out on the bed. The windows would be open and she'd hear the distant train whistle. He'd sigh and agree that it was a lovely sound, tell her how he also loved riding on trains. They would do that on their honeymoon, once he was free of Diana.

He'd touch her then, long slow caresses. As he touched, she'd feel herself swell and her wetness increase. In the light from the bedside lamp she'd watch his cock grow, thickening and lengthening until she knew he was ready.

He'd take his time, rubbing her wet folds, caressing her clitoris, making sure she was ready for him. She would be eager for him and he'd slowly slide into her, taking a long time before he came. And she'd climax, too, just a moment after he did.

The dream had flashed through her mind in only a few seconds, but when she returned to the present she lamented the time wasted and quickly rushed up the walk, idly waving to a few of her neighbors, sitting on lawn chairs on the grass, surrounded by children. As she turned her key in the lock, she heard only the wail of Maxie, her male Siamese, and the galloping feet of Minnie, her coal black female alley cat. No, she was a mixed breed, a domestic short hair like they said on Animal Planet. And Minnie wasn't just a domestic short hair— she was much more. She was a friend, a confidante. When she couldn't talk to anyone else, she could talk to Minnie. She flashed on the three women she'd met earlier. Maybe . . .

Eve opened the door and scooped Minnie up before she could slip out. Maxie turned his back and sauntered toward the kitchen as he always did, as if to say, "Okay, so you're home. Where's my treat?" but Minnie rubbed her cheek against Eve's and started to purr.

Cradling Minnie in one arm, Eve dropped her purse on the chair, walked into the kitchen, and glanced at the answering machine. Nope, no message. Had he called and just hung up when the machine answered? She wouldn't know unless she asked him. She realized that she could give him her cell phone number, but that seemed so public and impersonal, and anyway she was home all afternoon every Saturday and Sunday. No, the cell phone wasn't intimate enough. When he called she wanted to be at home.

The kitchen was tiny but immaculate, bright floral dishes put lovingly in the cabinet, a tea kettle shaped like a cat on the narrow stove, three cat-shaped magnets on the refrigerator holding the phone numbers of the building's superintendent, her family doctor, and the vet. Well-washed, spatter-patterned tile covered the floor. Although there was limited counter space, when she saw them at a garage sale, Eve couldn't resist the canister set—each of the three containers shaped like a fluffy, black and white Persian kitten—which now occupied a place of honor beside the stove.

Maxie jumped onto the counter and settled there, washing his paws as if he hadn't a care in the world. Eve dropped Minnie beside him, then got two kitty treats from the box in the cabinet and gave one to each. She kept a restraining hand firmly on Maxie and watched Minnie daintily eat her tidbit. If she didn't watch, Maxie would push Minnie out of the way and eat both treats. Men. Wasn't that the way.

Over the next hour Eve changed into jeans and a T-shirt, tidied her already tidy apartment, vacuumed the simply furnished living room, plumped the cushions on the ersatz colonial sofa, and straightened the matching chair and tables. She ran a soft cloth over the frames of the old romance movie posters that filled the walls, lovingly dusting Humphrey Bogart and Ingrid Bergman in *Casablanca* and Errol Flynn and Olivia de Havilland in *Robin Hood*. Then she gathered a load of laundry that she'd take to the laundry room in the next building that evening, when she knew Mike wouldn't call. He never called after five. Family time with his wife and kids. No, she wouldn't think about that part of it.

For lunch she opened a can of tomato soup. While it heated, she thought about which movie she'd watch. She looked over her large collection, but she realized that she already knew what she wanted. She pulled the *Picnic* tape from the shelf and stuffed it into the VCR. When the soup was almost ready she put a bag of popcorn in her small microwave and listened to the comforting sound of the popping. Finally, an oversized mug of soup in one hand and a bowl of popcorn in the other, she wandered into the living room and pressed play on the remote. As the film filled the TV screen, she dropped onto the sofa and the two cats settled themselves on her legs.

She fell into a light sleep and nearly jumped off the couch at three-thirty when the phone rang. Two startled cats dashed across the room as she picked up the cordless handset she'd placed on the floor beside the sofa. She stopped a moment to slow her racing pulse, and once sure she'd sound fully awake, softened her voice. "Hello?"

"Hi, sugar."

It was him. "Hi, Mike. I'm so glad you got a chance to call."

"Diana's out so I've got just a moment. How was your class?" She was in heaven. He'd actually remembered that she took yoga on Saturday morning. "Aerobics, right?" he asked.

"Yoga." Okay, he wasn't exactly right, but he'd remembered something. "It was really good. Angie is such a good teacher."

"That's great."

She pulled off her glasses. "Maybe next week, if you can call only on Saturday around lunchtime, you could use my cell phone. I really want to talk to you, but I might not be home. I might go out with some ladies from the class." It would be worth losing the sense of privacy to be able to sit with the others from the yoga class. Anyway, he didn't usually call until midafternoon, when Diana was out. She cradled the phone between her ear and shoulder.

"Sure. You'll give me the number on Monday. Does Tuesday lunch work for you this week?"

He knows it does, she thought. *He's my boss after all, but he always asks. So polite.* "Sure. I can't wait." She yanked the bottom of her T-shirt out of her jeans and took off her glasses.

"Me neither." He paused. "I think I hear the door. Gotta run. See you Monday morning."

"See you," she said, but the line was already dead. She breathed warm air onto the lenses and polished her glasses, then put them back on. She saw that the tape was playing the final credits so she stopped it, pressed rewind, and settled down to watch *Picnic* again.

As the opening shots filled the screen she scooped Minnie up and set her on her lap. "He's so wonderful. He says that in a few years he can get a divorce, once his children are old enough to understand." She scratched the cat's belly. "Won't that be wonderful, Minnie? Just Mike and me."

Minnie began to purr loudly and Eve pulled a brightly colored afghan over her legs and snuggled down to watch the film.

Chapter
5

Monica settled into her Lexus and turned the radio on. Contemporary soft rock flowed from the speakers. She pulled out her PDA and opened a "notes" page. She quickly listed the other three women's names and a quick bit about them so she'd remember everything next weekend. Remembering names and facts about people was one of the keys to her success in business. She closed the electronic organizer and heaved another deep sigh. She had to admit that she felt more relaxed than she'd felt in months. Except for that brief period after a particularly good orgasm, and that certainly didn't last.

The heat and humidity in the air promised that the temperature would hit ninety before the day was through, but she flipped off the air conditioner and opened all the windows. She closed her eyes and breathed in the damp, post-rain air. Wonderful. How long had it been since she had last just smelled the air? As her eyes opened, she watched cars pull out of the parking lot and hoped the three other women she'd just met would find time to get together after next week's class. "These women might be just what I need," she said aloud. "A little down time with no strings or stress."

Her first stop after class was her weekly appointment to

have her nails done. Hemorrhage red, or at least that was what it looked like, and not too long. Practical, yet classically sexy. She liked that. She picked up two business suits and a light jacket at the cleaners and drove to the local 7-Eleven to do her shopping. She used to go to the supermarket but in recent months she was home so little that she needed very few things. Bread, a box of tissues, instant coffee, and dog food. Lots of dog food. As she passed the sandwich area, she grabbed a turkey and tomato wrap and munched it as she paid for her purchases.

She thought back to the previous week and realized she'd only been home twice; the other evenings she'd had late meetings or dates and had used the corporate apartment. As senior account executive at Conroy & Bates, one of the largest advertising agencies in the country, she was entitled to lots of perks and took advantage of them all. *Why the hell not?* she thought. *After all, I probably bring in more business than any two other account execs.*

At what cost? Okay, she had to pander to the needs of corporate advertising bigwigs who had nothing better to do than dangle a multimillion-dollar media account so she'd jump through any of the hoops they held. Whatever. Her face graced the business pages of newspapers and magazines and when she spoke, those who mattered listened. She thought she might be able to crack the glass ceiling at C & B and that energized her. She might eventually make partner, but for now she was happy being a force in the industry.

She put her groceries into the trunk, then headed home. To get to her town house, she drove down Sheraton and gazed at the expensive houses with their mile-long driveways and carefully manicured lawns. From time to time she'd considered buying one of them, but why? For show? She had no need for six bedrooms and a three-car garage. Oh, an in-the-ground pool would be nice, and maybe a sauna, but really. Why? Her town house was more than enough for her: three large bedrooms, living room, dining room, den, and spacious kitchen. What more did she need?

As she pulled into her cul-de-sac in Evergreen Estates, the super high-end condo development she'd bought into three years before, she glanced at her watch. Almost two. She'd take a few minutes to do the few things that Hillary, her cleaning woman, hadn't done, then attack the pile of work she'd brought home. How little time she got to relax wasn't important. *Coronary.* She'd work at a bit more leisurely pace, but she had to get this stuff done for a meeting Monday morning.

Sam, her forty-five-pound Dalmatian, greeted her at the door with his exuberant barking. As she leaned down to rub his chin she marveled at the fact that he got just as excited when she'd been gone two hours as when she was gone all day. The dog quickly rolled onto his back and Monica spent several minutes scratching his belly, causing Sam to spasm in delight.

"Okay, love, get your leash. We can manage a quick walk." Wagging most of his body and almost grinning, Sam skidded across the off-white Spanish tile on her kitchen floor, ricocheted around the refrigerator, grabbed his leash from its shelf, and bounded back to the front door. "Sam, sit," she said, and the dog sat facing her with his bright blue leash in his mouth, wiggling with barely restrained glee. "Give," she said as she reached out her hand. Sam put the leash gently into her hand and she hooked it to his collar.

"Good dog," she said, marveling yet again at how well behaved he was.

Two years earlier she'd gone to the animal shelter with her younger sister Janet and her family to look for a dog for them. When Monica saw Sam's face behind the bars, however, she'd fallen in love immediately. "It's so impractical," she'd said. "I'm gone all day and that's not a good thing to do to a dog."

"You have a fenced yard out back," Janet had answered

with a twinkle, "and there's probably a neighbor who could take care of him when you're gone."

"I know, but . . . " An hour later Sam had joined her household. She quickly discovered that he'd been well trained by his previous owner and was a pleasure to own. When she was out late or stayed in the city overnight, as she often did, Craig, her next door neighbor's fourteen-year-old son, was delighted to come over, play with Sam, then feed him and leave him in the house until he could let the dog out again in the morning. In return, Monica paid him twenty-five dollars a week, a small price to pay for good care for Sam.

Now she hooked Sam up, opened the front door, and followed him outside into the steamy midday sunshine. It was amazing that the streets were completely dry despite the downpour of a few hours earlier. "Let's have a nice calm walk," she told the dog. She usually took him out for just a few minutes but as she strode through the visitors' parking lot she deliberately made herself slow down. *Coronary.* She pulled her cell phone from her pocket and pressed a speed dial number.

"Bonnie? Hi, babe."

"Hello yourself," her older sister said.

Now that she'd called, she felt a bit awkward. "It's been a while."

"It sure has. How the hell are you?"

The two made small talk for several minutes while Sam sniffed at every bush and tree around her block of town houses. Finally, Monica said, "I was wondering whether you guys were free sometime soon. I've been thinking that I haven't seen you, Jake, and the kids in quite a while."

"We're barbecuing tonight. Why don't you stop by for dinner? Come early. I know everyone will be tickled to see you."

Just what she needed. Although she and her sisters had little in common, she genuinely liked both Bonnie and Janet, and they had so much history that they were seldom at a loss for conversation. "Are you sure I won't be putting you out?"

"Not at all. I've got plenty. I'm going to hang up now so you can't say no. Dinner's around six. Be here! 'Bye!" The line went dead.

Monica snapped the phone closed. She was making changes in her life. If she could only keep it up. "Hey, Sam, we're going to Bonnie's house later. You get to play with everyone."

At four-thirty, having spent a couple of hours going over mounds of paperwork, Monica showered and dressed in a pair of lightweight summer jeans and a soft yellow blouse. She opened the car door and Sam bounded into the backseat, ready for an adventure. Not wanting to arrive empty-handed, Monica stopped at her favorite pie shop and picked up a crust full of blueberry calories and a quart of the shop's special vanilla-fruit-swirl ice cream, then drove the nine miles to her sister's quiet neighborhood. The raised ranch house was of moderate size and comfortable, with a huge oak tree in the front yard that caused Jake to lament that he couldn't get grass to grow beneath its branches. It wasn't at all like the ones on Sheraton, but more than sufficient for Bonnie and her family.

At thirty-six, her sister was three years older than Monica and had been happily married for almost thirteen years. "Auntie Em," her niece Lissa yelled as she saw her aunt's car pull into the driveway. "Auntie Em."

Auntie Em. She'd been called that since the first time Lissa, now aged eleven, had seen *The Wizard of Oz*. At first Lissa thought it was a big joke, having an aunt whose name began with M, but the nickname had stuck and now all of her nieces and nephews called her that. "Did you bring Sam?" Lissa said, skipping over to the car as it pulled to a stop.

To answer, Monica opened the car door so Sam could gallop toward the giggling girl. "Auntie Em's here, with Sam," Lissa yelled, and answering boys' cries of, "Here, Sammie," echoed from the backyard.

Monica spent the next hour sitting on her sister's deck, enjoying large glasses of sangria and large doses of family life, eventually watching Jake fiddle with the outdoor grill. Later, filled with hamburgers and hot dogs, she extricated herself and arrived back at her apartment at around eight, slightly sunburned and scratching three mountains that some hungry mosquito had built on her left ankle.

As she wandered into her bedroom, she realized that times like this left her with deeply conflicted feelings. She was envious of her sisters. Marriage, kids, the security of at least some steady person as the years passed, all sounded so comfortable and wonderful. But she was also contemptuous of them. They were both bright, college-educated women. How could they settle for suburbia, crab grass, and part-time jobs? Sure, Jake made more than enough money as an attorney, and Janet's husband Walt was a stockbroker, but what did Bonnie and Janet do all day? She remembered Eve's comment earlier that afternoon. What would she do if she didn't have her job, and what skills would her sisters have if something happened and they had to go back to work? Sure, Jake and Walt were all right, but men in general were unreliable and would skip out the minute things weren't going well. Her father was a prime example, leaving the family when Monica was in her early teens to do what he'd always "needed" to do, see the country with his new girlfriend, Doreen. Monica had listened to her mother in the years following, calling her father every name in the book, and a few she made up herself.

Tempted as she was to pick up the stack of work still undone, she stretched out on the bed and flipped on the TV. When her cell phone rang, she pressed the mute button. "Hello?"

"Hi, Monica." She recognized Trent Lockhart's voice immediately. He was the assistant media director at the skin care division of a large cosmetics firm, and she'd been trying to convince him to let C & B pitch his account.

Lowering and softening her voice, she said, "Well, hello stranger. I haven't heard from you in weeks."

"I've been busy. You know how it is."

"I sure do. To what do I owe this call?" She'd given him her cell phone number "just in case."

"I've got a free evening Wednesday and I thought we might get together and talk about"—he paused—"things."

Things. She knew exactly what things he was referring to. She had been dangling sexual favors in front of him just as he'd been dangling the account in front of her. Another unfaithful married man. "I'd love to talk about"—another pause— "things. Over dinner?"

"Sure. How about Peter Luger's in Williamsburg?"

"Seven o'clock."

"I'll bring my car. Why don't you come in a taxi and then I can drive you back to the city?"

"We'll see how it all works out," she said, knowing her meaning was perfectly clear. No pitching the account, no fucking. It was that simple. Actually, Trent was a really sexy guy and she would have done him just for the hell of it, but that wasn't the way the business ran, at least for her. And God, was she hungry. She'd been celibate for almost a month, longer than she'd gone in years. She pictured Trent: soft, country-boy blue eyes, razor-cut sandy hair, and a nicely turned out body. She wondered what he'd be like in bed. Aggressive, she hoped, and she'd find out soon. It was only a matter of time.

Monica had no qualms about trading her body for whatever she needed at work. She'd had brief affairs with several of the senior partners. Everyone understood that they were just short, feel-good fucks but they accomplished what she wanted. She got noticed. She knew no one would really *do* anything extra for her and she never even hinted at a *quid pro quo*, but she got considered for new accounts and found out about opportunities before most others.

What was the problem with that? She wasn't hurting anyone. She enjoyed sex in all forms, and with a few exceptions, had as good a time as her partner.

For a moment the image of the guy from the yoga class flashed through her mind and she wondered what he was like in bed. Nah. Too complicated. It was so much simpler when everyone knew what was what.

As she undressed after her call from Trent, she looked at herself in the full-length mirror on the back of the bathroom door. Not bad, she thought, sucking in her stomach, lifting her ribs, and arching her back slightly. Not bad at all. *So I'm not a kid anymore,* she thought, lifting her breasts with her hands. *I'm experienced and damn good in bed. Every man I'm with gets the best I can give.*

She sometimes wondered whether she should be ashamed of her behavior, but she wasn't and had never been. She quickly removed her lightly applied makeup and smoothed moisturizer into her face and neck. Then, feeling unusually good and even a bit relaxed, she slipped beneath the covers and listened to Sam shuffle up the stairs and settle comfortably beside the bed.

Reaching down to scratch Sam's head, she picked up an old issue of *Advertising Age.* She didn't read enough, keep up with who's who and what's what. Okay, it wasn't pleasure reading but it wasn't exactly work either. She was amazed at how good she felt, just reading. She had a pile of work for the next day but for tonight she'd just chill.

Chapter
6

On the eastern bank of the Hudson River, across from the Palisades, the town of East Hudson, New York, is a thriving bedroom community about thirty-five miles north of New York City. Like most Hudson River towns it sprang up soon after the pilgrims arrived at Plymouth Rock, when Otto Jenks built a small ferry to transport men, horses, and supplies across a slightly narrower section of the river. Otto called the area East Bank of the Hudson, quickly shortening it to East Hudson, abandoning the Native American name, which has been lost to history.

Mostly ignored by both sides during the revolution, East Hudson settled into a farming lifestyle, growing fruits and vegetables on small family farms, and raising thousands of cows, transporting their produce and livestock down the Hudson River by barge to the constantly hungry city at its mouth. Grapes became a substantial cash crop once a serious vintner named Elias Peters arrived and started the East Hudson Winery in the middle of the nineteenth century. Grand homes flourished, some for summer getaways, others for year-round flight from the heat and cold of New York City. Not as grand as the cottages of Rhode Island, they were still large and opulent.

When the railroad overspread the area, factories took advantage of inexpensive power from Niagara Falls and cheap transportation to sprout like mushrooms up and down the Hudson, making everything from hats to shoes, from stoves to elevators. A mixture of German, Italian, and Irish immigrants slowly moved north to provide cheap labor and many of the large East Hudson farms and estates were broken into smaller homes and apartments for the newcomers.

Early in the twentieth century, manufacturing slowly moved south and west, leaving deserted buildings and run-down railroad sidings all along the river to decay and rust. When the area railroads electrified, making short haul commuting practical, East Hudson found its true calling as a refuge for tired New York City workers. With stations in Tarrytown and Mount Kisco to the west, Croton to the south, and Peekskill to the north, the commuter railroads created a firm foundation for the entire county of Westchester, and the river towns gentrified.

Now a mixture of income levels and ethnicities, the town of twenty-five thousand boasted several main shopping areas, three large strip malls, and an easy commute to White Plains to visit Lord & Taylor's, Saks, and the hundreds of up- and down-scale stores located there. While cookie-cutter middle-income housing developments grew all around, the older section remained the center of town, with two good Chinese restaurants, three newer Oriental take-out places, Carvel, McDonalds, and two Italian restaurants with countywide reputations. The veal parmesan–eating public was strictly divided—those who frequented Antonio's and those who flocked to Villa Moretti. Fierce arguments arose, each group extolling the virtues of their favorite antipasto or chicken specialty.

The center of town life, however, was the Hudsonview Diner. It had gone through several owners before Nick and Maria Micklos took it over several years earlier, and for the last two years the Greek specialties had steadily improved until the pasticcio and lamb kabobs could be praised in the same breath as Antonio's chicken marsala and Villa Moretti's veal saltimbocca.

Now, late Saturday morning, one week after the sudden rainstorm, the four women sat in a booth by the large windows. They'd declined menus and just ordered coffee as they exhausted several subjects: how wonderful the yoga class was, the heat wave, now in its sixth day, and the latest episode of a Monday evening reality show that it turned out all of them watched, at least occasionally. The waiter arrived and put a heavy white mug in front of each woman. Eve carefully put her cell phone beside it.

"I'm delighted your husband agreed to watch the babies for you this morning," Monica said, adding a packet of Sweet 'N Low to her cup.

"As he should," Cait said, sipping her black coffee and wincing.

"He didn't bat an eyelash," Angie said, looking a bit surprised, "but I don't want to be gone too long."

"Hey, they're his kids, too," Monica said, "and you're entitled to a small amount of time off."

"I know," Angie said, reaching into her gym bag, "but he works so hard all week that he's also entitled to his down time." She pulled out her wallet. "I've got new pictures." She opened to several photos of the twins, dressed in matching navy and white outfits. For the next several minutes the women oohed and aahed over the adorable babies.

"What does your husband do?" Eve asked when Angie had put the photos away.

"He teaches English in the South Bronx. It's a really tough high school—you know, lots of drugs and gangs. But he loves the teaching and he tries to steer clear of the other stuff. It scares me a little."

"Has there been lots of violence in his school?"

"From time to time there's a fight or one of the guys brings a knife or gun to school. I think Tony's stopped telling me about that part of it."

"So why does he stay in the city?" Eve asked. "There must be jobs up here somewhere."

"It's not that easy," Angie answered. "He submits applications all the time, but there are so many good teachers looking to get out of the city that there are hundreds of résumés for every job. He just hasn't gotten lucky yet."

"That's tough," Cait said, reflexively smoothing the polish on her index fingernail with her thumb.

No wonder she's so frazzled, Monica thought. *Schoolteachers don't make nearly as much money as they should.* As Cait said, it was probably really tough for them to make ends meet. "How about you, Eve? You said you work, what do you do?"

"I work down in the garment district. I'm the executive assistant to the head of logistics for a shoe importer."

Monica's attention was suddenly riveted on Eve. "Shoes? My favorite thing. Which brands do you bring in? With my wardrobe, I probably own some of your company's imports." *Shit*, she thought, glancing at Angie. With all of Angie's financial difficulties, she shouldn't advertise how much she had.

As if reading her thoughts, Angie reached over and patted her hand. "You look embarrassed. Tony and I get along fine. Don't worry." She turned to Eve. "Yeah, which ones?"

Eve mentioned the names of several high-end brands. "No shit," Cait said, her eyes widening. "I have several pair of those, especially a wonderful little black slingback with a small rhinestone clip off to one side. I just love them."

"I'm glad. I don't do the buying, of course, but I'm glad they're going in the right direction."

"What does a person in charge of logistics do?" Angie asked.

"We take care of getting the shoes into the country from the Far East, customs, duties, tariffs, then filling orders from wholesalers, like that."

"What about you, Monica? What do you do?"

Over the last few moments Monica had considered how to answer that question and had decided to play it low-key. She suddenly realized that she didn't want to seem like some powerful Madison Avenue type that these women wouldn't be able to relate to. She liked this little group and wanted to feel part of it. "I'm with C & B."

"C & B?"

"Sorry. Those in the business are so used to the abbreviation. It's Conroy and Bates. That's a big ad agency in the city." One of the top five, actually.

"What does that mean you do, exactly?"

"I deal with big corporations who need to buy TV time and print space to advertise their products. I set up media plans, work with the creative guys, and approve commercials, like that. I also try to convince them to buy more and spend more."

"Phew," Angie said. "From all I've seen on those cop shows on TV, being in the advertising business is a lot of high pressure."

"On *Law and Order*, advertising people work twelve-hour days and sweat a lot over the possibility of losing an account," Eve said.

"You got that right," Monica said, trying to release the tension she suddenly felt in her jaw. It was always her jaw that felt it first. "That's why I'm taking this class. I've got to get rid of some of this stress."

"Well, yoga's good for that," Angie said. Her face softened and Monica realized that she was quite pretty, or would be if she'd do something about herself. She also realized that with twins, finding time to have her hair or nails done was probably out of the question. And there was always the money.

"How about you, Cait? You said you don't work?" Monica winced. "Maybe that wasn't the most tactful way to put that."

"It's okay, Monica. I don't work, per se, but I'm busy all the time. I'm on the board of several large charities and it seems we're going and doing all the time. I paint, work out, and my husband and I do a lot of entertaining."

"What does he do?" Eve asked.

"He's a partner in his family's real estate firm. American Properties."

"Wow. They've got signs up everywhere," Angie said. "Does he sell a lot of houses?"

"The firm does," Cait said. "Actually he's on the corporate side, selling or renting entire buildings to big businesses, Fortune 500 types."

"Where did you get the name Cait? I mean, spelled that way. I've never heard of it before."

She told them about her teacher and the two other Caitlins.

"Why didn't they call you 'Red'?"

"My hair wasn't quite this color back then," Cait said to Angie, tucking a strand behind her ear with a charming, slightly embarrassed grin. "It has a little help about once a month now."

The three other women giggled. "Ah," Eve said, becoming serious again. "I've been admiring that color. It looks so fabulous with your face."

"Actually, it would look great on you, Eve," Angie said. "You might consider doing something like it. You could use one of those wash-in products, and if you didn't like it, it would just disappear slowly."

"I don't think it would be right for me. Cait's so polished, so upscale, that it really looks perfect on her. Me? I don't think so."

Cait looked uncomfortable with the compliments. "God, this coffee's really dreadful," she said, quickly changing the topic. "I love this diner and I have lunch here a few times a week. The food's really good, but their coffee . . . " She made an ugly face. "I think it sits in those pots until it cooks down to gunk."

Eve put her half-full cup down. "You're right, Cait. It really is sludge. A gal at the office makes dreadful coffee like this.

My boss calls it cawful, for awful coffee." She paused and her face softened for a moment. Then she said, "Anyway, this qualifies as cawful."

Monica took a small swallow. She'd noticed the lightning quick change in Eve's mood but didn't comment. She hadn't really focused on the coffee since she'd been trying to cut down, but as she took another sip she couldn't help but agree with the other women. "I'm such a coffeeholic that I seldom notice what hot, brown liquid I'm drinking, but this really is the pits. I'd be afraid to let the spoon sit in the cup too long." She grinned. "It might dissolve. Cawful. Great term."

Angie sipped hers. "I'm just happy I can drink coffee again. You can't have caffeine while you're nursing, you know."

"Oh, right," Monica said. "That and no wine, were my sister's biggest complaints. Well, morning sickness, of course. And being unable to roll over in bed, and toward the end, no sex."

Angie groaned. "Not much sex afterwards either." Then she looked startled, as if surprised that the words had come out of her mouth.

"God," Cait said. "I couldn't get along without sex, good, bad or indifferent."

"Me neither," Monica said.

"Oh," Angie said, "I thought you weren't married."

"And your point is?" she said with a leer. "You don't have to own the cow to enjoy the milk."

"A woman I have to admire," Cait said, grinning.

"You sound just like Tony did before we were married," Angie added with a giggle. "He'd had enough of marriage."

"He'd been married before?" Cait asked.

"Jordanna," she said with forced lightness. "They were married for three years."

"Exes are the pits," Monica said. "My parents were divorced when I was thirteen and my mom never let me or my sisters forget what a shit he was."

"Oh, Jordanna's not that bad. We used to have lunch occasionally."

Monica caught a tightness in Angie's voice. "Used to?"

"Well, now with the babies and all, it's difficult for me to get out."

"She doesn't visit you?" Eve said, then paused. "Well, I guess that would be a bit strange."

"Very strange. Tony sees her from time to time." Angie looked down at her watch. "Listen, guys, I have to get going. I really enjoyed getting out. Maybe next week?"

"Sure," Monica said. She was surprised to realize that she had thoroughly enjoyed herself. Such an odd combination of women, but somehow they seemed to fit.

As Angie picked up her gym bag and took out some money, Eve's cell phone rang. She looked at the screen, and when she obviously recognized the phone number, Monica watched Eve's entire expression soften and a small smile light her face. She grabbed the phone and her purse, pulled a couple of singles from her wallet, and dumped them on the table. As she pressed the button to answer the call, she said, "Gotta take this call outside. Let's meet next week. Okay?"

"Sure," Cait said. "Do you have to rush off?"

"Yeah," she said, then whispered, "Just a minute," into the phone.

"Okay, see you next week."

Eve rushed out with Angie following more slowly. Cait and Monica stood up, and after leaving a few more bills on the table, Monica hugged her quickly. Then, leaving Monica behind, smiling at the spontaneous gesture, Cait too headed out into the heat.

This is becoming something really nice, Monica thought. She asked for the check, counted the money already on the table, added what she needed to, and walked down the ramp toward her car, a wide smile lighting her face.

Chapter
7

Eve had seen the familiar phone number on the screen of her cell phone and had hustled out of the diner. Mike. "Hi," she said into the phone. "Hang on a minute." Dashing across the street to the 3Cs parking lot, she unlocked her car and almost tumbled in. "Hi, baby." The interior was boiling hot so she started the engine and turned the air conditioner on full blast.

"Well, hi yourself," the familiar voice said. "What was that all about?"

She tried to catch her breath. "I was having coffee with a few of the women from my yoga class. You remember. I told you about that. That's why I suggested you call on my cell."

"Oh, yeah. Right. Listen, I only have a minute. Tuesday?" *What do you think?* "Of course, baby."

"Good. While I'm at home over the weekend I like to look forward to our little get-togethers."

Get-togethers? Why do I do this to myself? "I look forward to them, too."

"Okay. Gotta run. See you in the office on Monday."

"Call me again if you get—" But he'd already hung up.

Why indeed? She thought back to the previous Tuesday. The desk clerk at the small hotel they frequented knew them well and quickly supplied her with the key to their usual room. Mike's company credit card number was already on file. She unlocked the door and set her purse and a paper bag on the dresser. The room was a little seedy but the air conditioner worked and the beds were comfortable. And, she thought with a small smile, they didn't squeak. The furnishings were strictly utilitarian, the standard flowered bedspread with matching drapes, pale tan ersatz wooden dresser and nightstands, and industrial brown and beige carpeting.

The bathroom was plain white tile, with the usual individually wrapped soaps and little bottles of shampoo. From time to time, Mike took a quick shower, always forgetting to bring the toiletries into the stall. "Hand me the shampoo. That is, of course, unless you can't find real poo." Then he'd laugh at his joke for the dozenth time.

Today she'd brought delicatessen, pastrami on rye with cole slaw and Russian dressing for Mike, and roast beef on rye for herself. She pulled two diet sodas from the bag, and leaving the door slightly ajar, went to the end of the hall and filled the ice bucket.

When she returned Mike was already digging into the second half of his sandwich. "We've only got about half an hour," he said, his mouth full. "I've got a meeting with the Madrid people at one-thirty."

Of course, she knew about the meeting. She'd arranged it. "I know, but even just a half an hour is worth it."

Mike crammed the entire remainder of his sandwich into his mouth. Sitting on the edge of the bed, he looked so cute, Eve thought, with his receding hairline and black-framed glasses. *Maybe he's not much, but he's mine every Tuesday.* Slowly she pulled her plain black sweater off over her head and watched his eyes. She knew she was a little chubby but he seemed content with her body, looking her over, his gaze heating.

"Oh, Eve, I love watching you undress." He started to

stand but she pressed down on his shoulders, keeping him seated. "Mmm."

She slowly unzipped her skirt and allowed it to fall to the floor. Now she was wearing only a lacy black bra and panty set she'd bought the previous week just for him, thigh-high stockings, and a pair of three-inch spike heels she'd borrowed from the supply of samples they kept on hand in the stockroom. She folded her glasses and put them on the bedside table. She loved it when he looked a little fuzzy while they made love, sort of like seeing him through an oiled lens, as they did in the movies sometimes.

He reached forward and cupped his hands over her hips, slowly drawing her toward him. "You look great," he said, making her feel like a million dollars. "Really great."

He buried his face in her belly, inhaling deeply, obviously enjoying the scent of her body. When he unhooked her bra, her large breasts spilled out. As he filled his hands with her, kneading her flesh and pinching her nipples, she couldn't keep the grin from her face, knowing how much he loved the feel of her breasts. She leaned down and he took one nipple in his mouth, suckling, pulling hard, driving shafts of pleasure through her body to her now-wet crotch.

As sucking sounds filled her ears, he pulled down her panties and buried his fingers deep inside her, making her knees buckle with ecstasy. He knew just how to please her, now rubbing her erect clit while placing wet kisses all over her bosom. Although the pattern of their lovemaking was always the same, her body responded to it as if it were the first time, opening to him, igniting all her senses.

As he drove his fingers into her she unbuttoned his shirt and removed his slacks, reveling at the look and feel of him. Even his scent was intoxicating. Quickly they were on the bed, Mike naked, with her wearing just her thigh-high stockings and heels. "Do it for me, baby," he growled.

She knew exactly what he liked so she scrambled over him and licked the length of his cock, making him slippery. Then she knelt above him and cradled his erection between her breasts. She rubbed his shaft in the deep valley over and over, frequently licking drops of pre-come from the tip. She reveled in his moans of pleasure.

She knew just how much he could take before he came between her breasts, so she pulled away and grabbed a condom from where she'd put it on the bedside table. She unrolled it over him, then lay back as he climbed on top of her. When he was fully lodged inside of her, she felt his fingers between her legs, finding her clit and stroking. He was such a considerate lover, always making sure that she came before he did. Since she was so aroused, it only took a moment until spasms rocked her and had her entire body pulsing around his large cock.

"I love it that you're always so ready for me," he said, panting. "Makes me feel like quite a stud."

"You are, baby," she said, barely able to gasp out the words.

"Tell me," he said, thrusting and withdrawing slowly.

"You're so good, so hot, so big. I just love feeling you inside me."

"I love your big beautiful tits and I love your hot pussy. My cock in your pussy." His voice rose as his four-letter words had their effect on him. "I love fucking you." Then he screamed as he came.

When he'd calmed a little, he said, "God, baby, that was fabulous. You make me so hot that it's hard to wait." He chuckled. "Hard to wait. I get hard, all right." He waddled into the bathroom, grabbed a handful of tissues, and cleaned himself up.

He showered and dressed quickly, finally zipping his pants. He poured soda into two glasses, added ice, and handed one to her where she lay, still stretched out on the bed. He downed most of the contents of his glass, stared at his watch, and headed for the door. "I've got to run. You don't need to be at this meeting so take your time getting back." He blew her a kiss, opened the door slowly, looked both ways down the hall, and slipped out, gently closing the door behind him.

Eve lay on the bed, slowly decompressing from her satisfying orgasm. *Oh, Mike, if only . . .*

She remembered how it had all begun, a sudden, emergency overnight trip to a wholesaler in southern New Jersey. She realized at the time that her presence wasn't really necessary. Sure, she took notes of problems and made a few useful suggestions but a phone call from Mike to her in the office would have done just as well.

After several hours of meetings, faxes, and e-mails to suppliers and shippers, they had gone to a local Italian restaurant for lasagna and Chianti. Over salad he'd suggested to her that it was getting too late to drive back to the city that evening. As the meal progressed, the silences had become longer and charged with sexual tension. He'd held her hand and made it obvious that he was interested in more than just business.

At thirty-one she wasn't a virgin, nor was she naive. During dinner she read all the signs and wondered whether she could do something so totally out of character. But she was lonely. She had few friends and little family. Would this be so bad? Okay, he had a wife, but according to him they didn't have much of a relationship left. They stayed together for his kids. He told her that he was lonely, that he hoped she understood that he'd never done anything like this before either. "Eve, I know this isn't fair to you but I want you. I've wanted you for a long time. Can I hope that you feel the same way?"

They went to a local hotel and he got them adjoining rooms. They never used hers. Had he planned it that way? She never asked. They went directly to his and he was gentle and tender, so loving and patient with her. He'd slowly removed her clothing piece by piece, kissing each part of her overweight body, looking at her as though she were something special, precious. He'd paid particular attention to her large breasts, kissing and sucking. As some point he'd said that his wife was so small. She'd hated his reference to his wife but in the sexual haze she'd overlooked it. They'd made love and she'd enjoyed it. She hadn't climaxed but she hadn't minded. It had been fabulous.

The following week Mike had suggested "funch" at a small hotel near the office, and they'd been meeting almost every week since. That had been almost a year earlier. Now, sitting in the 3Cs parking lot, she wondered whether she was making the same mistake as she had sixteen years before. But she wanted him, needed him. Soon she'd be thirty-three and then what? With a deep sigh she started her car and headed back to her apartment.

As Cait pulled out of the community center parking lot she was gratified by her new friends' reaction to Logan's job. American Properties was a big name in the northeast and their black, white, and gold signs could be seen in front of all the best houses. It would be nice if it were Johnson Properties, but Johnson was such an ordinary name and when Marshall Johnson, Logan's grandfather, had founded the company almost fifty years before it had been just after the war and anything labeled "American" did well.

In the fifties, the era of the baby boomers, the real estate business in Westchester soared and American Properties and Marshall became legends, breaking up many of the large estates into half-acre lots, each with a new split level home to be sold. Then Palmer, Logan's father, took over and branched out into commercial properties. Now Logan was following in their footsteps.

Logan's business had been keeping him away from the house more and more lately, but although she was a little suspicious, Cait had decided not to think about it too hard. She cared for Logan but slowly it was evolving into a sort of brother/sister thing. She was curious about his life away from her but as long as he left her pretty much on her own, she didn't really care very much what he did. She had all the money she could spend, all the clothes she could wear, and her computer. As she drove through the steamy streets of East Hudson, she thought about sex. Actually, if she were to admit it, she thought about it a lot these days, and her thoughts seldom revolved around her husband.

She'd known Logan only a few months before he proposed. They'd both been in their mid-twenties and met when she applied for a job at the local real estate office. They were attracted to each other almost immediately. After only a few dates they professed their love for each other and then went to bed together several times before they began to plan the wedding.

Their lovemaking was, at best, ordinary. He'd already be erect, touch and fondle her for a few minutes, then plunge into her and climax quickly. But sex wasn't everything, and for Cait his marriage proposal was a dream come true. Caitlin Gaffney from Omaha would live on the best street in town. Logan's parents gave them the house they were still living in eight years later as a wedding present. Maybe it wasn't the biggest house in the area but it was the one she knew that all the neighbors envied, with a large, heated, in-the-ground pool, a built-in sauna and spa, five bedrooms, and a sumptuous living area created by the best decorator in New York City.

Sex. It hadn't gotten any better and in the last year it had deteriorated significantly, until now they didn't make love at all. Even back when they had, it had inevitably been unsatisfying. She used to slip out of bed after Logan was asleep and masturbate in the bathroom.

Then, several months earlier, she'd discovered the Internet. With her new screen name, Loverlady214, she began to prowl. At first, the goings-on were merely a curiosity. Four-letter words flying everywhere, as if by saying fuck and cunt and pussy often enough it made everyone a stud. All the guys were supposedly twenty-five and muscular, all the women were twenty-five and a 34DD. Looking down at her 36B chest was depressing. However, in the anonymous world of the Internet, she didn't have to be her real self. She could be anyone she wanted to be and Loverlady214 became twenty-five with long raven hair and a large chest.

It soon became addictive. She lurked, staying in the background, and sometimes getting turned on by a snippet of conversation. She'd gone to private rooms from time to time, but had logged off when things went too far. But "too far" had gotten farther each time.

Several months before, as she watched two people discuss what they'd do if they were together, she had slipped her fingers between her legs, and when the talk got hot enough, she'd climaxed. It had been wonderful, and anonymous. She didn't need Logan, or anyone. It was legal, moral, and so exciting. She wasn't cheating on Logan since there was no real contact. Cheating for her had never been a viable option, although when things had reached their dullest, she'd actually considered it. No, she admonished herself often, she wasn't like that, but she needed something and this might just be it. The 'Net filled her bill.

One afternoon while Logan was at work, she had logged on as usual and had been invited into a private room by a guy named JaketheSSSnake. When she lied and told him she'd never actually climaxed on-line before, they'd spent a delicious fifteen minutes driving each other higher and higher. She'd climaxed so violently that she'd been unable to type for several minutes. He'd laughed and signed off. Now she spent most of her at-home time on the computer. She'd researched ways to keep her activities secret by wiping any bits of data and cookies, whatever those were, from her hard drive, and she had purchased a program that did so each time she logged off. She was sure Logan was unaware of what she was doing, and she wasn't sure whether he'd care anyway.

Lost in thought, Cait pulled into the three-car garage and

was surprised that she'd been so distracted that she had to touch the brakes. "Hi, honey," Logan said, striding into the garage. He was tall, dark, and thick. That was the only way she'd ever described him. His body was well-developed but tended to be straight up and down, with wide hips and narrow shoulders. His dark hair was combed straight back and carefully razor-cut, his moustache and beard neatly trimmed every week by a barber. He wore tennis whites, and she had to admit, didn't look half bad.

"Hi, hon." He grabbed her as she climbed out of her car and gave her a bear hug, then rubbed his bristly moustache over her cheek. "How's my girl?"

"I'm good, Logan," she said, combing her fingers through her auburn hair. "Where are you off to?"

He released her quickly. "Tennis with Mark Petrie. How about meeting me at the club later for drinks?"

She tried not to sigh. "Sure. That sounds good."

"Why don't you wear that new bikini I like so much?" He waggled his eyebrows. "Maybe we can think of something to do later." His leer left little to the imagination. Maybe they'd actually have sex later, unless Logan drank too much and fell asleep immediately, as he usually did. Nah. Probably not. He talked a good game, especially around his friends, but when they were alone in the bedroom he wasn't the least bit interested.

She wondered whether he really meant that he wanted to have sex, or was his sexual byplay just a sham? She'd be just as happy to pass and was sure he would as well. "I'll see you later," Cait said as Logan kissed her on her cheek and climbed into his Mercedes convertible, leaving the seven-passenger van they seldom used in the third spot.

"See you," she said, waving as he pulled out. She glanced at the license plate. LOGAN1. Hers was LOGAN2 and the van was LOGAN3. She'd love a CAIT1, but why fight it? As she walked into the house, she grinned. She had plenty of time to log on.

*   *   *

Angie drove home wondering how, in only two encounters, she'd become so comfortable with the other three women. Sure, she hadn't wanted to get into her relationship with Jordanna, but all in all, they were really friendly people and she hoped that their Saturday morning meetings would continue.

She thought about the three other women. While Eve seemed to be so soft and shy, Cait and Monica seemed so strong. Would they put up with Tony's weekly visits to his ex-wife the way Angie did? It made her so unhappy yet she didn't want to say anything. Don't make waves. Be a good sport. That was what she'd been raised on. She hated scenes and confrontations so much that, back when she'd been the secretary to two local insurance brokers, she'd never balked at doing whatever demeaning job they'd asked her to do. She'd picked up laundry, made coffee, even baby-sat for one partner's three rambunctious sons so he and his wife could look at a piece of property.

Jordanna.

Angie and Tony had gone to high school together, and although he hadn't known that she existed, she'd been half in love with him. When he went off to the state university, Angie started to work, first at the local office supply store, then for Danny and Tyler Shultz and their insurance business. When Tony returned to East Hudson with his wife Jordanna, Angie was devastated. "See. What did I tell you?" her mother had said. "He's not for you. He obviously wanted something more than a small-town girl with only a high school education. You've seen that college girl wife of his, putting on airs all over town. She's class."

Thinking of her mother made her huff out her breath. What had she known? She'd stayed with her father through all his drinking. Angie had idly kept track of the couple for the next few years, watching Jordanna parade around town like the

queen of the May while Tony got a teaching job in the city,
then took a second job, moonlighting at the local convenience
store two nights and one weekend day each week. Angie
stopped in for gas occasionally and she and Tony reminisced
about old times like two good buddies.

Tony and Jordanna had been married for three years when
they split, amicably it was said. One afternoon almost a year
later, Tony was pulling out of a parking space at the mall and
backed into the rear bumper of Angie's car as she was backing
out of the space behind. No real damage was done to either
car, but, while examining the situation, they got to talking.
One thing led to another and they were married just a year
later.

Their relationship had been wonderful and the sex explo-
sive. At first, much as Angie tried to discourage such talk, he
lamented his lack of good sex with Jordanna. "She was such a
cold fish," he had said. "Not like you." He kissed her deeply,
hands roaming over her back, eventually finding their way beneath her top and unhooking her bra. He'd loved her body,
spending long minutes stroking and kissing her skin. They'd
get undressed and tenderly make long, leisurely love. It had
been the best ever for her. Then she'd gotten pregnant.

They were ecstatic. A baby. They talked about names for
hours and made plans to decorate one of the bedrooms in their
new little over-mortgaged house as a nursery. They wandered
through the mall admiring tiny clothes and being amazed at
how much Pampers cost.

When they learned she was having twins, however, they
were shocked, then dismayed. How would they stretch Tony's
meager salary? He'd quit his hated job at the minimart and he
enjoyed his leisure time, getting more and more involved in
his first love, computer games. They both vowed he'd not go
back to working so many hours. She'd work more time for as
long as she could and he'd get some part-time work with his
brothers in their construction business. It would bring in more

money for fewer hours. Jordanna had objected to the mere mention of Tony's doing manual labor but Angie thought it was a great idea. They'd sock away as much as they could before the birth, which wasn't much.

The stresses of her advanced pregnancy totally destroyed their sex life. She couldn't get comfortable, and in her seventh month, when she had to give up her job, they'd also given up sex. As she thought back, she realized that it was about then that he'd started to spend time with Jordanna, who still lived in her small but luxurious condo about five miles away from the Cariri house.

At first it had been a plumbing problem. Since they'd shared the condo before their divorce, Jordanna thought Tony might be able to solve the problem without expensive repairs. The fact that the repairs should have been the condo association's problem hadn't occurred to Angie at the time. Two months later the air-conditioning unit began to leak and then the washer broke down.

Tony had seemed delighted by the birth of MaryLee and Brandon, and had been some help around the house while she juggled laundry, meals, cleaning, and nursing two rapidly growing babies. As the spring approached, however, it seemed that he was going over to Jordanna's more and more often. Her mother, whom Tony adored, was ill, and Tony said they'd been visiting her in the hospital.

Were they having an affair? At first Angie would have vehemently denied it. Now she wasn't so sure. She wanted to ask Tony to be with her more but she didn't want to make waves. A good relationship with one's ex was important, but God, how she hated it.

She pictured Monica or Cait in her situation. "Listen, buster, it's time you spent come quality time with me instead of her. Got it?" No, she couldn't do that. Not a chance. But she smiled at the thought.

Chapter
8

After her coffee with her new friends Monica had her nails done and grabbed a bite of lunch. She was glad they hadn't gotten any more deeply into what she did for a living; she didn't want her title and six-figure salary to intimidate the other three. Actually, Cait's bank account was probably as big as hers but she had married into it, not clawed and scratched her way to the top. Oh, yes, and fucked her way there, as well. Earlier in the week she'd looked Cait up in the phone book and had driven past her house. Sheraton and Willowbrook, the very highest rent district of East Hudson. A most impressive area, and from what Monica could see from the road, Cait's house was one of the most impressive. At least five acres of land, about half of it wooded, a brook in the back with a decorative bridge over it, a sprawling house with a three-car attached garage, a small dining porch off of what was probably a huge kitchen, and a large in-the-ground pool at the side with cabanas and carefully groomed landscaping around a small waterfall. Angie and Eve were lightweights, but Cait . . .

She had never actually met Cait's husband but she knew him from his reputation around town. Rich and successful, he probably made as much money as Monica did, but the other two were not in her league. She didn't want to come across as the high-powered, hundred—no, she vowed—eighty-hour-a-week executive she was, and she certainly didn't want to get into the myriad ways she lured and kept clients.

Monica pulled into her driveway, waved at one of her neighbors, and thought over the pile of work she had for the weekend, prioritizing and organizing. As she pressed the remote to close the garage door behind her she pulled out her PDA and made a few notes. When Angie said there was a lot of pressure in her job, she didn't know the half of it.

As she wandered from the garage to her front door she looked around at things she seldom noticed. While heat radiated off the streets, the well-tended grass and plantings didn't wilt, even in the midday sun, watered by the extensive sprinkler system that came on in the wee small hours. Tall maples, sycamores, and birch were planted at carefully calculated intervals to give shade and comfort to the residents while stands of pine and cedar dotted the area.

In the distance she could hear the sounds of balls being hit on one of the tennis courts and children playing in the pool. She sighed. The common charges were exorbitant, but she loved Evergreen Estates, the most expensive town houses along the river. You could see a section of the Palisades from the clubhouse that she'd only visited a few times for owners' meetings. If she had the time she could play bridge or chess there—if she played bridge or chess. She could learn and it might be relaxing. Her overly long workweeks were what allowed her to afford all this, however. If she slowed down just a bit, she wondered, would her income suffer much? She had to slow down. *Coronary.*

Sam was waiting for her so she ruffled his fur, then snapped on his leash and headed for the edge of the complex where most of the residents walked their animals. Only one dog or two cats per residence, the house rules said, and she knew that notices went out, then fines were levied if anyone disobeyed.

As Sam sniffed at much-used trees and bushes, she allowed her mind to focus on the media plan she was working up for a breakfast cereal.

"Well, hello," a male voice called from about ten feet away, causing her head to snap around.

It was the hunky guy from the yoga class, walking a gorgeous golden retriever. The dog was tugging at his leash, giving Sam the once-over while the guy did the same to her. She had to admit that he was truly candy for the eyes, with a great body, now barely hidden in khaki shorts, a tight red T-shirt, and well-worn loafers. His ebony hair was long enough to be caught at the back of his neck with a leather thong and his piercing blue eyes had long dark lashes that any woman would envy.

She tried to post the "not interested" look on her face but he grinned anyway, his white teeth emphasizing his smooth, lightly tanned skin. God save her from men who thought that because they were gorgeous and they'd seen you occasionally from a distance, they could do the "get to know you better" bit. This dame wasn't buying it! "Hello," she said, tugging, trying to get Sam to move on. He'd seen the golden, however, and wanted to get a closer look. "We have to get along, Sam."

"They just want to get to know each other," the guy said, and Monica didn't miss the double meaning.

Oh, what the hell, she thought. *Let's do this and get it over with.* "Is letting them get together safe?" The golden was giving the guy a difficult time, despite the rippling muscles in his shoulders and arms. "Your dog looks like quite a handful."

"It shouldn't be a problem. Sadie's fixed."

"Well, that's good. So's Sam." Monica allowed her Dalmatian to get close enough to give Sadie a thorough sniff. Once they'd become comfortable with each other, the dogs went back to investigating the nearby shrubbery.

"Sam and Sadie. Sounds like a comedy act," the guy said with a smile. "I'm Dan. Dan Crosby. We met at the yoga class."

"Oh, yeah." *Like he doesn't expect everyone to notice him.* "Nice to meet you, but I've really got to be going," Monica said with a bit of impatience, deliberately not giving him her name.

"I'm sorry if I disturbed you. I just wanted to say hi."

Realizing she was being intensely rude, she softened. "I'm sorry. I guess my mind was elsewhere. Do you live up here?"

"No. This is my sister's dog. She and her family are out of town this week so I volunteered to take care of Sadie. You?"

"Yeah. I'm on the next block."

"I'll be around quite a bit this week so maybe we'll see each other again."

Torn between enjoying looking at the guy and wanting to keep her distance, she said, "Sure. Maybe we will." Would it hurt to see him "around?" She liked the KISS system—keep it simple, stupid—and personal relations were always complicated. In her relationships with her clients, hot and sexy though they might be, everyone knew the rules. You rattled each other's chain, warmed the sheets when you wanted to, and each partner tried to give as little and get as much as he or she could. Keep the clients and potential clients happy—no more and no less. She didn't have the time or energy for extra-curricular activities. Monica pulled at Sam's leash and they started back toward her driveway.

Tuesday evening she actually made it home while it was still light. Dressed in her city duds, as she thought of them, a white linen business suit with a bright kelly green sleeveless blouse beneath, she took Sam out for his evening constitutional. Again, she encountered Dan, walking his sister's golden retriever. "Hi there," he called from across the street. "I thought we'd probably run into each other again."

The two dogs pulled toward each other so she had no choice but to approach. God, the man was beautiful, this evening wearing light tan slacks, a black polo shirt, and the same well-worn loafers he'd been wearing when she last saw him. His long hair was loose, ruffling in the warm summer evening breeze, and although she felt like a fool even thinking about it, she longed to learn whether it was as soft at it appeared. *With a body like that he's probably got an ego to match and the brains of a snail.* She used this as a mantra to keep herself from responding to him.

"Hi." She was trying to think of something to say when she realized that she was tongue-tied. This never happened to her. "It was really hot today." *Great line, Monica.*

"Yeah, it really was. I never did get your name?" He extended his hand.

She took his hand, which was warm and dry, with a good firm grip. "Monica. Monica Beaumont."

"You're right about the heat, so I'm going to wander over to the pool for a dip. Would you like to join me?"

"I'm afraid I have work to do."

"Work? It's after seven. Surely you're off duty, whatever you do."

"I work for an ad agency and I'm afraid I'm not often off duty." Actually her dinner had been rescheduled so she'd taken advantage and hustled onto Metro North with a briefcase full of media rates she needed to look over.

"Ridiculous. Come on, Monica. Put on a bathing suit and join me. Actually, if you don't want to join me that's okay, too, but you really must take advantage of the pool once in a while and unwind."

He was right. How long had it been since she'd enjoyed a swim in the pool she paid such exorbitant common charges to support? He sounded like her doctor had when he'd used the C word—*coronary.* This could be part of her new plan to relax more, not an effort to get to know Mr. Dan Gorgeous. What the hell. "You know, I hate to admit it, but you're right," she said. "Maybe I will do just that."

"Great. I'll be over in a few minutes. If you want to sit with me, great. If not, that's fine, too, I'll understand. I'll feel I've done my job just getting you out of your house."

An early evening after a hot August day drew adults to the pool area. The children who usually monopolized the water and diving boards were already in bed and the teens were off doing their own thing, so the bulk of the people in the pool area were commuters trying to cool off after their trek home from the Big Apple. The area was well maintained, lounge chairs and tables kept scrupulously in tip-top condition, the oversized main pool clean and smelling lightly of chlorine. Steam rose from the hot tub and a small fountain played in the six-inch-deep kiddy pool. Several couples paddled around in the shallow end of the adult pool, while three men swam laps. Several lounge chairs were occupied with people pouring drinks from multicolored pitchers, the tables beside them covered with sandwiches and bags of chips. The smell of grilling burgers and steaks wafted over from the picnic area.

All the way home with Sam she'd debated with herself, then finally allowed as how she wanted to see what Dan was really like and dispel any fantasies she might be building. She had several bathing suits, and after worrying about the message she might send, she finally selected a one-piece, wriggled into it, and slipped on a pair of sandals and a light, lace cover-up. She stuffed a towel, her passcard, and keys into a small tote and walked the two short blocks to the pool area. Dan lay several feet from the gate, eyes closed, stretched out on a lounge chair. He really was something to look at, although she was surprised that he wasn't wearing a skimpy Speedo. Rather, his suit was dark brown and looked more like a pair of shorts. He did give the term six-pack abs new meaning, however, and she tried not to drool.

Why was she so fixated on his looks? she wondered. She snorted as she walked toward him. She never judged people on their outward appearance. She was attracted to him, however, and had decided to find out things about him that would end this fixation. *Beauty is as beauty does*, she thought yet again.

"Hi," he said, looking up from beneath his baseball cap. "I wasn't sure you'd show up."

"I wasn't either," Monica said, putting down her canvas tote and settling into the seat beside him, "but you were right about my needing to relax so I decided to join you for a few minutes."

"I'm glad. I like that suit."

She felt uncharacteristically vain, proud that she'd picked a deep violet concoction that seemed to consist of two pieces laced together up the sides and cut high on the hips. "Thanks." *It better get that look*, she thought. It had cost the earth. "So," she said, "tell me a little about yourself." *Like, are you married?* He wasn't wearing a ring but you never could tell. She'd been hit on by more married men than she could shake a white picket fence at.

"I'm not married, never was."

A bit miffed that he seemed to be reading her mind, she said, "That's not the first question that came to my mind."

"I'm sure it wasn't, but I thought I'd get it out of the way. You?"

"No. Like you, never was and maybe never will be. Why not?"

"Not what?"

"Married. I can't imagine it was from lack of opportunity." *Oops. That says I've noticed how gorgeous you are. Now we'll hear some come-on stuff like "can't find the right woman."*

"It's just difficult for me to make time for the dating scene so I'm content to let it go for now."

"You sound like a busy man. What do you do?"

"I maintain large networks and computer systems for a major Internet service provider. I've got a sizeable staff but if I'm not at some site around the country, I'm online."

Well, stereotype number one down the drain. He's obviously got brains beneath that gorgeous gift wrap. Okay. Make conversation. Keep it light and distant. "Sounds like it takes up most of your time. What brings you out here this evening?"

"I decided, like you did, to shut down my computer and chuck the whole thing for an hour. I need the space to clear my head. How about you? What do you do?"

"I'm with C & B. That's an advertising agency."

"I know. Conroy and Bates. One of the biggies. Account exec?"

Surprised that he hadn't assumed she was a secretary, she nodded. Well, secretaries couldn't afford town houses in this development without family money, so she guessed his was a logical assumption. Still, she was reluctant to admit how high up in the food chain she was. "Lots of pressure."

Dan sat up and reached down to the concrete beside him. "I brought a pitcher of lemonade and an extra glass. Can I offer you some?"

Over a few glasses of lemonade they talked about everything from sports, about which Monica knew very little, to politics, about which they both knew a lot.

At one point a boy of around seven ran ahead of his mother through the gate, into the pool area. "Hey, Dan, where's Trevor?" the boy asked with a bright smile.

"He and his sisters are off on vacation." Dan reached out and ruffled the boy's hair. To Monica he said, "My sister's kids. Trevor's seven, Marly is nine, and Alexa is ten."

The boy's face dropped. "Oh yeah. He told me last week." Then he brightened. "Will you come in and play with me? I brought my beach ball. We could play volleyball in the big pool."

Dan turned to Monica. "We bat the ball around sometimes." His gaze returned to the boy. "Sorry, sport. I'm talking to this nice lady." Dan raised his eyebrow at the boy, who

turned to her with sparkling blue eyes. "Hi. I'm Cameron."
He extended his hand. "Nice to meet you."

"Nice to meet you, too, Cameron. I'm Monica." They
shook.

A man of about thirty in a red Speedo came through the
gate leading a boy of about three, followed by a woman wearing a terry robe over a demure one-piece black swim suit,
pushing a stroller. "Hi, Dan," the woman said. "Don't let
Cameron bother you."

"He's not. Monica, these are the Pascoes, Rob and his wife
Serena. They're close friends of my sister and her husband."

"This is Brad," she said, indicating the three-year-old, "and
this is Mark."

"He's still a baby," Cameron said, "and so far he's okay."

"How is their vacation going?" Rob asked.

"Since I haven't heard from them, I assume it's going fine.
If everything goes as planned, they'll be back on Saturday."

"Say hi if you hear from them before we do." The man
turned to his son. "Come on, Cameron, and don't bother Mr.
Crosby."

"He's not Mr. Crosby," Cameron said triumphantly. "He
said last time I could call him Dan."

Rob and Serena laughed and Rob headed for the kiddy pool
with Brad. "Say good-bye to Dan," Serena said. "Nice to meet
you, Monica."

"'Bye, Dan. See ya."

"See ya, Cam."

Another stereotype shot to hell, Monica thought. He was
obviously good with kids. "Your nieces and nephews are just a
bit younger than my older sister's kids," she said when Serena
was gone. "Bonnie's are thirteen, eleven, and nine, spaced almost exactly two years apart, and all have birthdays in May. I
guess the August heat gets to Jake."

"I guess so," Dan said with a laugh. "Nieces and nephews.

Another thing we have in common." When she looked puzzled, he continued, "In addition to yoga, of course. How did you happen to take this course?"

Monica told Dan about her conversation with her doctor, surprised at how easy it was to be open with him. "So I decided that I have to do something to relax. I saw the ad in the Pennysaver and considered it an omen."

"Your doctor's right. My job's probably as stressful as yours. I am Mr. Troubleshooter. When something goes wrong with the network anywhere in the U.S., I get sent to God knows where, God knows when. So I quickly decided that, if I'm going to work hard, I play hard."

"What do you do when you 'play hard'?" Monica made quoting motions in the air.

"I do whatever appeals to me at the time. I bowl a pretty good game, I play a little tennis—badly I will admit—I love computer games, but I guess that's sort of like a busman's holiday. How about you?" Dan asked. "What do you do to play?"

There was nothing overtly suggestive in the comment so Monica gave it serious thought. She couldn't think of a thing she did just for fun. She saw plays in the city, but those were usually with clients, as were her dinners out. On the weekends she worked. Until her visit with her sister the previous Saturday she hadn't gone out just for the hell of it for months.

"Gotcha," he said. "Work hard, play hard. Give me time, I'll convert you."

Give him time? Did she want to? The conversation was lively, and it was another hour before she noticed that the Pascoes had left, the sun had set, and the lights in the pool house were on. Mosquitoes were out in force and she'd reflexively slapped at a few. She glanced at her watch and was surprised to see that it was after nine. "Listen, it's getting buggy and I've still got work to do." She grabbed her tote and stood.

He stood as well. "This has been nice. Maybe we could do it again sometime. Over dinner?"

"I don't know. I'm really busy in the city most evenings."

"Me, too. Maybe we could meet there or do something one Saturday, after yoga? I love to walk so maybe we could just wander one afternoon. Blue Mountain Reservation is just beautiful this time of year. I'll give you a call."

Startled at his knowledge, she said, "Where did you get my number?"

"Okay," he said with a boyish grin he probably practiced in front of a mirror. "I'll 'fess up. I looked you up in the phone book while I changed into my trunks. Can I call? It's not often I find someone so good to talk to."

"Me, too," she said before she censored her words. "I don't usually let guys pick me up."

"Is that what I did? I thought we had lots in common: the house here, the dogs, the yoga class. We're hardly strangers."

He was so outrageously charming she had to laugh. "Right," she said, but her voice had no edge to it.

"Come on, Monica, don't be such a stickler. Let's see whether this thing we've got has any legs."

"Thing we've got?" He was difficult—no, impossible—to resist. "Okay, sure." She pulled a small card from her tote and scribbled on it. "Here's my cell number. I'm easier to reach this way."

"I'm pretty busy this week so if I don't speak to you before, I'll see you next Saturday. At class."

"Right. See you." She walked down the sidewalk toward her house with a light step. Why not? she wondered. Why was she so reluctant to attempt a lightweight relationship with him? She sighed. It was just that business dating seemed so much easier. Everyone knew the rules. *With Dan I'm not sure there are rules.* That feeling made her extremely uncomfortable.

Although he seemed really nice and genuine, in her experience most men were rotten to the core. She regularly went to bed with guys who were cheating on their wives, and that merely reinforced her negative ideas about the male of the species. She didn't need entanglements, and as she walked back to her house she thought that Dan might become a definite entanglement.

Chapter

9

The Hudsonview Diner had been built in 1968, and remodeled several times since to make it appear lighter and airier. Instead of the tiny railroad-diner-style windows and deep burgundy ersatz leather upholstery that kept the interior dark, now the windows were wide and tall, covered only with vertical blinds. The benches in the booths and the chairs in the dining room were smooth tan vinyl and the tables pale cream. Although the wait staff's slacks were always black, the top part of their uniforms changed yearly, first formal white tuxedo-type shirts with black vests and bow ties, then burgundy or forest green polos, now pink denim-looking short-sleeved oxfords for the women and all black for the men.

The following Saturday, the four women sat in the same booth on one side of the large dining area gazing at menus, with the mid-August sun blazing through the window beside them. "As always, I'm hungry and trying not to think about it." Cait slapped her menu onto the table and used her long fingers to tuck her hair behind her ear. She'd slipped on a pair of lightweight sweatpants over her leotard.

"I've stopped worrying," Eve said, gazing at the list of sandwiches, her cell phone on the table beside her. She was still wearing the cotton knit shorts and well-washed T-shirt she'd worn to yoga.

"Yeah, me too. I took this yoga class to help me control my diet," Cait moaned. "It's not working."

Angie frowned. "Yoga isn't meant to help with your weight, just relax you." Today her T-shirt said, 'Ask me about my twins.'

"Yeah," Cait said, shaking her head, "relax me so much I won't care how much I weigh."

"Don't talk about weight with me around," Eve said softly, looking down at her chubby arms.

"No coffee this week," Monica said, quickly changing the subject. Eve seemed so unhappy about herself and it was a shame. She wasn't a bad-looking woman, but she seemed to take no pride in her looks, did nothing to improve herself. She wore no makeup, her hairstyle was seriously unbecoming and although Monica had only seen her workout clothing, she didn't have particularly good taste in that either. "It took me days to recover from the cup I had last week." Actually it hadn't but it was something she could say that would unite the women, and that had become important to her.

A tall waitress with fluffy brown hair and a bit too much lipstick came over, pad in hand. "What can I get for you, ladies?" She looked at Cait, who sat on the inside, her back to the door.

"Tuna on white toast and a Diet Coke." Cait turned to the others. "I have it on good authority that if you have a sandwich and a diet soda they cancel each other out, calorie-wise."

Monica, who sat across from her, was amazed at how so much seemed to revolve around diets. Cait couldn't have been a pound over her ideal weight, with a perfect figure, long legs, and a slender waist.

The waitress looked at Monica expectantly and she decided to indulge herself also. "Give me a grilled cheese and an order of fries, very well done."

"Don't let me have any of those fries," Cait said.

"And to drink?" the waitress asked.

"Just water will be fine."

Angie, who sat beside Monica, ordered only a diet soda while Eve, seated on the outside, beside Cait, asked for a small salad and a club soda. "I try to watch my weight," Eve lamented, then added with a small smile, "and it's so easy to watch since there's so much of it."

The others laughed and some of the sadness left Eve's eyes.

"I saw you talking to the hunk after class," Angie said to Monica. "I guess we should really call him Dan."

"Really?" Cait said, her head swiveling to stare at Monica. "Got something going on with Mr. Stud?"

Suddenly Monica was embarrassed. Why, she couldn't fathom, but the idea of the others knowing about her talking to Dan made her uncomfortable. It was out of character.

To the three women sitting with her she said, "We met during the week walking dogs and just said hello this morning. It's nothing more than that." Actually, it had been more than that. He'd asked her to dinner that evening. She hadn't given him an answer, rather suggested that he call her at home later.

"Mr. Hunk, uh, Dan, is quite something," Angie said. "I've never been a leg kinda girl before, but he's got great ones. Must play a lot of tennis or run or something."

"Actually," Cait added, with a twinkle, "I'm a big fan of his behind. He's got the most squeezable buns I've ever seen. You could do a lot worse than sharing a bed with those glutes."

"Okay, ladies, enough," Monica said, staring at her napkin. "I'm not going to share a bed with his glutes, or any other part of him. Let's change the subject." She turned to Angie. "How are the babies?" Monica relaxed as the conversation turned to Angie's twins. Why did talking about Dan make her so uncomfortable? Why did Dan make her so uncomfortable? He was just a nice man who'd asked her to dinner. He probably had a girlfriend who was out of town for the weekend. Men. She shook off the storm cloud and turned back to the other women.

By the time their orders arrived they had seen the latest pictures of the twins and heard about their efforts to walk. "It's called cruising and they're just about ready for it."

"Cruising?"

"That's the new term for walking around still holding on. I think Brandon will be first to strike out on his own," Angie said, as the waitress placed dishes and glasses on the table. "MaryLee seems to be content to crawl around and play with her toys. And his."

"A typical woman, and it sounds like a good life to me," Cait said, picking up her sandwich. "Angie, time to make more babies?"

"Bite your tongue. I always wanted a big family, but not all at once. I'd like to wait at least two years before we stop using condoms."

"Condoms? How quaint. Aren't you on the pill?"

"I tried them when Tony and I were first married. I gained twenty pounds and I was nauseous all the time so I stopped." She looked sheepish. "I never learned to put the diaphragm the doctor suggested in right and we think that's where the twins came from. Now, we both take responsibility so it's condoms for us." She hesitated and ducked her head. "I can't believe that I'm talking about birth control with all of you. It's pretty private."

"Funny," Cait said. "We do seem to have gotten beyond private very quickly."

While they ate, they chatted about a juicy piece of society gossip and the persistent drought throughout lower New York State. Sadly, the sporadic summer rains weren't having much effect on the rapidly depleting reservoirs. "If I hear one more politician tell me to shut off my water while I brush my teeth I'll scream," Monica said.

"Short showers and no car washing or lawn watering," Angie said. "Like I have time to wash my car or water my lawn. I think my grass is going to dry up and blow away."

"Like I have any effect on my condo association's sprinklers," Monica said.

After Monica related an incident from work and Eve talked about the following year's shoe styles, Angie said, "Did you hear that the lottery is up to almost two hundred million?" Angie said. "I'm tempted to buy a few tickets."

"Do you know what the odds are against winning it?" Monica said.

"I know, I know," Angie said, chewing quietly, "but I love to think about it."

"It's really not that much money," Monica continued. "If you take a lump sum it's only about one hundred, and after Uncle Sam takes his cut, you only get to keep fifty."

"Fifty million. Mere pocket change," Eve said dryly.

"What would you do with all that cash?" Cait asked Angie.

Angie gazed off into space, contemplating. "What wouldn't I do? I'd get a van with lots of room for the kids, and a bigger house. Tony could stop commuting to the Bronx and stay around here. I'd put a lot of it away for college for the twins, and then I'd get day care for them and go back to college myself."

"Why college?"

"I've always envied people like you, Cait, educated, poised, able to handle everything. I wanted to go after I graduated from high school, but there wasn't enough money so I went to work."

"You envy me," Cait said with a sigh. "I'd love to have your life, kids and all."

"Don't envy my twins. They're wonderful and I love them dearly but they're an incredible amount of work."

"I know that, but I'd love to have them."

"See me some afternoon and I'll give them to you."

"What about you, Eve? What would you do with all that money?"

"I don't know. I'd love to travel but without anyone to travel with, I don't know."

"Would you quit your job?"

"Of course not," she said quickly, then snapped her mouth shut. After a slight pause, she asked, "What about you, Cait? What would you do with the money? You seem to have a lot as it is."

"As you've all gathered, I'd love a baby. Maybe Logan and I could adopt—nah, he'd never go for it. I don't know what more money would change for me. Monica?"

"You know, this seems really silly but I'd love to buy one of those huge RVs and travel around the country. You know, stop where you want, stay where you want, move on when you want. No worries, no responsibilities. That would be my idea of heaven."

"I've always wanted to travel," Eve said, looking dreamy. "For me, it's trains. I've always wanted to go to Europe, get a Eurail pass and go everywhere. I even want to eat and sleep on one. Like the Orient Express."

"No people?" Cait asked.

"Probably not. Just me."

"Speaking of Mr. Hunk," Cait said when there was a lull in the conversation. "Has he asked you out?"

"Were we speaking of Dan?" Should she admit that he'd asked her out? Monica wondered. Somehow this group was becoming important to her, even with all the teasing. She allowed herself to smile. "Yeah. For dinner tonight."

"Fabulous. You're going, of course," Cait said.

"I don't know."

"God, if I weren't married, I'd jump at the chance. Actually, I think I'd jump him."

"What's he like?" Angie asked, sipping her soda.

Monica related all she knew about him, sticking to the facts.

"So he's not married, bright, charming, and as we've all agreed, beautiful," Cait said, taking a bite of her sandwich. "What's the hang-up?"

"I don't know. All the guys I date are work types. Just short-term flings. Nothing important. This feels different, and I don't think I want it."

Eve adjusted her glasses, then reached for Monica's fries. Angie slapped her hand, so, with a grin, she withdrew her fingers. "Feels different how?" Eve asked.

"I don't know. I like things easy, light, where everyone knows that nothing's going to get serious." *And nobody's going to let you down.*

"It's just a dinner, Monica," Cait said, wiping her fingers on her napkin. "He didn't ask to marry you."

"I know, and it sounds silly when I say it but I don't think I'm going to go. Too many possible problems."

"If that's the way you feel, just say no," Eve said. "Call him up and tell him you're not interested."

"Yeah. I guess that's best."

They talked while they finished their food, the conversation often getting back to whether Monica should date Dan or not. Eventually Angie reached beneath her feet for her tote bag. "Much as I'm enjoying this, I think I'd better get going."

"Relax, Angie," Cait said. "Tony can watch the babies for a little while longer. We're just getting started here."

"Started giving Monica a hard time about Dan," Angie said, finding her wallet and putting some money on the table. Then she sighed and rested her elbows on the table. "Anyway, I don't know how much longer I'll be able to meet with you guys like this."

Eve looked crestfallen. "Why? I really enjoy these girls' days out."

"Me too, but weekends are going to become really hectic once school starts."

"School? How come?" Cait asked.

"Tony's been working with his brothers all summer. They're in construction and Tony's been earning some really good money."

"Okay," Cait said. "So?"

"Either Frank or Paul has been able to pick him up so I can have the car during the day. It's hectic getting the babies out, but I can get most of my errands done while he's at work. Once he's back commuting to the Bronx, I'll be carless all week, and there are just so many things to do that I'll need both days to catch up."

"He drives to the South Bronx?" Eve said.

"There's no good public transportation and the neighborhood's not good to walk in. They have a gated parking lot for the teachers so he takes the Ford."

"You only have one car?" Cait seemed incredulous.

Angie slowly nodded. "Yup. I've been angling for a used van but we just can't swing it right now. So, sadly, once Tony's back at work I'll need all the weekend time I can get to do all the things I need to."

"Listen," Cait said. "That's totally out of the question." She tucked an errant strand of hair behind her ear and steepled her fingers. "I'm not willing to give up on our lunches. What do you say, ladies?"

"Not a chance," Monica said.

"No way," Eve said softly, adjusting her glasses on the bridge of her nose.

Cait brightened. "I can't see why I can't drive you wherever you need to go, say one day a week until we figure out this car thing."

"Thanks for the offer, Cait," Angie said, ducking her chin, "but that's not an option."

"Why not?"

"You've never tried to get anything done with two ten-month-olds. It's a nightmare that I can't inflict on you."

Cait sipped her water. "You wouldn't be inflicting it on me. I'm volunteering, so don't make any snap decisions. We have a few weeks to think about it and I know we can work this out. Anyway, I'd love to get to know your twins. In case Logan ever gets me pregnant."

"Is that a possibility?" Monica asked.

"Not with our sex life," Cait said with a toss of her head. "We tried for quite a while and it didn't happen, but lightning might just strike and I want to be ready." She quickly turned to Angie and added, "Look at it as taking on a teaching assignment."

"Cute," Angie said, "but no. Anyway, I've still got a few weeks to meet you guys like this. And Monica, next week you'll have to let us know about your date. We could all use a little vicarious hot sex." She stood up and grinned. "Well, at least I could. Good sex for Tony and me is just a fond memory."

"I can imagine," Monica said.

"Yeah." Angie sighed. "We've barely got the energy for a quickie before one of us falls asleep. This has to get better, right?"

"That's what I gather from my sisters," Monica said. "The first year is the worst, but then they only had one at a time to deal with."

"See you all next week?" Angie said, brightening.

"Of course," Cait and Monica said simultaneously.

Eve stared at the screen of her cell phone, shook her head, then dropped it carefully into her pocket. She glanced at the check and fumbled in her purse for her wallet. "Me, too. I'll be here. Next week, same time, same place."

When the two other women were gone, Cait looked at Monica. "What do you think's up with Eve?"

"What about Eve?"

"She puts that phone beside her plate and glances at it just about every minute. Last week, when it rang, she ran out of here like her ass was on fire. Think it's a guy?"

"Don't jump to conclusions. It might just be she's expecting a call from a friend or some family member."

"Ten bucks says it's a guy. We'll have to find out next week."

"Don't make her crazy pumping her for information. If she wants to keep things private, that's her right."

Cait pulled a few folded bills from her pocket. "It's my right to see what I can find out." She stared at the check and counted the money Eve and Angie had left. She added her money to the stack. "What are you going to do about Dan? He's really too good to just dump."

"I don't know what I'm going to do."

"You know it's not a long-term decision. Maybe you'll have dinner together and discover you two have no chemistry. No bedding potential. Then you can just drop it."

Monica felt her nipples tighten at the thought of Dan in her bed. "Oh, there's chemistry all right. That's not the problem."

"You're overthinking this, Monica. Just go for it. How often do you meet a nice guy with potential?"

Monica sighed. "How often indeed?"

Chapter
10

That afternoon, as Monica was going over a stack of media guides, she found herself debating whether to go out with Dan. When her phone rang she was ready to say yes. "Hello?"

"Hi, Monica, it's Bonnie."

Expecting to hear from Dan, she was surprised to hear her sister. Once she rearranged her brain, she heard the catch in Bonnie's voice. "You sound terrible, sis," she said, suddenly frightened. "Is one of the kids sick?"

"No. Nothing like that." Monica heard her sister start to cry. "Oh, Monica. Jake's leaving me," she said, hiccupping. "He's got a girlfriend."

"He's what?" Monica rubbed her temples. *Here we go again. Just like Mom and Dad. I was just with Bonnie and Jake last weekend and everything seemed so good. It just proves that you never know. It can come like a bolt out of the blue.*

"Calm down, babe. Take a few deep breaths."

She heard Bonnie inhale and let her breath out slowly several times. "I've been worried for the past few months. He's been distant, spending more time at work, you know, all the symptoms. I couldn't believe it. Thursday he called and told me that he had to stay in the city for a late meeting and they'd put him up in a hotel." Monica heard her sister take another deep breath. "He didn't sound right so when he got home from work last evening I asked him. Right out. 'Is there someone else?' I said. He said yes. He's been doing one of the junior attorneys. Carly McDermott. I know her. We've talked at company functions." She broke down again. "How she must have been laughing at me. It's humiliating. She's ten years younger than I am and wears skirts cut up to her thigh." Bonnie was crying again. "She's so good-looking, I don't know, like the district attorneys on *Law and Order.*"

"Calm down." When she thought her sister could go on, Monica said, "So what happened? What did he say?"

"He said he'd been seeing her for almost three months. I carried on like a banshee but I didn't know what to do. I told him he was a shit and he agreed, but he said he loved her and that, since I now knew everything, he was moving out. Into her apartment in the city."

The weeping was almost too much for Monica to bear and she felt her eyes fill. "Oh, sis. I'll be right over."

"No, don't come over," Bonnie said, regaining some of her composure. "I'm taking the kids to Mom's for a few days while I sort some stuff out."

Their mother lived in eastern Pennsylvania in a house easily large enough to hold Bonnie and the three children. "Do the kids know?"

"We told them together a little while ago. Funny, but they weren't as shocked as I thought they'd be. Maybe they're more perceptive than I am. They've all got friends whose parents are divorced so it's not as much of a surprise to them as it is to me."

"Oh, Bonnie, I'm so sorry."

"I know. Me, too. I figure that it will all look better after a few days in the country."

"I'm sure you're right. Is there anything I can do?"

"We can talk at length when I get back but right now I'm

having trouble holding myself together. There is something you can do. Call Janet for me, will you? I can't bear to go through this one more time. I told Mom, then you, and that's all I can deal with. Would you call her for me? Please?"

"Done."

Again crying softly, Bonnie said, "Can I call you in a few days?"

"Of course, sweetie. I'm here for you whenever you need me, whatever you need me to do."

"I love you, sis."

"Back at you."

As she pushed the off switch Monica thought about Jake. He was a nice enough guy but then weren't all men a bit sleazy underneath? Although she had a briefcase full of work, she went to the kitchen and opened a Sam Adams. Drinking the beer directly from the bottle, she quickly dialed her other sister's number, and when Janet answered Monica filled her in on all the details.

"God," Janet said. "That sucks. I always thought of them as the perfect couple."

"Yeah, me too, but it seems that no marriage, no relationship of any kind, is safe nowadays. Every guy cheats and they all lie."

"Not everyone. I know that Walt's all mine."

"Then you're one of the lucky ones. The very few lucky ones."

"Maybe I am but it does make you wonder."

They spent several more minutes talking, then, vowing to support Bonnie in any way she needed, ended the conversation.

When Dan called an hour later, Monica declined his invitation. "Okay," he said, "but be aware that I'll ask again."

"I'm really sorry. I just can't."

A few minutes later, Monica was on the phone again, her voice almost abnormally bright. "Hi, Gerry, I was just confirming our meeting Wednesday." She knew Gerry Petrowski would be in his office on Saturday. A media buyer for a large auto dealer, he was almost as much of a workaholic as she was. Their "meeting" Wednesday was at a hotel in the city for a quick, no-strings evening of drinks and probably sex.

"Sure, hon. I'll see you in the bar at seven. Dinner, drinks, and maybe a little hanky panky."

"I'll bring the panky, you bring the hanky," she said, her voice artificially bright. "Maybe we'll use that hanky for a blindfold."

His rich laugh was warming. Each knew exactly what to expect from the other. "Sounds like a plan to me."

At home a mile away, Dan Crosby sat in his recliner, the phone still in his hand. So Monica had thought better of having dinner with him. He wondered why. They had spent such a delightful time sitting by the pool and talking about everything and nothing. They seemed to enjoy the same things. She told him about her job with the advertising agency, amusing him with anecdotes about her clients.

When he'd mentioned that he was a computer geek, she'd grinned and given him the once-over. He knew he was good to look at. It was difficult not to when women went all silly around him, but she had seemed different, enjoying looking at him but taking a more serious interest in him as a person. As he gave her a brief introduction to the UNIX operating system, her eyes didn't glaze over and she asked a few insightful questions. She wasn't a computer person, but she obviously knew how to use her company's systems and get the most out of them. All in all, a very interesting woman. That morning after yoga class she'd given him all the right come-on vibes, but she'd just turned him down flat. Could he have been that wrong?

He had no idea why he was so hung up on this particular woman but she appealed to him in some indefinable way. She seemed charming, bright, interesting, and he was curious to find out why she was sending such mixed messages. He leaned farther back in his well-worn lounger and pictured Monica, naked on his lap. Sexy? Sure, and that was important to him, but there was more. Well, he told himself, he'd find out why the sudden brush-off and then . . . He wasn't about to give up on her. Not just yet.

Cait spent Saturday afternoon at a Friends of the Library fund-raiser and arrived back at her house a little after four. As usual, Logan was gone, but he'd reached her earlier on her cell and told her that he wasn't going to be home until after six. She quickly logged onto Paul's Place and found that Hotguy344 was also logged in. She wondered whether he did anything but sit on his computer, cruising for willing women, but found she didn't care. Getting her kicks was all she was interested in.

Once she and Hotguy344 were in a private room, she dragged her blouse off and began to caress her breasts.

Hotguy344: You seem to be in a hurry today.

Loverlady214: My husband will be home soon and I want some time with you.

Hotguy344: You're married?

Loverlady214: Yes, but he's not important. Why should you care?

Hotguy344: I just like to think I'm the only one for you.

Loverlady214: I know I'm one of many for you - no problem - just kicks.

Hotguy344: So what time is it where you are? Do we have enough time?

Loverlady214: It's almost five so we have time.

Hotguy344: Oh, then you must be on the east coast of the US or Canada. I'm in Fairbanks Alaska - It's early afternoon here.

Cait relaxed. For a moment she had worried that she'd told him too much, but since he was so far away it didn't matter. Alaska. She'd never been there but she and Logan had talked about taking a cruise on the inland waterway someday. Maybe she'd ask Hotguy a little about it. Another time.

Loverlady214: No wonder you need hot times to keep warm.
Hotguy344: You got it, although now it's really hot here.
Loverlady214: In Fairbanks?
Hotguy344: Yeah. It gets hot here in the summer but that's pretty short.
Loverlady214: Here in NY it's really hot today too.
Hotguy344: So let's heat it up in here.

For the next half hour, she and Hotguy344 played. She climaxed twice, and by the time Logan arrived home and they dressed for dinner, she was totally mellowed out.

In Paramus, New Jersey, less than an hour from Cait's house, Nick Montrose, aka Hotguy344, sat with his fingers on his keyboard. Loverlady214 interested him. Sexually she was open and easy to please, ready for playing in different realms. Just his type. And they were practically neighbors. Maybe he'd find out exactly who and where she was and they could get together for real, husband or no husband.

He spent a good deal of his time on-line. As a night watchman for a trucking company, he had a great many seriously boring hours at work. At forty-two, he was short and stocky, dark complected, with big hands, a thick moustache, and a full, slightly shaggy beard. He'd thought of shaving several times, but the beard fit the Alaskan mountain man persona he wanted to convey.

He'd been playing in chat rooms for several years and occasionally ferreted out personal information about his on-line partners. Several times he'd arranged to meet a woman "up close and personal" and had some "interesting" experiences. A few times things had gotten a bit heavy, but he always made sure that his Alaska identity was intact and that the women never knew his real name or even the state he lived in.

As time passed he'd found getting personal information easier and easier. A carefully phrased question here, an innocuous statement there, and bingo. He knew all he needed to know to use the Internet to find out the rest. It had become ridiculously simple.

Alaska. That was a really great ploy. He'd discovered that women were much freer with information if they thought he was so far away. No danger here, they'd reason. No possibility of being found out, of someone telling her husband, of meeting Hotguy344 in the supermarket. He'd even read up on life in Fairbanks, wandered several Web sites to get the flavor of the place. That business with the temperature was courtesy of weather.com.

Before he'd chosen Fairbanks he'd thought a lot about where to "put himself." He wanted to be about as far away as he could manage but he quickly decided that outside the U.S. wouldn't work. He didn't know enough about Europe or Asia, and anyway, he'd reasoned, the time zones were too different. Fairbanks, however, was just four hours earlier than the East Coast and only an hour earlier than the west.

It had worked like a charm. Two months ago, when he was Superstud1234, he'd visited a willing thirty-year-old single woman in western Pennsylvania. He'd told her he was visiting a relative in the neighborhood and they'd set up a meeting at a local restaurant. As usually happened, she wasn't the thirty-year-old blonde she'd told him she was. Rather, she turned out to be forty if she was a day, with the gray starting to slip into her hair. He wasn't the twenty-five-year-old stud he'd made himself out to be either. He'd warned her that he didn't really look the way he'd described himself in their chat sessions and had been charmingly honest about his age and looks. She'd said that it wouldn't matter. It hadn't.

They'd adjourned to her house right after dinner. She'd said she was interested in bondage and so he'd tied her to the bed, then fucked her over and over for more than three hours. The sight of her soft white body immobilized made him crazy. He'd slapped her around a little, and although she'd asked him to stop he'd known that she really wanted it. He had given her just a few more slaps, watching the red splotches appear on the insides of her thighs, and she'd cried. He'd loved the power that he'd felt at that moment.

He savored the feeling for a while, then he'd untied her and apologized for getting carried away. He'd given her some bullshit about her being so sexy that he'd just lost control. She'd reluctantly forgiven him, but she'd told him she didn't want to see him again. Oh, well. Easy come, easy come. There were so many fish in the sea, or on the 'Net, as it were. Now he was Hotguy344 and he thought Loverlady214 just might be a possibility. She was married, but they could get around that without too much difficulty. She said she was twenty-five but he figured she'd deducted a few years. Or maybe added some. Maybe she was very young and fresh. He'd quickly realized that women usually pretended to be something they weren't. Was she really married? Probably. People were much more honest when they just blurted out information. Well, he'd just see what he could discover about her and maybe . . .

He returned to Paul's Place, and as he watched the list of "who's logged on" he saw that Up4ItAll had just logged in. Ah, Up4ItAll. They had often had fun together. The last time they met, she'd told him her name was Eileen and that she was into rape fantasies. They'd talked for hours about inventive ways he might tie her up and then, when he was really hot, he'd jerked off while she described how powerless she felt. He wanted to picture Loverlady214 tied and at his mercy but he didn't know enough about the way she looked. Convincing her to buy a camera was one of his next tasks, but it would wait. He had lots of patience.

Hotguy344: Hi, Eileen wanna go private?
Up4ItAll: Sure Set it up

Angie and Tony spent the afternoon at his brother's house. Everyone raved about the twins as they played in the small sandbox in Frank's backyard, and they all watched Frank and Linda's three cavort in the small above-ground pool. While the women talked about the kids and made salads and snacks, the men warmed up the grill and chatted about their latest construction project, converting a large, detached garage into a studio apartment.

On the way home Tony mentioned that he might stop in to see Jordanna after they got the twins to bed. "After all," he said quite reasonably, "you'll fall asleep quickly anyway. I want to see how her media room is shaping up."

Be a good sport. "Okay. If you want. I was hoping to have some time just for us."

"We've got the whole day tomorrow," Tony said.

Yeah. With two ten-month-olds. Through slightly gritted teeth, she said, "You're right. Just help me get the babies down, then say hi to Jordanna for me."

Chapter

11

E ve's phone didn't ring until early that evening. She was
stretched out on her bed watching the DVD of *An Affair
to Remember* with a cat curled up against either side of her legs.
She liked to call her bedroom "country casual" with a red,
white, and blue crazy quilt bedspread and cute curtains with
blue and gold stars all over them. The air smelled of the pot-
pourri she kept in small floral dishes around the room.

She pressed the mute button on the TV remote, picked up
the receiver, and stared at the familiar number of Mike's cell
phone.

"Hi," she said. "It's great to hear your voice."

"It's great to hear yours, too," he said, sounding unusually
soft and sexy.

"Mmm," she purred. "You sound all warm and fuzzy. Are
you at home?"

"Diana sent me out to the video store to pick up a film for
us to watch tonight, and for once the kids didn't want to come
along. I'm parked in the lot at the elementary school and I'm
free to talk for a few minutes."

She kicked the cats off the bed and curled up. "That's wonderful. How was your day?"

"Fine. Where are you?"

"Home, silly. You called me here."

He chuckled. "I know that. I meant, are you in your bedroom?"

"I'm on the bed watching a movie. It's Cary Grant—"

"What are you wearing?" he asked, interrupting.

"Wearing?"

"Sure. Are you in your nightgown?"

"I'm wearing shorts and a T-shirt. Why?"

"I want to be able to picture you."

"Why?"

"Stop asking why and just roll with it," he snapped. "I'm sitting here with a raging hard-on and I want to be able to picture you."

"Oh."

He paused, then said softly, "I'm sorry I was a little short with you just now. Since we can't be together next week I thought this might be the next best thing."

"We can't?" she said, realizing that she was sounding like some kind of idiot. *Pull yourself together.* "Oh, right. You're going to be out on the coast all week." In the past he might have taken her along, but this time he was going alone.

"Right. So I got to thinking about us and . . . well . . . I wanted to be with you, if only by phone. Would you do something for me?"

"Sure." *What in heaven's . . . ?*

"Would you take your T-shirt and underwear off so I can picture your beautiful breasts without anything covering them?"

Phone sex. He was doing phone sex. It should have felt a bit sleazy, but as she pulled her shirt off, she realized that her body was responding. "Okay. I took off my shirt and my bra." She had no idea whether she was supposed to be saying anything.

She heard his long, soft sigh. "Yeah. I love your tits. I can see them now, all white and full, with those beautiful nipples."

Her nipples puckered in response to his words. She tried to think of something to say now but she was totally tongue-tied.

"I'm really hot for you right now," Mike said, his voice slightly hoarse. "My cock's very hard. Does my talking like this turn you off? Be honest."

"No," she whispered, realizing it was true. She didn't mind, as long as he was getting pleasure. And she was, too.

"Does it make you hot?"

Should she admit it? "Yes."

"That's great. Why don't you take off the rest of your clothes?"

On the screen Cary Grant and Deborah Kerr were standing at the rail of the ship trying to appear uninvolved, but she knew that the purser had pictures of them together. She heard Mike's heavy breathing and pulled off her shorts and panties. "I did it."

"Are you wet?"

"That's sort of embarrassing, you know."

"Yeah. It's supposed to be. Are you wet? Tell me."

"Yes," she admitted.

"Good. Very good. I'm unzipping my pants and taking my cock out. It's so hard and I can feel the warm air on it. It's extra exciting, knowing that someone might be walking their dog and see me."

"You have to be careful."

"I am, but I'm really horny for you. Would you touch your breasts for me? That way I can dream that they're my hands on you."

Come on, this is silly, she thought as one hand touched her flesh. It was soft and warm. She felt her breathing quicken but she pulled her hand back.

"Touch them like you do when you're alone and hungry."

Masturbation. "I never have." She knew that most women masturbated, but not her. It wasn't something that nice girls did and she didn't know how. She felt humiliated and her enthusiasm for this phone sex thing was waning.

She could hear his gasp. "You've never masturbated? You're such a hot, sexy woman and you're always so aggressive with me that I just assumed."

"Well, you're wrong," she said, feeling tears gather. She wasn't like other women. It was okay when she was pleasing him but doing something just to please herself was wrong. Anyway, there was probably something wrong with her. If only there were a female equivalent of Viagra . . . "I just never did." It wasn't the kind of thing nice girls did. *But I'm not a nice girl*, she told herself. *I'm dating a married man.*

She heard his laugh through the phone. "That's wonderful. Masturbation is so much fun. This can be your first, and I'll be here with you, if only at long distance. You'll love it." She swallowed hard. When she remained silent, he continued, "It's your body and you can touch it if you want to. There's nothing bad about it. Guys do it all the time, and I think most women do, too. Why not you?"

Why not? It just wasn't nice. "I don't know," she said, her voice tiny and shaky.

"There's no reason why not. So are you touching your tits?" Should she admit it? "If you aren't, please do it. For me."

Tentatively, she reached for her breast again. She stroked her flesh, swirling her fingers over the white skin the way Mike did, staying far away from her nipple. That seemed dirty somehow.

"Now pinch your nipple."

She trembled, torn between the need she felt and the shame. "I can't."

His voice got lower and softer. "Of course you can. Think about last week and how you love it when I play with your tits."

A thrill went through her despite herself. "I wish you wouldn't use that word."

"You mean tits? It's a great word. And quite dirty. Would you prefer boobs?"

She huffed out a breath and smiled in spite of herself. "Of course not."

"Okay, so pinch your tits. Do it for me."

She pinched her nipple and gasped as a shard of pleasure darted through her, making her lower lips swell and her juices flow. It was okay. She was doing this for him.

He laughed again. "I can tell from your breathing that you did it. Does it feel good? Admit it."

"Yes," she said softly.

"Great. I'm touching my cock, wrapping my hand around it. It's so hard. Would you slide your fingers between your legs for me?"

No way! "I couldn't."

"Why not? You're excited, wet, hungry, and you know what you want. Why can't you do it for yourself?"

Why not? "I don't know."

"Right. Again, no reason. So do it."

Her hands still trembling, she slid her fingers through her pubic hair and found her wetness. *God, this is so bad, but it's for Mike. And it feels so good.*

"Can you feel your clit? Find it and stroke it while I stroke my cock."

Clit. Cock. Tits. She never used them, but the words were making her hotter and hotter. She needed this, and she let her fingers explore. When she touched her clit, lights exploded in her head.

"Does it feel good?"

She was beyond caring what he thought or what was right. "Yes," she purred. "Oh, yes."

"Good girl. Find what feels the best and do it. My cock is

dripping and I'm getting close to coming. Do you think you can make yourself come?"

She came so easily when Mike stroked her that a few strokes of her own fingers and she knew she was close to orgasm.

"Come on, baby," he purred. "Do it for yourself. Rub your fingers over your beautiful cunt."

"Stop saying those words," she said, panting.

"Why? They make you really hot. I want to get you off."

Her fingers had taken on a life of their own, rubbing faster and faster. Her body shook so hard she could barely hold the phone. Despite her initial reluctance, she was going to come.

"I'm so close," Mike purred, "but I know how to hold off, keep myself on the edge. I'll be able to hear from your breathing when you come, and I know you're close, too. Rub, baby, rub your beautiful pussy. Do you want to stick your fingers in? Prop the phone on the pillow beside your head and stick your fingers inside while you stroke. Trust me, I know just how you like it."

She did as he told her to, pushing two fingers of her other hand into her channel. Then she came, hard, spasms rocking her entire body, a small moan escaping into the phone.

"I can hear you come. Oh, baby, so good," he said, his breath making hoarse sounds through the phone. "I'm going to come . . . right . . . now!"

As her body slowly quieted she heard rustling as Mike settled. "That was fabulous, baby," he said. "And your first time, too. God, that was great."

It was, but she wasn't sure she wanted to admit that to anyone right now so she remained silent.

"This will give us something to do in the evenings while I'm away. I can't wait. Gotta run now. I'll try to call you Monday evening from my hotel."

She didn't know what to say. Part of her was deeply troubled by the feelings he'd awakened, but another part wanted to giggle at how good it felt. She settled for, "Okay. Good night."

"Good night, baby." The line clicked in her ear. When she calmed she noticed that Minnie had climbed back onto the bed and curled against the bare skin of her legs. She'd never noticed the softness of Minnie's fur against her skin before but now it was as if all her nerve endings were super sensitive.

What had just happened to her? She wasn't like that, or hadn't been in almost seventeen years. But even then she hadn't been such a wanton. She heard Mike's words echoing in her head. *It's your body and you can touch it if you want to. There's nothing bad about it.* That made so much sense, but all her upbringing yelled in her ears. *It's bad, dirty, disgusting.* It wasn't. It had felt good. She'd have to think about it. Later. Right now, she just wanted to dream about Mike, who somehow morphed into Cary Grant. She un-muted the TV, and in a haze of sexual fulfillment, watched the man on the screen, her fingers idly playing in her pubic hair.

Chapter

12

"So how did your date with Dan go?" Cait asked the following Saturday, only seconds, it seemed, after they settled into what was becoming their regular booth. "I saw you and him chatting it up before class this morning. Is he as gorgeous in real clothes? Or without them?"

"My date with Dan didn't," Monica said. Part of her regretted that she'd talked about Dan to her friends—yes, she'd started thinking of these three women as her friends in just a few weeks—but she was also glad she had someone to talk to. She'd spent several hours with Bonnie after she got back from her visit to their folks, and more on the phone with Janet. It seemed that the situation between Bonnie and Jake was terminal. "My sister and her husband have split."

"Oh, Monica, that's tough," Angie said, reaching over and grasping her hand. "I'm so sorry."

"Yeah, me too," Eve said, getting her cell phone from her purse and putting it on the table beside her. "I can imagine what the family's going through. Kids?"

"Three, all school-aged. Lissa is taking it hard. She's eleven and hasn't really talked to either Bonnie or Jake since they told the kids last weekend. At nine, Mark seems to have accepted things pretty easily, but Josh, he's thirteen, spends all his time on the computer, and who ever knows what a teenaged boy is thinking anyway?"

"God, that sucks," Cait said. "Is there anything you need?"

Cait seemed to be a fixer. Whenever any of them mentioned a problem, Cait was the first to volunteer to help. Nice woman, if a bit "upper crust." "I'm afraid there's nothing much anyone can do."

"What happened?" Eve asked.

"Jake's had someone else for a few months and finally got around to telling Bonnie. Some bimbo from his office. He's moved into her apartment in the city."

"It won't last," Angie said, sounding knowledgeable. "With twins, I watch a lot of talk shows, and everyone knows that the first partner after a breakup is just a Band-aid and seldom becomes permanent."

"That's comforting, but it doesn't really matter," Monica said, taking no solace from what Angie said.

"Maybe he'll reconsider and come back," Angie continued.

"He's a jerk and she's better off without him."

"Is he really a jerk," Cait asked, "or is that your opinion since you found out about the other woman?"

Startled by Cait's perceptiveness, Monica gave that comment a bit of thought. "If I were being honest I would have to admit that I always really liked him. He seemed steady and solid. So much for my opinion, and that's scary. He's a jerk." She chuckled. "Forget the nice language. He's a shit."

Cait took Monica's hand, and Eve's. "Grab on, Angie. We'll make a pact." When all hands were joined, Cait said, "We all hate Jake."

"And all men are jerks," Monica added.

Angie broke the circle. "I can't agree to that," she said. "Tony's not a jerk."

"Oh?" Monica said, feeling bitchy. "And what about the lovely Jordanna?"

"She's nothing."

"Really?" Monica said, raising an eyebrow. "You've told us very little about her but every time you mention her name your temperature drops a few degrees."

Angie squirmed in her seat. "She's okay."

At that moment the waitress arrived and the four took a few moments to decide on what to order. Eventually the waitress disappeared to get Diet Cokes and order their sandwiches.

Cait leaned forward and rested on her elbows. "Tell us about Jordanna."

"You're really pushy," Angie said. "Maybe I don't want to talk about her."

Cait lowered her head, looking contrite, and said, "Sorry. I do get a bit pushy sometimes but it's just that I care."

Angie let out a long breath. "I know, Cait. Sorry. Jordanna's a sore subject and I don't think I want to talk about her. Let's just leave it that she's okay."

"Fair enough. We don't have to hate her but we do hate Jake. Right?"

"Right," Angie agreed.

"Anyway, not all men are skunks," Cait said. "Logan's a really nice guy."

"He's in real estate?"

"His grandfather founded American Properties and his dad still handles individual houses and new developments. Logan's in charge of the corporate side and they're very, very successful. He's a perfect husband and couldn't be more attentive."

"Oooh. A perfect husband. Methinks the lady doth protest too much," Monica said, still irritated by the idea of "nice" men.

"Don't be bitchy, Monica," Eve said. "There really are some good guys around. I'll bet Dan's one of them."

"Well, I'll never find out. I'm not letting anything get started. It will only end up in the toilet and I'm not ready for that.

What about your boyfriend?" Monica asked Eve, aiming her barbs to hurt the way she was hurting. "Is he one of the good guys?"

"Boyfriend?"

Monica indicated the cell phone beside Eve's hand. "The phone. You gaze at it as if waiting for it to ring. Gotta be a boyfriend."

Phew, Monica's in quite a mood today and these women are much too perceptive, Eve thought as their sandwiches arrived. She wondered whether she wanted to discuss her relationship with Mike. Well, they didn't have to know he was married. That would be all Monica needed to thoroughly validate her opinion of men. Eve blushed, then grinned. "Yeah. He's a good guy. He often calls me on Saturday afternoons just to tell me he loves me."

"Oh, that's sweet," Angie said. "Sometimes Tony will call on his cell like that. It's really great when he does."

"Angie, you seem to have found one of the good ones," Monica said.

"My folks have been married for thirty-three years and are still happy," Angie said. "So are Tony's folks and both his brothers."

"Yeah," Eve said, glad to get the topic of conversation off of Mike. "My folks, too."

"So tell us about the boyfriend," Monica said.

God, Eve thought, *she's obviously not letting the subject drop.* "Okay," she said, resigned to having to give them something. "His name's Mike and he lives on the Island. He's actually my boss."

"On the Island? How often can you see him?"

Every Tuesday afternoon, Eve thought, but she said, "Oh, we get together during the week sometimes."

"No weekends? Is he that far away?"

"He's in Huntington, about an hour and a half by car."

"So why no dates on the weekend," Monica said. "Is he married?"

Eve couldn't control her blush. "Well . . ." She bit into her egg salad sandwich and hoped someone would change the subject. She wasn't that lucky.

"Gotcha," Monica said. "Has he been giving you that 'we stay together for the sake of the kids' routine?"

"That *is* why he and his wife are staying together."

"That's crap. I told you. All men are shits."

"All men aren't shits," Angie said, "and Eve doesn't have to talk about all this unless she wants to. Just because you're in a funk, Monica, that's no reason to pick on her. I don't like the idea of this becoming the Spanish inquisition. I like our lunches and I don't want bad feelings to louse it up. If Eve doesn't want to talk, that's her business."

"The woman has claws. I'm really sorry," Monica said, looking at Eve. "I'm in a lousy mood and I'm taking it out on you." She raised her gaze. "All of you, and I'm sorry." She reached over and squeezed Eve's hand. "Really. No hard feelings?"

"Of course not." Eve made a decision. She had almost no friends and these three women were quickly becoming important to her. She'd been longing for someone to talk to about Mike. She'd once mentioned him to her mother, only to get the third degree about his looks, his net worth, and his marital status—about which she'd lied. None of these women had any chance of ever revealing her secret to anyone who mattered, so maybe she could finally have someone to talk to. "It's all right. I haven't got many friends, except my cats, of course, and I'd really like to talk about him." She stalled a minute as she cleaned her glasses and settled them back on the bridge of her nose. "Monica's right. He's married."

"Ah," Cait said. "Tricky."

"Yeah, that's a good word for it."

"How did it start?" Cait asked.

Eve looked for censure in Cait's eyes and saw nothing but

curiosity. She told her friends—yes, friends—about the business trip that had ended in bed. "That was almost a year ago."

"So how do you manage it? Do you take trips together often?"

"There were a few early on, but recently not as often as we'd like. It just hasn't come up. So mostly now it's lunchtime quickies." She felt herself blushing. "And the occasional phone call."

"Phone call?" Angie said.

"Phone sex?" Cait asked, and Eve nodded.

"Oh. Any future in the relationship? Is he separated, or like that?" Angie asked, reaching out and grasping Eve's hands and gazing into her eyes, a deeply concerned look on her face. "It might work out."

"He keeps saying that he and his wife stay together for the kids and he swears that when the children get old enough . . . He's been saying the same thing for almost a year."

"How old are his kids?"

"They're young but he doesn't talk about them much."

"Where did you say he lives?" Eve could see an angry edge in Monica's eyes. It didn't seem to be directed at her. Rather at Mike. Eve smiled when the picture of Monica appeared in her mind. Lance in hand, she'd walk up to his front door and skewer him. "No, you can't take him on. As I said, he's out on Long Island."

"I'm sorry, Eve," Angie said. "It must be tough. I guess you love him a lot."

Love him a lot? Did she? Talking to these three wonderful women about him, she wondered how much was love and how much was habit and loneliness. She nodded slightly and felt Monica pat her hand. "Well," Eve said, "that certainly put a crimp in my appetite. I always knew Mike would be good for something."

"Listen, sweetie," Monica said. "I'm really sorry for my attitude before and no one's going to judge you here. If he makes you happy, go for it."

Make her happy? Did he? "I don't know whether he makes me happy or not. It just is."

"So be it," Cait said. "So many things in life 'just are.'"

They talked for almost half an hour, then Cait said, "I've got to get going." She got out her wallet. "Monica, be sure to let us all know whether you make the big move with Dan, will you? Those of us who are married need a few vicarious thrills."

"Not happening."

"You know, Monica," Eve said, adjusting her glasses, "sometimes it's worth a little risk. Nothing good in this life comes cheaply. I'm not totally blind and I know Mike might hurt me, but the fun of 'now' is worth the risk."

"I know, but I remember what it was like when my folks split. I was just about Lissa's age and it sucked. I don't want that for my kids."

Cait laughed. "Kids? Dan asked you for a date, not a long-term commitment. You need some good sex to clean out your pipes, you know. Otherwise you start to rust. Eve's getting hers." She winked.

"Don't knock it until you've tried it, Monica," Angie said, "although for me good sex is a fond memory."

"Oh, I get mine," Monica blurted out.

Three heads snapped toward her. "You've got someone you haven't told us about?" Cait said. "So you're playing the single, working, too-pissed-off-at-men-to-bother woman and all the time you've got something going."

"Nothing regular, just the occasional date in town."

"No one special, just casual fucking?"

Monica grinned. "Lots of casual fucking, and that's much simpler than"—she made quoting motions in the air with her fingers—"a relationship."

"For you, maybe," Angie said. "I'll keep my relationship with Tony, thank you."

Cait glanced at her watch. "I've got a meeting that I'm already late for so I've really got to go. Don't tell them anything about your casual sex, Monica," she said, indicating the other two. "Next week you'll tell us all about it together. Okay?"

"She doesn't have to tell us anything," Eve said.

"I know that," Monica said. "But it's really sort of a lark. Anyway, I've got to run, too. I'll tell you everything next week, same time, same diner."

Chapter

13

When Monica arrived back at her car after lunch, she found Dan sitting in a small black convertible parked beside her Lexus. "It's a beautiful day," he said, climbing out of his BMW, "and I thought I'd kidnap you."

He'd asked her out again before class and again she'd politely refused. She'd slipped out quickly afterward to avoid any temptation. "Excuse me?"

"Remember my motto, work hard, play hard. We're going to the zoo." He opened the passenger side door. "Get in."

He terrified her because he tempted her. "I'm not going out on a date with you. I thought I made that clear."

"You did, but this isn't 'a date', it's going to the zoo."

That logic eluded her. "That's *out* as far as I'm concerned."

He got a little-boy sheepish look. "Okay, it's outside, but it's not really out. Not as in date. I want to go to the Bronx Zoo and I want to take you with me. When was the last time you visited the lions, and tigers, and bears, oh my?"

She shook her head in amazement at his gall. "I have work to do, and you're insane." She glanced around and saw Cait strolling toward her Honda. Behind Dan's back, Cait curled her fingers in an OK sign, pulled off her sunglasses, and made an exaggerated wink.

"No, I'm quite sane, and I'm going to the zoo. With you. Get in."

What was she going to do with him? The day was unusually gorgeous for New York in August, an almost painfully blue sky with only a few fluffy clouds, low humidity, and temperatures in the low eighties. She considered all the reasons she should get into her own car and go home: gobs of work, the danger of being with Dan, the need to talk to her sister as she'd done several times during the week.

He'd obviously been home to change out of his yoga sweats and now he looked handsome in white, butt-hugging shorts and a yellow polo shirt. She sighed as she remembered Angie's comments about his great legs. He did have great legs and nice feet. He wore sandals and she noticed his straight toes. *Now I'm looking at feet. What's come over me?*

"I can't go running off at the drop of a hat," she said. Could she?

"Remember what your doctor said. Think of today as medicine."

"I can't just take off. I'd have to shower and change, and make sure Sam has enough food and water." *I guess I can have my nails done tomorrow.*

"Okay, fair enough. I'll follow you home and haunt your driveway until you come out again. Where the zoo's concerned, I'm a very determined man."

She shook her head in exasperation, then resigned herself to spending an afternoon with him. What was the harm? They'd spend a nice afternoon together, relaxing. She'd look at it as part of her doctor's prescription. That would be all. Somewhere, a small voice said, *Why are you deluding yourself? You're very attracted to him, and it's okay.*

He put on a pair of oversized sunglasses and as promised, drove behind her in his little sports car, then pulled up in front of her house. He remained behind the wheel listening to the radio while she took a very quick shower, pulled on a light blue short-sleeved shirt and a pair of lightweight white jeans, and took care of Sam. Fifteen minutes later she locked her door behind herself.

"You're a speedy woman," Dan said, and the brightening of his face warmed her more than she wanted it to. With a shrug, she folded herself into the tiny car.

"I hope you like Ella Fitzgerald," he said as she became aware of the mellow voice coming from the CD player.

"I'm not really familiar with her music," she said, then listened a moment, "but it's nice."

"Nice? I'm a bit of an old-time jazz fan, Ella, Dizzy Gillespie, Count Basie, like that, but there's a box of CDs in the back. Pick something else if this isn't your taste."

"Not at all. I'm enjoying it." She wasn't just saying it, she thought. It really was nice, and a change from the country music station she usually listened to.

As they drove south on Route 9, the wind made conversation impossible. Her hair would be a disaster, she thought, but the feel of the warm air on her face was sensual. She hadn't been in a convertible since Harry Polito took her for a drive in his father's car when she was in high school. She counted. That was fifteen years ago. *One of these days, when I fly somewhere warm, I'll have to rent one. It's a gas.*

Half an hour later they turned off the Bronx River Parkway and parked in the zoo's lot. Dan got out, came around, and opened the door for her. Nice manners, she thought. He offered her his hand, and since she couldn't gracefully get out of the low-slung vehicle without help, she took it. "That's a good girl," he said. "Now," he added as they strolled toward the zoo entrance, "why the sudden about-face last weekend?"

He'd obviously realized that she had been about to agree to go out with him and then abruptly changed her mind. "I just had other things to do."

He shook his head. "Wrong answer. If you tell me you don't want to discuss it, that's okay, but please, don't lie to me. We'd all but made plans, and then when I called your voice sounded like it had been frozen. My ear was frostbitten by the time I hung up."

She had to laugh at the picture he painted. "It wasn't that bad."

"Was too," he said, whining like a five-year-old.

"Was not," she said, now laughing. "Okay, I guess it was. I was just down. I'd gotten some bad news."

Dan's face was suddenly serious and they stopped walking. "I'm so sorry. I didn't mean to pry."

She sighed, resigned to telling him. "My sister's husband has decamped."

His concern looked genuine. "Kids?"

"Yeah. She's the one with kids of similar ages to your sister's."

"Shit. That sucks." He was silent for a moment, then said, "I'm just picturing how I'd feel if Sarah's husband did that. God, it's like a shot in the gut. No wonder you were swearing off men."

She was surprised at how immediately perceptive he was. She nodded ruefully. "I might ask you, why the persistence?"

She watched his shoulders rise and fall. "I don't really know. While we were sitting by the pool that evening I felt something I'm not used to with women. Friendship."

She wanted to be insulted. He should feel lust. But as the thought echoed through her brain with lightning speed, she realized that friendship was a good thing. That was what she felt with Cait, Angie, and Eve, and it warmed her. "Friendship," she whispered.

"Oh, that's not to say I didn't want to throw you down on a lawn chair and have my wicked way with you." As she spoke, he mimed twirling a long moustache like the villain in an old silent film.

She couldn't help it. She burst out laughing. He was charming, impossible, delightful, and difficult. Yes, difficult. And very,

very dangerous. She turned her face up to the heat of the sun, then looked at him. "I think the lions and tigers and bears, oh my, are waiting for us."

They spent several hours wandering through the various exhibits. As they walked out of one, she said, "I haven't been in the House of Darkness since elementary school. It's terrific."

"I know. I bring my nieces and nephews here. The boys and the younger girls love it, the older girls think it's yucky." His voice squeaked, "Ooooh, bats," then returned to its normal deep timber. "I've no idea where those yucky feelings come from but then I've no idea where anything teenaged girls do comes from. They are a complete mystery."

"None of my nieces are teenagers quite yet, but Josh, he's thirteen, isn't taking my sister's separation well at all. According to her he's sullen and almost completely uncommunicative. Lissa is only eleven but she's mastered the 'harrumph' that says, 'Mother, you just don't get anything.' I think she blames Bonnie for the split." As she spoke, Monica realized that she was able to discuss Bonnie's troubles with Dan without the immediate pain it usually caused.

He chuckled. "I know just the female teen attitude. Sadly, it will only get worse."

"I was never like that," Monica said. "I was the perfect child."

"Like hell."

She dropped onto a bench in the shade. "Why do you say that?" she asked, puzzled.

He sat beside her. "You were brighter than most of your schoolmates and probably bored to tears—"

She had been just that.

"—so you probably went away." When she started to defend herself, he said, "Oh, not in the physical sense. You just stared out the window and paid no attention to what the teacher was saying."

"That's true." She smiled at the memory. "Mr. Fishbein, in seventh grade science, kept trying to catch me daydreaming, but somehow my brain was recording everything he said, even though my conscious mind was elsewhere. He'd snap a question at me. 'Ms. Beaumont, what's the answer?' giving me no clue as to the question. I found that I could merely rewind the tape and give him the answer he wanted. The kids all laughed and gave me the thumbs up. When I'd done that three or four times, he gave up."

"I knew it."

"How?"

He smiled ruefully. "Because I was like that, too. School drove me to distraction, not because I wanted to go out and play sports, but because, after a week, I knew what the teacher was going to say before he or she said it. That was until I got to MIT. The inner workings of computers fascinated me. I'd read everything I could get my hands on in high school and built my own desktop when I was fifteen. Then I programmed my own browser to surf the 'Net. It was better than anything out there then, but the Web was much smaller, too."

"I'm impressed."

"Don't be. It's just the way my mind works. Anyway, I tested out of a few of the basic classes and finally got to something both fascinating and challenging. I've been fascinated and challenged ever since." He stood. "End of life story. Let's find the seals."

The rest of the afternoon sped by, and by the time they returned to Dan's car she was footsore and filled with hot dogs and slices of pizza. "So, now that I've bought you dinner," he said, starting the engine, "can I have my wicked way with you?" He had bought the junk food after a short argument about who would pay. Finally she'd relented and allowed him to spend fifteen dollars on "dinner."

He was nuts, and she wasn't ready for anything more serious than an afternoon at the zoo. "I'm really sorry but that will have to wait." Why had she put it that way, implying that something would happen in the future? "I didn't mean it that way."

His laugh was unrestrained, rich and full, and she found she loved the sound of it. "Don't fumble over words. I, for one, had a delightful afternoon and I want to spend more time with you, no strings."

"I hate to admit it, but I had a great time, too. But I have a briefcase full of work waiting for me and I really do have to get home." She wanted to see him again. "Maybe another evening?"

He suddenly looked sad. "I have to admit that I had an ulterior motive for kidnapping you today. I'm leaving for San Francisco tomorrow morning and I won't be back until Friday. I didn't want to wait another week to have our first date."

"You said this wasn't a date."

He looked sheepish. "I lied."

"I knew you couldn't be trusted," she said with a twinkle.

"You were right. How about next Saturday evening? Dinner? Our first real, planned-beforehand, getting-dressed-up date?"

Oh, what the hell. "I'd love to."

"Logan," Cait said the following Monday evening, "I'd love to get a camera-phone thing for my computer. You know, the kind where I could talk to your mother or my sister-in-law. I could keep up with the kids and stuff. Mary already has one," she said, referring to her brother Fred's wife, "and so does your mom. Mary says it's great. Like being there. With her new baby on the way . . ." *Calm down and don't talk too much*, Cait told herself. *Don't sound as if it's too important. Just a lark.* The previous evening Hotguy344 had again suggested what fun it would be if they could see each other. When she'd asked, he'd assured her that they'd just log on with screen names and remain as anonymous as they'd always been. "I understand your fears—I've got them, too. No problem."

Just the thought of seeing him, watching him jerk off, made her hot. She took a deep breath and tried not to fidget.

Luckily Logan, as usual, was so preoccupied with the contracts he was reading that he didn't have the foggiest idea of what was going on. "Sounds interesting," Logan said, looking up, "but do you know anything about hooking it up? A guy at work mentioned that he has one so he can talk to his brother in Chicago, but he said it was a bitch to get it working the first time."

"No, I don't know a thing. Maybe I'll do a little research and talk to someone in the computer store. I know your family would get a kick out of it."

"Sounds fine to me, but I'm afraid you can't count on me to help. I probably wouldn't be able to figure it out anyway, but in addition I'm going to have trouble getting home at a decent hour over the next few weeks. I've got a big deal cooking with a brokerage firm. They might take over an entire building in White Plains."

As Logan babbled on about his "big deal," Cait tuned him out. A camera would add such a delicious new dimension to her chats with Hotguy.

By Friday she had bought what she needed, installed the hard- and software, and had had a picture conversation with Mary and her kids. It really was as simple as the guy who'd set it up for her said it would be. She'd just signed on, and with a few mouse clicks she'd been talking to Logan's sister, and watching as her kids played behind her. She'd called her mother-in-law and they'd marveled at the advances in technology. His mother regaled her with stories about old, five-digit phone numbers, operators, and party lines until Cait was ready to scream.

She wanted to tell Hotguy that she'd gotten the camera and

let him know that she didn't look exactly like the person she'd portrayed in their chats, but she was afraid Logan might arrive home unexpectedly. If he walked in on her while she and Hotguy were chatting the old way, it only took a mouse click to shut him down, and she'd just tell Logan that she was too hot for a robe. Now, when she planned to dress in her sexiest undies and perform for the camera, it would be a lot more difficult to bail out quickly.

Logan finally called to tell her he'd be late again, and when she told him about the camera and her conversation with his mother he'd been thrilled. Anything to keep his parents happy. He informed her that he wouldn't be home until at least nine and she tried not to show how delighted she was. After a few last pleasantries, she hung up, changed into her sexiest lingerie, just in case, and logged into Paul's Place. She was bitterly disappointed to see that Hotguy344 wasn't logged on.

As she sat staring at the list of chatters, Cait wondered how things with Logan had deteriorated so much that she looked forward to the evenings when he didn't come home. She thought about Monica's sister. Was Logan fooling around? At this point in her dismal marriage she found she didn't really care. No, she thought as she watched conversations scroll down her screen, she did care, but not as a wife might care that she was being cheated on, just as a friend who cared about her husband and wondered what was going on. Friends. That's kind of what she and Logan had become.

Early in their marriage Cait had hoped to become pregnant and fill her life with children, but although she and Logan made love frequently, it didn't happen. At first, each month she was bitterly disappointed when she got her period, and when she was a day late, she secretly rejoiced, only to be let down again. They let it slide for several years, then they decided to find out why she hadn't conceived. They were tested, invaded, poked, and prodded, but the doctors could find nothing physically wrong with either of them. Although they then tried several courses of fertility treatments, everyone, including both her family and Logan's, had eventually adjusted to the fact that they weren't going to produce grandchildren and had stopped asking about it. Thank God.

Logan, however, had remained determined until about six months before, when the whole baby thing had finally come to a head. For what seemed like the dozenth time that week, Logan had moaned about not being able to give his father a grandchild, specifically a male one. "Neither of my sisters has produced a boy and I had so hoped to give my dad his first grandson." He glared at Cait as though it were her fault, and there was a hint of desperation in his voice. "Maybe there's another doctor."

"No more doctors, Logan!" Cait snapped, finally done with the whole thing. "I've had enough." She stood and paced as she ranted. "No more thermometers. No more hormones." She'd come to terms with it all, and wished Logan would just leave her alone. "No more having mandatory, strange-position sex when the 'time is right.'" She made quote marks in the air with her fingers. "No more. Can't we just have normal sex for a change?" Strange-position sex. Several months before Logan had told her that they might have better luck with her on her knees and Logan behind. She didn't mind the position per se, but since foreplay had become almost nonexistent and in this new position Logan hardly touched her during sex, he had to use lots of lubricant. It had all become messy and impersonal. It wasn't lovemaking, it was procreation, and they didn't even have that unless it was her time to conceive. Sex with Logan had become a chore, not a pleasure.

After an hour of fighting, weeping, and cajoling, Logan finally agreed that conception would be put on hold. Since then, despite what she'd told her yoga friends, she'd been happy that there had been no sex at all for her. Except on-line.

When Hotguy344 finally logged on it was almost eight-thirty. When they were in private, she said:

Loverlady214: I got my camera.

Hotguy344: That's great. I can't wait to see you.

Loverlady214: Me too. I won't look exactly the way I described myself.

Hotguy344: <laughing> Me too. I'm older and not so good looking.

Loverlady214: I'm laughing too. I'm a bit older and I'm a redhead, not a 'raven haired' temptress.

Hotguy344: Hair color be damned. You are a temptress.

Loverlady214: Can you tell me how to make this thing work in the chat room?

Hotguy344: I can't right now - I'm logged on at work and I haven't got a camera here. I don't have much privacy either.

Loverlady214: You're working? I thought you worked nights.

Hotguy344: It's late afternoon here and anyway sometimes I pick up overtime by taking someone else's shift. Can we arrange a time to meet tomorrow?

Loverlady214: Sure. That's probably better. My husband will be home in a half hour anyway.

Hotguy344: That will give us a little time anyway. What's your real name? Calling you Loverlady, especially once I can see you, is too impersonal.

Cait wondered whether it would be a good idea to give him her name but then decided to stop worrying about every little thing. What could it hurt?

Loverlady214: Cait. It's short for Caitlin.

Hotguy344: Mine's Brett.

Loverlady214: Nice to meet you, Brett.

Hotguy344: Nice to meet you, Cait.

Nick Montrose sat in the small booth at the gate of the trucking company where he worked, staring at the screen of his laptop. He had told her part of the truth. He did pick up extra shifts from time to time. He'd almost slipped about the time difference but he'd covered all that quite nicely, if he did say so himself.

Cait. Interesting name. *I need your last name and the city where you live.* He couldn't wait until he could see her and see everything around her, too. He'd know whatever he needed to know very soon. He continued typing.

Hotguy344: Cait what?
Loverlady214: I don't think I'm comfortable giving you my
  last name.
Hotguy344: You're right, of course. Well, mine's Sullivan if
  you care.

He'd used the name Brett Sullivan before.

Loverlady214: You sound like you're pouting. Of course I care.
Hotguy344: <smiling> I know you do. Sorry.
Loverlady214: It's Johnson.

Gotcha. One more piece of the puzzle. Hungry, lonely women were pretty easy to manipulate. Nick smiled. Time to change the subject before she got too curious about why he wanted to know her name. *Maybe I can fog her mind a little. This might be a good moment to get into something a bit more kinky.*

Hotguy344: Have you ever been submissive during sex?
Loverlady214: No, Logan's not much for creativity.

Logan? Logan Johnson. Her husband. More and more in-formation. *Don't press it for tonight.* And maybe the 214 was her address. Or her birthday. Most people used one or the other as the number after their screen name. Patience, Nick. It would all happen in good time.

> Hotguy344: Well, what if you were tied to the chair you're sitting on. Let's pretend that your wrists and ankles are tied, but you have a voice system that allows you to communicate with me.
> Loverlady214: Sounds kinky.
> Hotguy344: And what's wrong with that? Does it excite you?

There was a pause, then she typed:

> Loverlady214: Yes

He had her. First times with him in the dominant role were especially exciting. He'd watch her initial enjoyment of being under his control. He felt his cock grow. A shame he couldn't take it out and jerk off but he never knew when a trucker would need something more from him than just waving, entering the code numbers in the log book, and opening the locked electronic gate. He put his small computer on his lap so he could feel its warmth and press the plastic against his hard-on. He might just be able to come that way.

> Hotguy344: If you were restrained I could touch you whenever I wanted - I could pinch your nipples, finger your snatch.

He'd never talked quite this dirty with Loverlady214 before but he sensed she'd be up for it.

> Loverlady214: I guess you could.
> Hotguy344: I think, right now, I'll fill your sweet pussy with my fingers - I know you'd love that - you'd love the power-

less feeling - I can do what I want and you can't do anything about it.

Loverlady214: <breathing heavy> No, I guess I couldn't.

God, she was fabulously responsive. Some women he'd tried this with had been turned off. A few just logged off and he never got to chat with them again. But Cait—he loved knowing her real name—seemed to be enjoying it.

Hotguy344: I'm sucking on your nipples and fucking your cunt with my fingers - Feel good?

Loverlady214: Oh yes. I can feel what you're doing. I'm trying to use my hands but I can't.

Hotguy344: Wonderful. My cock is getting so hard. I'm going to take it out and make you suck it - Open your mouth.

He almost typed "Open your mouth, bitch," but he stopped himself. Not too far. Not yet. Cock, cunt, pussy. That was enough for tonight.

Hotguy344: Now suck me off.

Loverlady214: I'm so hot - this talk makes me really excited.

Hotguy344: Do yourself while I fuck your mouth.

He paused, both for effect and to log in another eighteen-wheeler.

Hotguy344: I'm going to come in your mouth.

Loverlady214: Going to come too.

Hotguy344: Right now!!!!!!!!!!!!!!!

Loverlady214: And me!!!!!!!!!!!

He waited for several moments, knowing she'd think he was too far gone to type. Actually he'd pressed the heel of his hand into his erection so hard he had cooled himself off. Finally he put his hands back on the keyboard.

Hotguy344: I'll see you tomorrow. I mean really see you.
Loverlady214: Damn!!!!!!! I forgot. I can't do it tomorrow. Hubby and I are going away until Labor Day weekend. Do you celebrate Labor Day up there?

Where did she think Alaska was, the moon?

Hotguy344: <really sad> We celebrate here too. Two weeks?
Loverlady214: Yeah. It sucks but I have no choice.
Hotguy344: You got me all hopeful. I can't wait to actually see you but I guess I'll have to.
Loverlady214: Maybe waiting will make it better.
Hotguy344: I'll log in as often as I can on Labor Day weekend, looking for you.
Loverlady214: We'll be back that Sunday and I'll log on as soon as I get some privacy. Then you'll tell me how to get this camera thing working and we'll do it.
Hotguy344: We'll do it all right <lol>

Soon, they both logged off and Nick stood up to adjust his underwear. Shit. He'd have to wait for two weeks. Oh, well. He was patient, especially with such a delicious reward on the horizon. Eventually he'd know enough about Mrs. Logan Johnson of Somewhere, New York.

He couldn't wait to see her. Of course, she might turn out to be a dog and he could let go of the idea of meeting her in person. Maybe not.

Chapter

14

Although it was mid-August, the weather in East Hudson, New York was dismal, cool and gray, and threatening to rain as the four women took the same seats they always took in their booth at the diner. Eve slid in beside Cait, and after Monica wiggled over to the window, Angie settled beside her. They caught up on the now almost eleven-month-old babies, both able to walk, holding on, where they wanted to go. "They're not quite ready to strike out on their own yet. Brandon's always been the adventurous one so I think he'll be toddling before MaryLee. I don't know why I can't wait, since I know once they're totally mobile everything will get totally chaotic."

Cait looked at Monica. "How's your sister Bonnie?"

"She's still staying at my mother's and adjusting, slowly. Jake called her during the week trying to arrange to see the kids but setting things up will take a few weeks. Right now, the kids don't want to see him."

"That's so sad. The children are always put in the middle," Eve said.

"I told Bonnie not to ask them to take sides. They should see their father and try to make the best of everything."

"You're so right," Eve said. "That's the best way to handle it."

They placed their orders, sandwiches and diet sodas for Cait and Monica, a salad for Eve, and just a cup of tea for Angie. "It's so yucky out that it seems like hot drink weather, but no diner coffee." They all laughed as they always did. The coffee in the diner really wasn't as bad as they made out, but it had become a running joke.

While waiting for their food, they revisited a television show that had taken a strange turn the previous evening. When the conversation slackened for a moment, Cait said, "I'm really going to miss you guys but I won't be here the next two weeks. Logan, his folks, and I are going to Paris. Actually we're leaving tonight and coming back the Sunday of Labor Day weekend."

"Paris!" Eve said. "You're so lucky. You'll have to tell us all about it."

"I've been meaning to tell you that I can't make it next week either," Angie said. "I've got to dash right after class. Tony's folks are having a big barbecue, and getting the kids and Tony organized is a major project."

"I've got a problem with Labor Day weekend," Eve said. "My company's closed the week before Labor Day and I've got plans to visit my family back in St. Louis. I'll be back that Monday afternoon."

For several minutes they pumped Cait about her trip and discussed all the places they'd heard about and always wanted to see. Finally their food arrived. "We'll miss you, Cait," Monica said, "and I'll miss our foursome. I don't know about all of you"—she ducked her chin with a bit of embarrassment— "but I've really come to enjoy our little bull sessions. Our—" —she put on a thick British accent—"ladies' luncheon." The other women giggled.

"Well," Cait said, still smiling, "I propose that we meet at

Huckleberry's on the Monday evening of Labor Day weekend. I think we all deserve a 'girls' night out.' I know I will after spending two weeks with my in-laws. Neither Monica nor Eve will be working that day so . . . could you all make it?"

Huckleberry's was a local watering hole with a restaurant at one end and a sports bar at the other. "I should be able to be there," Eve said. "Girls' night out. Sounds too good to pass up."

"Me, too," Monica said, "and Angie, even if you have to bring the twins, you're going to be there."

Angie grinned and raised her hand to her forehead in a military-style salute. "Yes, ma'am. Actually, I think Tony will be able to watch them."

"Think?" Monica said.

"Okay. Tony will watch the babies."

"Great," Cait said. "Okay, now down to business. We've waited long enough. Monica, tell us about Dan. I saw you two standing beside that cute little BMW Dan drives after our lunch last week. Did you two finally do the deed?"

"If by do the deed you mean sex, of course not. We did, however, spend a great afternoon at the zoo."

"The zoo?" the three women said in unison.

Monica smiled as she remembered. "It was all totally unexpected. He waylaid me as I went to pick up my car, and kidnapped me. We had a really nice time."

"A really nice time," Cait snorted. "What a wimpy comment. Come on, 'fess up. We all know that he's quite a hunk. Is he a jerk?"

"Surprisingly, no. He's a really easy guy to spend time with." She told them about their afternoon, his family, his interest in jazz. "I actually went out and bought a few CDs. Ella Fitzgerald, Duke Ellington. It's really good stuff."

Cait looked at Eve and Angie. "That's it. She's gone. Buying CDs of his music is just the first step but we all know

where this is leading." She raised her glass. "To those first delicious, tentative steps." Eve and Angie clinked their glasses
against Cait's while Monica's face reddened slightly.

Monica didn't mind the teasing, but she wasn't sure about
how to react to what Cait had said. Had she taken some kind
of first step? When Dan hadn't been in class that morning, her
disappointment was much greater than she'd expected. He'd
warned her, of course, when they'd talked from his hotel late
the previous Wednesday evening. "They've set me up with a
meeting Friday morning so I'll probably miss my flight and
have to red-eye back Friday night."

"Do you want to call off our dinner Saturday?"

"Not at all. I'm not letting you get cold feet and decide
again that you're too busy or something else silly. I sleep
pretty well on planes and I'll catch a nap Saturday afternoon, if
I have to. I shouldn't be too much of a basket case."

Monica returned to the present and looked at her three
friends. "Dan's an unexpectedly comfortable man. I'm going
to take it one day at a time and that's that."

The women spent the next hour talking about matters as
diverse as the weather, the president's current tax proposal,
and the most recent developments in a sensational celebrity
trial. Monica had never been much interested in TV shows or
movies, but since Angie was a walking celebrity news bureau
and Eve was heavily into old movies, she now paid attention
to the entertainment news on TV so she could talk knowl-
edgeably. When the time came for them to separate, the four
women exchanged hugs and assured each other that they
would meet at Huck's two weeks hence.

The first Monday in September, at exactly seven, Monica,
Angie, Cait, and Eve met in the parking lot of Huckleberry's,
a freestanding family restaurant in the heart of East Hudson.
Although Monica hadn't been to the place often, she drove by

it several times a week and had watched it evolve through its multiple ownerships.

The building had originally been built about ten years earlier to house Gringos, a Mexican restaurant. Lots of people dined there at first since TexMex food was then a novelty. Sadly for the owners, the menu was limited and the food mediocre. Gringos died within a year. Tokyo Nights, a Japanese sushi bar, never caught on and hadn't made it a full year. The building was renovated again, and Kansas City, a steak house with delusions of grandeur, opened with great fanfare but mixed reviews in the local paper. They had a steady flow of customers but not enough to grow beyond local notice, and the Sunday brunch was overpriced and didn't start until noon, long after the churchgoers were home and already fed. After the broiler in the kitchen caught fire and much of the back of the restaurant was destroyed, the building had stood empty for six months.

Then Huckleberry's Family Fare had arrived with good, uncomplicated food at reasonable prices. To lure families, the owners had redecorated the dining room, recovering the seats in the booths and the chairs in bright colors, painting the walls pale beige, adding large windows and a patio with outside tables. They had crayons and coloring books for the kids and even a small play area with a TV that played a continuous loop of cartoons. The menu consisted of almost a dozen different kinds of burgers, along with the standard, home-cooking fare that families with kids and small budgets would enjoy. They turned the far side into a sports bar with several big-screen TVs and a slightly rowdy crowd on weekend evenings. Once Monday Night Football began, Monica realized, the joint would be jumping.

Although it was toward the end of the normal dinner hour, the place was still crowded, noisy with the sounds of children playing and the TV from the bar showing some sporting event. The four women were shown to a booth at the far end of the room, and they took seats in the exact same positions they always took at the diner, Cait and Monica on the inside, Eve beside Cait and Angie beside Monica. The hostess handed them each a menu, then disappeared. "One thing I've always appreciated about this place," Monica said, "is the height of the sides of the booths."

"I never noticed," Eve said, "but you're right. They're so tall that you feel kind of private and don't hear the noise as much."

"That way we can talk about anything and not be over-heard," Cait said, making an exaggeratedly wicked face, "and we've got a lot to talk about. After all, it's been two whole weeks."

"You're up first," Monica said to Cait. "Tell us about your trip."

As she took a breath, their waitress arrived dressed in the Huck's uniform, a man-tailored shirt in a hot color—hers was kelly green—and black jeans. Cait looked up and said quickly, "I want a margarita."

"We can make it plain, strawberry, or the house special, with Cointreau and a touch of Grand Marnier."

"I'll have the house special, frozen, with salt."

"That sounds too good to pass up," Monica said. "Make it two."

Eve thought a moment, then said, "Okay, three."

Angie said, "I really shouldn't." A grin split her face. "What the hell? Make it four."

"And add a plate of your house special nachos," Monica said. The waitress made a note on her pad, then disappeared.

"You're mean," Angie said with a grin. "Those nachos are probably four thousand calories."

With an exaggerated wink, Monica said, "Yeah, ain't I terrible?"

Eve turned to Monica. "Before we interrogate Cait about her trip, how's your sister?"

"She's holding her own. Jake's living with his bimbo." Monica tried to look abashed but failed. "Sorry, she's probably not a bimbo but it's difficult to think good thoughts about a woman who dates a married man." Monica's eyes snapped to Eve who was looking embarrassed. How could she be so stupid? Eve was such a lovely soul and she'd just rubbed her face in her lifestyle. Dumb, dumb, dumb. To cover her blunder, Monica quickly said, "Okay, Cait, you're up. Tell us all about Paris."

For several minutes Cait told them about her trip. She was a gifted speaker, bringing life to the Eiffel tower, the Louvre, and the many fabulous restaurants the family had visited. She regaled them at length with stories of their drives through wine country and a trip to Versailles.

"It sounds like you had a great time," Angie said. "I envy you."

Cait huffed out a breath and her shoulders dropped. "Don't," Cait said, her voice low, her comment surprising everyone. "It was a lousy trip."

"Why?" Eve said. Monica saw that Eve was back to her usual self, with seemingly no hangover from her insensitive remark about dating married men. "You make France sound so beautiful."

Monica watched Cait's face cloud. "Oh, don't get me wrong, Paris was fabulous and the countryside was magnificent. It's the rest."

She looked like she was going to cry, so Monica reached across the table and took her hand. "Hey, Cait. We don't mean to make you unhappy. This is girls' night out, fun and games. We're here if you want to talk, but if not, we'll understand, too."

"It's the same old thing. I had hoped that while we traveled Logan would come back."

"Back? From where?"

Cait took a deep breath. "I haven't wanted to talk about it because it makes it more real somehow, but he's not with me anymore." The others remained silent, allowing Cait to talk at her own pace. "It's as though he's somewhere else, always deep in thought. Oh, he answers questions, talks about things, but there's a curtain between us. It's all muffled. I don't know quite how to explain it." The three women took Cait's hands across the table. "I'm worried that he's seeing someone else and that my marriage is over." The hands squeezed. "And I'm even more worried because I'm not sure I care anymore. Oh, I'd miss his company and his friendship, but the rest? It's like there's no love left.

"I'd hoped that while we were away from the business and in a new environment things would improve, but it was worse somehow. His parents talked, mostly to each other, and we were pretty much silent. Nothing."

"Oh, Cait, I'm so sorry," Angie said, and the others nodded.

"Is there anything we can do to help?" Eve asked.

"Having friends like you is all the help I need right now." She swallowed hard and blinked several times.

At that moment the waitress arrived with their drinks in oversized martini glasses, thick and frosty, with coarse salt covering the rims and thick straws poking up from the pale green-gold slush. She also put down a gigantic plate of chips covered with salsa, olives, beans, sour cream, and guacamole, and a few things Monica wasn't quite sure of.

"You ladies," Cait said when the waitress left the table, "and this"—she sipped her drink—"will help a lot."

The women took a moment to suck in the liquid through the straws. "Shit!" Eve said, wincing and holding her forehead. "Brain freeze!"

"God, I hate that," Cait said, seemingly glad to change the topic. They waited until Eve had recovered her breath. "So,

Monica," Cait said, taking a chip and scooping up some of the nacho goodies, "how are things going with Dan?"

Monica's face softened and she grabbed a chip. "Things with Dan are really wonderful. We've been out half a dozen times and he's still as nice as I thought he was after our first day at the zoo. It's surprising the hell out of me."

She flashed back to their first real date, three weeks before. He called that afternoon after he got home and suggested several places he thought she might enjoy, including a Japanese steak house, a good Spanish tapas bar, and a French restaurant, all in the city.

"Everything you've suggested means going all the way down to New York. There are lots of great places up here and we both commute all week. Maybe we should just relax and stay up here." She usually let her date pick the place to eat but with Dan she felt like an active partner.

They talked about several places and then the conversation wandered off into other topics. When she mentioned that she'd bought a few CDs and grown to like Duke Ellington and Count Basie, Dan suggested a small jazz club in White Plains. "It's got different groups each month, some good, some average. I don't know who they've booked for this weekend but we could give it a try. The food's pretty good and if the music sucks we can leave."

"Sounds great. I think we've got a plan."

Unlike her usual self, Monica spent quite a while debating what to wear, and finally selected a pair of slender tan linen slacks, and a tan and teal striped summer sweater with a matching cardigan in case it got chilly. As the hour Dan was to pick her up approached, she found that her heart was pounding and her palms were sweating.

She heard his car pull into the driveway and to get past the "meet at the door" moment, she walked out to meet him. He looked really good in khaki linen slacks, a cocoa brown polo

shirt, and dark sunglasses. She was surprised that he'd arrived
at her house with the top up on his little car. When she ques-
tioned him, he said, "I can put it down if you like, but I
thought you might worry about your hair." *God, he's quite something,* she thought. It would be easier if he had some flaws.
Would perfection gnaw at her after a while? "Anyway, it's difficult to talk with the top down."

They left it up. On the way to the club, they talked about
everything and nothing. The conversation never faltered,
each anxious to add something or relate an anecdote. When he
mentioned a film he'd seen recently, she felt totally comfortable telling him that she'd hated it. They debated and then
agreed to disagree. After half an hour, she was almost disappointed when he easily maneuvered his car into a small parking place in the heart of White Plains.

The club was small and dimly lit, with a tiny raised stage in
one corner for the performers who, according to Dan, would
start playing at nine. She looked at the menu and a list of the
specials, finally deciding on the cold salmon with the house's
special dill and cream sauce. "Want to share?" Dan asked. "I
was really debating between the salmon and the rack of lamb.
If you're a lamb person, we could go halvsies."

Since she'd been considering the same two dishes, she
gladly agreed. Dan freely admitted knowing nothing about
wine so he asked her if she wanted to make a selection from
the wine list. "What do you like?" she asked, flattered.

"You," he said with a twinkle, "but I'm sure that anything
you select from the wine list will be fine." She chose a Pinot
Grigio, and when it arrived he seemed quite pleased with it.

Through the salad course, an unusual combination of radic-
chio and bits of fresh peach with a balsamic vinaigrette dressing, they discussed the current situation in a drought-stricken
region of Africa, the sexual issues in the Catholic Church, and
the state of the economy. When the main course arrived, they

were debating the results of a recent study on cancer and coffee drinking.

When Monica had eaten half of her really delicious salmon and he'd finished half of his lamb, they switched plates. "It's the best way I know of to have your cake, or in this case lamb, and eat your salmon, too."

The jazz combo, a sax, clarinet, bass, and drums, arrived at about eight-thirty and spent the next fifteen minutes trotting between the back of the restaurant and the stage. Then they tuned up, making difficult squealing noises and adjusting the microphones. Finally, at nine, while she and Dan were drinking coffee and a really good brandy, the quartet started playing. The music was unusual, but wonderful. During the short silence between each number, Dan made sure Monica was still enjoying herself.

When the group announced their second fifteen-minute break at about eleven, Dan suggested that they leave. "I think we're both starting to overdose and I'm still getting over jet lag."

"Oh, Dan, I was enjoying myself so much that I forgot. You must be totally fuzzed."

"Not quite, but falling asleep behind the wheel isn't my idea of a great way to end a most delightful evening."

"Want me to drive?"

"Can you drive a standard shift?"

"Of course, and I'd love to get my hands on that little baby of yours."

He dug in his pocket and without hesitation, handed her the keys.

During the drive home, Monica worried about the awkward moment when they would say good night at her door. Since he was silent, she wondered whether he was wondering what would happen, as well. However, when she pulled into the driveway, she saw that Dan was actually asleep. "We're here," she said, softly awakening him.

"Oh shit," he said, jerking to an upright position. "I'm so sorry. Not the most romantic way to end an evening."

Monica's laugh was rich and genuine. "It sure gets us out of the 'come in for a drink' moment. Go home and readjust to New York time."

"Were you worried about that, too?"

With a rueful grin, she said, "Yeah. I'm not in any hurry. I think we just might see each other again."

His grin was easy to see, even in the darkness of the car. He reached over and cupped the back of her head. His lips were soft, warm, and undemanding. When the long kiss ended, they both climbed out of the car and Dan came around to the driver's side. "Good night, Monica. I'll call you."

"Are you okay to drive home?"

"Sure. Little short naps are so refreshing. Not polite, but refreshing. I'm fine."

"Good night, Dan." She pressed a light kiss on his lips, grabbed her purse, and walked to her front door, listening to Sam's frantic welcoming barks. She turned and waved, knowing he'd wait until she got inside before he drove away.

Chapter
15

"Since then," Monica said to her friends, "we've been out several times and had a lot of fun together."

"But no sex yet," Cait said.

"Back off, Cait. If sex happens I can assure you that you won't be the first one to know about it, but eventually I will tell all. I promise."

"There I go getting pushy again," Cait said. "Sorry, Monica. Let's change the subject." They were all working on their second margarita and tongues were a bit looser. "I've got a joke that's been going around the Internet. God has almost finished creating Adam and Eve so he tells them that he's got only two things left. The first is a penis and the ability to pee standing up. Adam waves his hand in the air, jumps up and down, and yells, 'Oh, please, I want that. Please, please, please.' So God gives it to him." Cait paused to sip her drink.

"Well, Adam's so delighted that he runs all over Eden, peeing on bushes and rocks and trees while God and Eve watch. Eventually Eve turns to God and says, 'Well, I guess I get what's left over. Exactly what is it?'"

She paused briefly, then said, "And God answered, 'Brains.'"

While the other three women burst out laughing, Cait picked

up her drink and sipped again. Through her laughter, Monica said, "I love it. It's so silly and so . . . so . . . men."

"Okay," Cait said. "Quick. Angie, what's the silliest thing you've ever done?"

"Anything?"

"Anything."

"I ate a sandwich of two slices of bread and a jar of the babies' strained apricots." When Eve raised an eyebrow, she continued, "Well, they smelled good and the babies love them."

"Good answer," Cait said, giggling. "Monica."

"I watched two hours of *The World Poker Tour* on TV when I was supposed to be working."

"I love you, Monica," Cait said, laughing harder. "Sometimes you just have to fuck work."

"Wait a minute," Eve said, giggling behind her hand. "I watch that show."

By that time the women were laughing so hard it was difficult for them to catch their breath. "Cait," Eve said. "How about you?"

"I got on-line, went to e-Bay, and bought a four-dollar phony diamond bracelet. Then I went to a pain in the ass party with a bunch of really snooty people I really hate and showed it off as if it were worth thousands. No one knew the difference. They gazed at it with envy all over their pinched little faces."

"You didn't," Monica said, leaning forward and dipping a chip into a pile of guacamole.

"I did. Even Logan was surprised, but he believed that I'd gone jewelry shopping when he wasn't around. He's such a snob sometimes." She paused. "I guess I used to be that way, too. As long back as I can remember I always wanted to live in a big house on Sheraton or Willowbrook. Now it seems so ridiculous." She chewed, then with relief on her face returned to the previous conversation. "Okay, Eve, you're not off the hook just because you watched poker on TV. Not silly enough. What's the really, truly silliest thing you've ever done?"

Eve got a dreamy look on her face and adjusted her glasses. "About six months ago Mike and I went to Pittsburgh to clear up problems with a wholesaler. I guess I didn't need to be there but we got to spend a night together.

"Anyway, the room had a stall shower that was really one of those glass enclosures on top of the tub. You know the ones?"

The three other women nodded.

"It was a Jacuzzi tub just big enough for the two of us, so after we made love I filled the tub with water and poured in a cap full of shampoo to make a bubble bath. Then we climbed in and turned on the jets."

With a dreamy look on her face, she continued. "Mike closed the doors so it was sort of like a cozy little room. We talked and touched until bubbles started to fill the tub, then rise up the shower stall. Soon we were in foam up to our necks." The three women chuckled.

"We climbed out of the tub in hysterics. It was so funny. We were both covered with bubbles." All at once Eve's face clouded. "Then it got ruined. His wife called on his cell phone and asked why he was laughing. He told her that he was watching something on TV."

Eve started to cry. "Don't hate me, Monica."

"I don't hate you, why would I?" She picked up her glass and took a healthy swig. She knew exactly what Eve was referring to.

"I'm the kind of woman you hate, dating a married man. When something like that happens I feel so guilty. About her, I mean. You have every right to hate the woman your brother-in-law's moved in with." She swiped at the tears now flowing down her face. "Monica, I love Mike. What am I supposed to do?"

Monica took her friend's hands across the table. "Oh, Eve, I didn't mean to make you so upset. I spoke out of turn and I'm so sorry."

"You weren't out of line, but try to see it from my perspective. I love him."

"Don't take this wrong, but do you really love him?" Monica asked, her voice purposely gentle. "If he were free, would you marry him?"

"In a minute," Eve said.

"And have him cheat on you, too? He would, you know. Once a cheater . . . "

"Enough of this," Cait said, interrupting. "Point made, Monica. We'll have no bad feelings tonight. I won't allow it. We're changing the subject. I'm just drunk enough to propose that we each tell about the best sex we ever had."

Angie frowned and took a chip from the plate, dipped it into the small bit of remaining guacamole, and said, "Count me out on that. I don't think I've ever had the kind of sex you people probably have had. I was pretty uneducated when Tony and I got married, and since then he's been my only." She frowned and took a large swallow, draining her second margarita. "He'd been with Jordanna, of course. She was probably better than me. Maybe she still is."

"Excuse me?" Monica said, putting her glass down with a loud clank. "What the hell does that mean? Do you mean to say that you think he's having an affair? With his ex?"

Angie immediately looked embarrassed and put her hand over her mouth. "I'm a cheap drunk and my mouth gets too loose. I didn't mean to say that at all."

Cait raised an eyebrow. "Truth, girl. You did mean it. Give!"

"Stop it, Cait," Eve snapped. "We're friends but that doesn't give any of us the right to pry. Whatever Angie meant is her business alone. That goes for all of us. I like you guys very much and I want to continue to hang out with you, but not if you give everyone the third degree every time something slips out."

"Phew," Cait said, "the woman has claws." She patted Eve's hand. "And I hate it when she's right. I really do get overly aggressive sometimes." She turned to Angie. "I'm really sorry, sweetie. I didn't mean to mess in your life."

Angie smiled weakly. "I know you didn't and I love you all for caring. I shouldn't have said anything, but Jordanna scares me."

"I thought you were sort of friends," Eve said softly.

"Yeah," Angie said. "I try to make everyone think that, but I really hate her guts." Again she put her hand over her mouth. "I shouldn't say that. I should be happy that she and Tony get along, but I'm so damned jealous of her I could scream." Her voice quavered. "He goes over there almost every weekend and talks to her on the phone at least once a week. She's gorgeous and classy, sort of like you, Monica."

"Thanks, I think," Monica said, flattered at Angie's classification of her but sad for her friend and her low opinion of herself.

"Jordanna's everything I'm not. She's been to college and has a great job. She's got her figure. No stretch marks or boobs that hang down to her knees. She wears great clothes that aren't always stained with baby beets and formula." Tears were running freely down Angie's cheeks. "She talks about international business and finance, things that Tony's interested in, not what some ten-month-old did today."

"She's a rat," Eve said, "and we all hate her."

"Thanks for the support, Eve. I love you for it." She paused. "Jordanna. Even her name is perfect."

"Angie's a nice name," Eve said. "It fits you."

"If your name bothers you," Cait said, "why not use Angela?"

"Angie fits me, small, comfortable." She looked completely miserable. "And anyway I can't use Angela. My name is really just Angie. It's like that on my birth certificate."

"Who's to know? Become Angela if she's more like the woman you want to be. You can be whomever you want."

"It wouldn't help."

"If she's so perfect, why did they split?" Monica asked.

"He doesn't talk about it much, but I gather that she dropped him. His sister-in-law talked about it one afternoon just after we were married. It seems that Jordanna thought Tony would get his masters, then his doctorate, and be a college professor. She loved the idea of being the wife of a professor. When it appeared that he wasn't interested in going further than teaching high school, she dumped him." Angie smiled wryly. "Kept the name, though. She's still Jordanna Cariri."

"Why did she keep his name if she dumped him?"

"She works with some financial services firm and has an identity as Jordanna Cariri, so she kept it. That makes me furious, too." From her expression it was clear that she was both angry and depressed.

Monica wrapped her arm around her friend's shoulders. "It's okay, honey. You're a wonderful woman, and other than these two," she said, indicating Cait and Eve, "the nicest dame I know. You're a great mom, a fabulous yoga teacher, and what's most important, a really good person."

"I second that," Cait said. "You're the best."

Eve looked at Angie and said softly, "Why don't you do something about Jordanna? Tell Tony that he shouldn't see her anymore."

"Oh," Angie said quickly, "I couldn't do that. He's got a right to see whoever he wants."

"Do you really think he's having an affair with her? I mean, if you were being brutally honest? Do you really think he's a cheater?"

Angie thought a minute. "No. I guess I just think that if I were him I'd prefer her to me. I wish I could compete."

"You can, if you want to," Cait said, rubbing the nail of her index finger with her thumb. "You could get your hair done, buy a few nice things to wear. It won't fix things if they're really broken, but it might make him look at you like a woman instead of a mommy."

"I've thought about it, but I don't have the time or the money to spend on myself. Anyway, it would be like putting makeup on a cow. I'd still be a cow."

"Cut that out!" Eve said. "Don't put yourself down that way. That attitude is what keeps you from doing anything about anything. I should know."

"In my humble opinion, if things are that way with Tony, I don't think you can afford not to make the effort. That alone will show Tony something." Cait took Angie's hand. "I told you several weeks ago that I would spend some time helping you with your errands, since you don't have a car at your disposal now that Tony's back commuting to the Bronx. We have a quest. We'll get your hair done, maybe your nails, too, and we'll find a few pieces of new, sexier clothing, even if we get things at Wal-Mart." Her eyes gleamed. "And we have to get some new, disgustingly frivolous, man-catching undies, too. We'll make good things happen for you, babe."

"I can't let you do that," Angie said, sticking her chin out. "I won't take charity."

Cait looked at her seriously. "If you had a lot of something and I needed it, would you give it to me?"

"Of course, but that's not the same."

"Why not?"

Angie paused, tears filling her eyes. "I don't know. Why would you do that for me?"

"Because we're friends and that's what friends do for each other. Right?"

"Right," the other two chimed in.

"Good. Then we've got that settled."

From the look on Angie's face it was obvious that it wasn't settled, but they let it pass. "If you do things on the weekend," Eve said, "I'd love to help. I could drive, or baby-sit."

"Me, too," Monica chimed in.

Angie was trying to wipe away the tears and smile at her friends at the same time.

"Okay, it's a plan. We'll work out the details during the week," Cait said, "and let's all agree to hate Jordanna."

"If I were being fair," Angie said, "it's not her fault. They have a lot of history."

"She's his past, and you're his present and his future," Cait said, "and we're going to turn you into something so much more." She reached out and fingered Angie's ponytail. "So much more. You'll be a regular Cinderella. If any three women can do it, we can. Right, ladies?"

"Right," Eve and Monica said together.

"Good. Any problem with that?"

With a watery smile, Angie shook her head. "Maybe."

"Okay, let's get back to good sex," Cait said. "Come on, Angie, think back. We need to hear good, hot things about Tony. Maybe on your honeymoon or the first time you and Tony did it?"

A small smile crept over Angie's face. "Well . . . "

"Tell us. Then we'll know what we're fighting for."

Angie thought back to when she and Tony had started dating after his divorce. He and Jordanna had been apart for almost a year, and he'd had a few short-time girlfriends but nothing that lasted. Since high school she'd had several boyfriends, too, none really serious, but she was content with her single life. She'd moved from her parents' house on Sycamore into a one-bedroom in the East Hudson Apartments. She'd enjoyed decorating it herself, with colorful paintings by never-to-be-known artists on the walls and comfortable, inexpensive furniture. She was a bit lonely in the evenings so she found a wonderful little brown poodle at the local animal shelter to keep her company.

After their cars tapped rear bumpers in the Hudson Valley Mall parking lot, she and Tony got to talking. As attractive as ever, he had a lean, muscular body and a deep tan, both of which he maintained doing construction part-time for his brothers' firm. They'd begged him to join the family construction business after their father's death and he'd been surprised to discover that he didn't hate it as much as he'd expected to. "I never wanted to work in the family business," he said, "and Jordanna thought doing construction was beneath me. Now that she and I have split I don't care what she thinks."

They started to date, and soon they were seeing each other every weekend and talking on the phone almost every night in between. On the second Saturday in September, about two months after they began seeing each other, a cousin of Tony's got married and they arranged to go to the wedding together.

She shopped for several weeks until she found the perfect dress, sheer jersey with a scooped neck, a slender ankle-length skirt, and a figure-flattering wide gold belt. She got some chunky gold jewelry and gold sandals with high heels. She had her hair done early that afternoon, a soft pageboy that flattered her face and showed off her new earrings.

When Tony arrived to pick her up, he whistled. "God, my folks will flip when they see you. You look so great."

Slightly embarrassed, but intensely pleased, she said nothing. At the party, she met so many of Tony's relatives that she quickly lost track of both names and relationships. "Don't let it worry you," he said. "I've been part of this mob scene for most of my life and I often forget who's related to whom and how."

After a sumptuous sit-down dinner, the band played dance music, everything from the cha-cha to circle dances. But it was the slow stuff that she liked best. Tony danced every one with her, holding her close and sighing hot breath into her ear. "I want you," he whispered late in the evening.

They had done some kissing and petting but hadn't yet been to bed together. "I want you, too," she'd said, the wine she'd consumed making her unwilling to resist.

"Let's get out of here," he said, and after saying good night to about a thousand people, put her in his car and wordlessly drove to her apartment.

He parked and pulled her to him. The kiss was deep and long, his tongue snaking into her mouth and stroking hers, his hands caressing her back through her coat. "Let's go upstairs," he said in a hoarse voice.

"Yes," she said. "I want you very much."

In the apartment, although she knew he was very aroused, Tony seemed able to take his time. He slowly removed her dress and slip, then slow danced with her as he removed his clothing until he wore only his briefs. He stroked her back and sides with his fingertips as he whispered, "You're so soft," over and over.

His kisses drugged her with need and his restraint gratified her. He nibbled her neck and lightly bit her earlobe, rubbed his palms up her arms, then slid the straps of her bra from her shoulders. As the cups fell from her breasts, he purred and kissed the upper slopes, then down to her nipples.

Without stopping his laving of her breasts, he removed her bra and slowly lowered her panties until she stood in only her thigh-high stockings and shoes. When he stepped away to gaze at her she wanted to hide, but the look on his face kept her still. "You're so beautiful," he said, his eyes roaming over her. "So beautiful."

She could tell from the large bulge in his briefs that he wanted her, and she was soaked and ready for him. She wasn't a virgin, but she was uneducated and very nervous. Would she be enough for him? After all, he'd been married to Jordanna who, no doubt, was an expert between the sheets.

"May I make love to you?"

The question took her by surprise. She knew that she was sending the little come-on signals that men usually looked for and assumed that, since she hadn't said no, he'd decide that she meant yes. Tony, however, was asking her right out. How could she deny him, even if she had wanted to? "Oh, yes," she sighed.

Quickly they went into the bedroom, and as she removed the rest of her clothes, he pulled the geometric-designed spread off the bed. As if she weighed nothing, he picked her up and lay her on the cool sheets. "My mind doesn't want to rush," he said, removing his briefs, "but I'm so hungry for you."

"I want you too. Protection?" she said softly.

"Of course," he said, dashing into the living room and retrieving a condom from the pocket of his slacks.

She couldn't tear her eyes from him as he unrolled the latex over his erection. His upper body was well-muscled from all the lifting he did and his upper-body tan was a dark contrast to his white hips and pale, tight buttocks.

They kissed, then he nibbled along her jawline and nipped at her earlobe. Although she was in a sensual haze and wanted it to go on forever, she knew he couldn't wait. She cupped her palms over his hips and urged him to mount her. Then he was on top of her, slowly entering her sopping body. She arched her back to meet him, and wrapped her legs around his waist to pull him more deeply inside of her. "God, baby," he groaned, "don't do that. It's difficult enough to hold back."

"So don't," she said, feeling bold and daring. "Do what feels good."

"But..."

She wiggled her hips so his thick cock moved within her until she heard his bellow as he came. Covered with a thin sheen of sweat, he collapsed beside her. "What about you?" he asked when he caught his breath.

"I'm wonderful." She hadn't climaxed but it was still the best sex she'd ever had.

"I know that people say the dumbest, most impetuous things after an evening like this, but I love you so much. Will you marry me?"

Shocked, she stammered, "We . . . I mean we've only just begun dating," she said.

"I know, but we've known each other since high school and I can feel"—he tapped his chest near his heart—"in here, how right this is."

In high school she'd loved him the way one teen loves another, but now she was older and loved him as a woman. This was sudden, but like Tony, she felt it was right, too. "I do love you."

His face radiated with the most brilliant smile she'd ever seen. "Then you will?" He sounded incredulous.

"Yes," she said.

Angie told her friends the PG-rated version of that evening, enjoying the dreamy looks that lit the other three women's faces. "And we were married three months later."

Eve said, "That's so beautiful, I want to cry."

"It sounds so fabulous," Cait said. Finally having heard the good side of Tony, she understood what Angie saw in him. "So romantic. I, for one, think he's a keeper." She leaned forward and looked into Angie's eyes. "We'll make this work for both of you. I mean it."

Angie's smile was crooked and a bit damp as she said, "Thanks. Okay, I want off this sex hook you've got me on. It's someone else's turn. How about you, Cait? You started this. What was your best sex with Logan?"

Chapter
16

Cait had already thought carefully about whether to tell her friends about Hotguy and had decided that it was too juicy not to share. Maybe that was why she'd brought sex up in the first place. "My best sex wasn't Logan."

"No? Who then? Someone from before?" Eve asked, picking up her drink, trying not to look too curious.

"Nope, not in the past. Someone from right now. This afternoon, actually."

"You're cheating on Logan?" Angie said, suddenly shocked. "Somehow that doesn't sound like you."

"I'm not cheating. Well, not exactly."

"Okay," Monica said. "Now I'm confused. What does 'not exactly' mean? Either you're having sex with someone who isn't your husband or you're not."

"I've got a cyberlover and we had our first on-camera encounter this afternoon while Logan went to his office and checked his e-mail."

The other three women gaped. When Eve regained her composure, she said, "A cyberlover? How does one do that? How did it start?"

Cait told them about her ventures into chatting, and then her discovery of Paul's Place. "I met Hotguy—that's his screen name, actually Hotguy344—one afternoon and we made love in a private room." She spent the next few minutes explaining about hot chatting and private places in cyberspace. "His real name is Brett. He told me he was handsome, but when I saw him I realized that he's not really very good-looking. But God, he's hot, hot, hot." She fanned her face with her hand. "And after all, I'm no babe myself." She munched a chip to create a theatrical pause.

"Isn't that sort of thing dangerous?" Monica asked. "I mean, what do you really know about him?"

"Not much. I know he lives in Fairbanks, Alaska, and that's about it. But he doesn't know much about me either, so where's the danger?" Cait was feeling really good and very sure of herself after her afternoon romp.

"I don't know," Eve said. "It sounds creepy to me." She blushed and ducked her head, a small smile on her lips. "Even if the sex is really good, but what do I know about any of that?"

"Hot chatting isn't dangerous if you're careful not to reveal too much personal information." She realized that Brett did know her name and what state she lived in, but he was so far away that it couldn't matter. Could it? A small shiver passed over her.

"You said you used a camera this afternoon," Monica said, leaning forward and chewing on a chip with salsa. "I, for one, am dying of curiosity. I have no idea what goes on on the Internet. Give!"

"It all started when I logged onto a Web site called Paul's Place." She found she enjoyed telling her friends about her escapades almost as much as having them in the first place. The looks of wonder and envy did her heart good.

"Sounds wonderfully kinky," Angie said. "I can't imagine myself doing it, but if I were single and much more experimental than I am, I just might."

Eve stared at Angie. "You're kidding, Angie. It seems so far out of my experience, and yours, too."

"Different and far out aren't necessarily bad," Cait said, enjoying amazing the women more and more. She was the expert and it felt good.

"You said you used a camera today? What about Logan? What if he finds out or walks in on you? It sounds like quite a risk."

"He knows nothing and doesn't seem to care enough to investigate. I don't feel bad about that. Anyway, to me it's not really cheating since there's no physical contact of any kind. Logan's not interested in having sex with me and I'm no saint. I have my needs and this scratches my itches without my having to pick up some guy in a bar or at a party."

"It sounds so reasonable when you say it, Cait," Eve said, "but I don't know how I feel about it. I'm trying to imagine how I'd react if my husband, if I had one, was doing what you're doing."

"Well," Cait said, "different strokes." She sounded almost cocky, but watching her friends' reactions, she wondered whether she was as sure of herself as she sounded.

"You bet," Monica said. "I'm dying of curiosity. Tell us about the camera thing. How does it work? You talk to each other live, too, right? It must have been the first time you've heard his voice or seen his face."

"It was." Cait smiled and allowed her mind to drift while she spoke.

She had found Hotguy344 in the chatroom at Paul's Place and they'd gone private. She told him about her camera and he gave her a short list of instructions to follow so they could see and talk with each other. It took a few attempts but finally she saw Hotguy344's image appear on her screen.

He wasn't at all what she'd pictured. The Brett she fantasized about, the one he'd described to her in their early encounters in the chat room, was in his mid-twenties, with blond curly hair and a great physique. The real Brett was much older, stocky, with dark hair and eyes. He had a neatly trimmed moustache and a bushy beard that he stroked with his large, long-fingered hand. He wore only briefs, and she could see that his body was covered with thick hair. "Not what you expected?" he said, and she could watch his mouth move as he spoke.

"Not quite, but I'll bet I'm not either." She'd warned him, and from the look on his face as he looked her over, he seemed pleased.

"Why in the world did you tell me all that stuff about being twenty-five with dark hair? You're sensational exactly the way you are." Cait glowed at his praise as he continued. "Stand up and let me look at you."

The camera sat on top of her monitor so she stood and stepped back so he could see her from knees to hair. She had worn a pair of tiny white shorts and a tight T-shirt. She hadn't worn a bra so her nipples showed prominently through the thin fabric. "I like your tits," he said.

A shiver echoed through her body. His voice was gruff and forceful, and it sliced through her. "Thanks," she said softly.

"I'd like to see them better," he purred, then said, "Why don't you take off your shirt?"

With a growing smile, she slowly removed her top. She treated it like a strip show, slowly pulling the hem of the shirt up, revealing her breasts only a bit at a time. She heard him laugh. "You like to tease," he said. "That's wonderful." She watched his palm stroke the length of the bulge in his small black briefs. "Ah, Cait, this is going to be so good."

She realized that he'd called her by name. Wasn't that a bit dangerous? Probably not. "Yes, Brett, it certainly is." She wanted to be more than just an object in this game so she said, "I love watching your hand on your cock." So far she'd only typed those words. Hearing herself say "cock" was almost as exciting to her as seeing Brett on her screen.

"Now the shorts and panties. Since this is our first time I'm really eager to get it on with you."

She took off the remainder of her clothing and sat in front of the camera, her heels on her chair. "Are you wet?" he asked. "I want to watch you stick your finger between your legs and tell me how wet you are."

She stroked herself. She was soaked, and she told him so. "I love that," he said, pulling down his briefs.

When she saw his cock for the first time, as thick around as her wrist, she said, "That's quite a piece of equipment you've got there." She tried for coy but it came out with a small catch in her voice.

"And it's all for you." He filled his palm with lubricant, then wrapped his hand around his dick and rubbed from tip to base. "I like to make it feel like I'm fucking you." He stroked again. "Does watching me make you hot?"

"I'm so hot already there's not much further to go." She realized that she meant it. She was so highly aroused that she could probably come from just a touch of her fingers, but she wouldn't do that just yet. She'd let the anticipation build for as long as she could stand it.

"Then watch me." He was obviously well practiced and knew exactly how to touch to make his cock swell and dance. As she stared, transfixed, he reached between his thick, hairy thighs and cupped his balls, squeezing and pulling on his sac. "I'm getting close, too," he said. "Spread your legs more and point the camera down so I can see your pussy." She adjusted the camera, shifted forward on her desk chair, and parted her inner lips with her fingers. "Ah, yes," he said as he rubbed the length of his cock, "your wet lips almost fill my screen." He leaned back and kept rubbing. "Now touch your clit. It's so swollen it's almost like you have a cock like mine. Rub it!"

It was as though he controlled her fingers as he told her exactly where to touch. "Slide your fingers to the left. Oh, yes, I can tell that you like that. Now rub the right side of your clitty with one hand and pinch your nipples with the other." She knew her body pretty well but listening to him give directions for her to rub here and stroke there made it all the better. Soon her pulse was pounding and her breathing was ragged. "Getting close?" he growled, and she watched him look around the area around her computer. "I can see a thick magic marker on the desk beside your keyboard. Take it and push it into your snatch. Fuck yourself with it. I want to watch."

Without hesitation she took the marker and used the blunt end as a dildo to fuck her pussy. It didn't fill her, and somewhere in her brain she made a note to go to an adult Web site and buy a thick dildo for herself for next time. While she slid the marker in and out, she rubbed her clit with her other hand. Her eyes never left Brett's hand and she soon realized that he was as close as she was. She'd done that for him. She'd aroused him, gotten him really hot. "I want to see you come," he said. "Do whatever it is that you do when we chat and make yourself come. When you do, I will."

She knew just the places to touch and in only a moment, she came. She knew he could hear her grunts and the mewling sounds she made and watch her head fall back as she fought to breathe. "You're a treasure," he said, rubbing his cock harder and faster. As she came down, she watched semen spurt from the tip of his cock and he caught it with his other hand.

They cleaned up, and finally he said, "We'll have to do this often. It's delicious and the closest I can come to fucking you in person—for the moment."

"I've got to go now," she said, still in a sexual fog. "I hope we can do that again soon."

"Can we make plans now?"

"I never know when my husband's going to be out so you'll have to hang around Paul's Place and I'll get there when I can."

"That will have to do. I'm logging off." She saw his fingers on his keyboard and then her screen returned to the logo of the Web site she'd logged on to. She quickly shut her computer down.

As she thought over their encounter, she smiled, then heard him say something about fucking her in person. What did his "for the moment" mean? Ahhh. Probably nothing, and she was too content to think about it too much. This had been both exhilarating and exhausting. The camera made it so much more exciting and she couldn't wait to meet him again. She hoped he felt the same way.

When she finished telling her three friends the slightly expurgated version of her encounter with Hotguy344, she was wet. Pleading too many margaritas, she rushed to the ladies' room and masturbated to orgasm. When she returned to the table her friends were looking at her in awe. "I can't believe you did that," Eve said. "It's like a whole new kind of sex."

"It is, isn't it? And it's going to be difficult for me not to log on daily."

"You're sure he doesn't know anything about you?" Monica asked, sipping her drink. "I worry about you, babe."

"Nah. I'm really careful." Careful enough? She picked up her drink. "Okay. Monica, your turn. Best sex ever."

"After that story of yours," Monica said, "I can't think of anything anywhere near as hot as that."

"My story wasn't that kind, either," Angie said. "I 'fessed up so now it's your turn. No punking out."

"Okay," Monica said with a resigned sigh. "I haven't had lots of long-term relationships and I think most of the really good stuff happens when two people grow to know and trust each other. Most of my sex is one-night stands. Most good, some not. It's difficult for me to single out one experience."

"Okay, how about we change the rules?" Cait said. "What's the worst you've ever had?"

A picture flashed through Monica's mind and she couldn't help but laugh. "That's easier. I did business briefly with a guy who worked for a slick woman's magazine, I won't say which one. We'd been talking on the phone for several weeks and eventually decided to get together for drinks. He wasn't a bigwig at his place, but had a little bit of power. He was young and kind of cute, so I was willing to hop into bed with him if that was what it took."

"I'm curious," Eve said. "Is there a lot of fooling around? You know, *quid pro quo* stuff? I know there is in my business. Since the government is so tight on money changing hands, although I'm sure some does, it's more favors for favors, with sexual favors at the top of the list."

Monica was nodding. "Yeah, in mine, too. I spend quite a few evenings with clients and sometimes it's assumed that sex will follow."

Angie's eyes were round. "You really do that sort of thing?"

"Sure, and don't look at me like that. I'm not a prostitute, I just do what I need to do to get things done. I don't mind. As a matter of fact, most of the time I enjoy it, so what's the harm? Most men think with their penises and if that means they'll think of me more often, more power to me."

"You have a very low opinion of men," Eve said. "There are lots of good ones out there."

"Like Mike?" The words slipped out and immediately Monica regretted them. "I'm so sorry, Eve," she said, taking her friend's hand. "I didn't mean that the way it sounded." She pushed her drink away. No more liquor for her.

"It's okay, Monica. No offense taken," Eve said. "I can understand how you feel. We are what we are. If we're going to continue to get together, and I hope we will, we have to cut each other a little slack. There's good and not so good in each of us and we need to take each other for what we are. I love you guys and that's that."

Monica did really care about these women and she felt her

throat closing and tears prick the back of her eyes. She blinked them away. "Hear, hear," she said, and the others agreed. Four glasses were raised, clinked, and sipped from.

"Okay, back to Monica's worst sex ever," Cait said.

"You know, I don't even remember his name, so I'll call him Tom. We went to his room and kissed and stroked, both still fully clothed. Tom had consumed a lot of alcohol and he was really plastered. Frankly, I think he was most of the time. Anyway, we went into the bedroom of his suite and I took off my clothes. He disrobed, too, mostly." She chuckled at the memory.

"Mostly?"

Her laugh was infectious and by this time the women had joined her. "He left his undershirt and his socks on. I didn't want to ask and upset him so we went at it to its logical conclusion. His sock-covered feet were so slippery on the sheets that he couldn't brace himself and kept slipping down the bed."

"Did you finally ask why the socks?"

Monica made a face. "He said his feet got cold. I think I was insulted that he didn't think I could keep him warm."

"Was that why he wore the undershirt, too?"

Monica's laughter got louder. "He said that he still took his laundry home to his folks and he wanted the semen stains to demonstrate to his mom that he'd gotten lucky." The laughter around the table was so loud by then that Monica was afraid they'd all be thrown out. "I swear to God. Needless to say he never got lucky with me or anyone I knew again."

"You're kidding," Angie said, through her tears of laughter. "No one could be that, that—well, I don't know what he was."

"Neither do I," Monica said.

"That's a great story," Cait said when she'd caught her breath. "I knew I loved you for a reason. Eve, how about you?"

"If you all don't mind, I don't have a good story either way, except for the bubble bath thing, so I'll opt out."

"No problem," Cait said.

Angie glanced down at her watch and blanched. "Damn. It's after ten. I've got to get home." She reached for her purse, but Cait stopped her. "Tonight's my treat. I haven't had such a good time in quite a while. This will come out of my entertainment money for the week."

Monica knew that Angie didn't have money to spare so she quickly said, "Well, thanks, Cait," hoping that if she agreed, Angie would, too.

"Well," Angie said, standing, "if you're sure."

Eve and Monica slid out of the booth and reached for their purses. "They're all sure," Cait said. "I'll hang around and take care of the check. You all go home, and we'll get together next week at the diner after class, right?"

"Absolutely," Monica said. "I think we should make girls' night out a regular thing, too, maybe once a month, or even more often."

"Yeah," Eve said. "We'll pick another date when we get together next Saturday. Maybe toward the end of the month. I really needed this evening out. My hair needs lots of letting down."

Everyone quickly agreed and Eve and Monica headed for the door. "I can't tell you how much I enjoyed tonight," Eve said as Monica walked beside her. "I don't want to get all mushy, but I don't know why we've become so close so quickly. It really feels good to have friends like all of you."

"That goes for me, too." They parted in the parking lot. "It feels like we've know each other for years. See you next week."

"You bet."

Back inside, Cait held Angie back as Eve and Monica walked toward the door. "Give me your phone number. I'll call you tomorrow and we can make plans to shop so you'll have your weekends free—or as free as they ever get."

"You don't have to do that. I can get everything done over the weekend."

"And have no time for Tony? Not a chance. I've got the car and the time. You bring the kids, the car seats, and the list. Sounds like a deal to me."

"Are you really sure?"

Cait squeezed Angie's hand. "I'm really, really, really sure." She took down Angie's phone number as she dictated. "I'll call you tomorrow and we'll figure out all the logistics. Deal?" She extended her hand.

With a slight hesitation, Angie took Cait's hand and said, "Deal."

Chapter
17

The following Wednesday, Cait drove her van over to Angie's house and parked in front. The simple split level was typical of the neighborhood. Painted a dark toast color, it sat on a quarter acre of grass, the yard neat, if a bit neglected. A sprinkler was set up to water the sparse collection of zinnias and salvia that straggled along in front of the foundation planting of small azaleas, andromeda, and evergreen shrubs that had probably come with the house. The most striking thing about the property was the huge oak tree in the backyard that dominated the area. As she peeked around the garage, she saw a tire swing hanging from a low branch.

Angie answered the doorbell wearing a pair of lightweight, well-washed jeans and a T-shirt that read, "God put me on this earth to accomplish a certain number of things. Right now I'm so far behind I'll never die." When Cait read it she burst out laughing. "I love that shirt, but let's make it a bit less true."

"Come on in, Cait. I made coffee and I think it's a bit better than the swill at the diner." Actually, Cait thought, the diner coffee wasn't really that bad, but it had become such a running silliness that no one had the courage to defend it. "Can I get you something else?"

"Thanks, no," Cait said. "I had breakfast with Logan before he left for work, but I'd love some coffee."

Angie poured two mugs of coffee, put a creamer shaped like a cow and a sugar bowl that looked like a sheep on the kitchen table, and the two women settled in comfortable leather-looking chairs. "Where are the babies?" Cait asked.

"Wouldn't you know that the one morning I wanted to be on some kind of a schedule, they chose to take extra long naps. I hate to wake them."

"Of course not. We've got plenty of time. If we let them get up when they're ready then they won't be cranky while we shop."

Angie beamed. "You always put such a good spin on things. Thanks. I just hate to waste your time."

"I've got nothing else to do today so we've got the whole day. Stop worrying. I can guarantee you that you're not imposing. What's with the tire swing in the backyard? Was it left by the previous owners?"

"Tony put that up," Angie said with a chuckle, "to celebrate the twins' six-month birthday. He can't wait until they can use it."

"He's quite a guy."

"Yeah," Angie said. "In most areas he's a doll. Have you been with Hotguy since the weekend?"

"Nah. There just hasn't been time."

Angie slowly shook her head. "I can't imagine what it must be like. It's so far from anything I've ever done."

"That was true of me until about six months ago." She poured milk into her coffee from the cow. "Before then I wouldn't have believed it of me, either."

Angie sighed. "Part of me longs for an adventure like that. My life is so dull I want to scream."

"Without a car I can imagine that the days get pretty tedious. Aren't there any women in the neighborhood with kids that you can make plans with some afternoons? Play dates and such? There must be folks within walking distance."

"Yeah, a few, but most of them are a bit intimidated by twins. I love the babies, but it's such a hassle to get them out of the house without help, too. By the time I get one changed, fed, dressed, and in the stroller, the other's crying or one of them spits up and needs clean clothes. I plan to take them for a walk but by the time I'm organized, it's later than I planned and it seems easier to stay here."

"Maybe you need to make the effort," Cait said gently. "I don't mean to sound like some amateur shrink here but maybe you need to just do it if only for your sanity. Put the kids into their stroller, dribbled-on clothing or whatever. Other mothers know what it's like. Just dump them in, before the weather gets too cool, and walk around. You might find there are more women looking for companionship than you think."

"Well, yeah, but . . ."

"Yeah, but. Sweetie, I think you're making some of your own problems. You've got to be stronger, more sure of yourself. You have nothing to lose."

"I know you're right. Once the weather gets cooler it's just going to get more difficult. It seems so good in contemplation, but in reality it never seems to happen. Maybe I'm just not good at this mother thing."

"Bullshit. You can be good at whatever you work at. You're so much more than you make yourself out to be. You know that old prayer, 'Give me the courage to change the things I can change, the serenity to accept the things I can't, and the wisdom to know the difference.' Take a stand about the things in your life that you can change." She sipped her coffee, hoping she wasn't coming on too strong. She'd been thinking a lot about Angie and envied her her babies and her settled, comfortable life. Granted, having cruising twins was a

hell of a lot of work, but it was also so rewarding. Cait wondered what she had that matched it. "That goes for
Jordanna, too."

"That might be one of those things I can't change. She just
is, and I'd be best off getting used to the relationship that
Tony has with her. They've got quite a few years of memories
that they share."

Cait paused. "You don't have to be a shrew as far as Jordanna
is concerned, but you can tell Tony occasionally that you'd
rather that he stay home instead of going to her house."

"I couldn't."

"Of course you could. You need to get a little backbone."

"Oh, Cait, is that the way I seem to you?"

"I don't mean to try to rearrange your life, but yes."

"You're so strong, so sure of yourself. Not all of us are like
that. You set out to get something done and it gets done. Like
this morning. I didn't want you to put yourself out for me but
you just rolled over my objections. I think about doing something and then I second-guess myself until I'm almost stag-
nant."

"I can understand your problems with Jordanna, but why
this 'little woman' mentality?" Cait sipped her coffee, now
afraid she'd said too much. "You're so much more than you
think you are."

Angie let out a long sigh. "I'm afraid that you see things in
me that aren't there. What if I see people and they don't like
me? What if they blow me off?"

"Has that happened often? All the people in the class love
you."

"I've been at Tony's family gatherings and lots of the women
are working, smarter than I am, with college degrees. We talk
about kids and house things but when it comes to anything
more intellectual, they pretty much ignore me and talk among
themselves. I just barely finished high school."

"Education isn't everything. I know lots of people with

only high school diplomas who are smart, witty, and charming. You've got so much to offer but you've got the self-confidence of a flounder."

Angie giggled as Cait continued. "You're warm, loving, generous, and a great friend. You have lots of poise and patience in front of a class full of yoga nincompoops like me.

"When I joined the class you went out of your way to make me comfortable and found time to show me the basics that everyone else already knew. You were wonderful and made me feel like I could learn everything. Why doesn't that translate into the rest of your life?"

"I don't know. When I teach the class I feel like I really know what I'm talking about. I feel"—she stopped and thought for a moment—"I feel bigger there."

"Well then, our job is to make you feel bigger elsewhere."

As Cait heard gurgling sounds from the baby monitor, Angie said, "Here we go."

It took only a few minutes for Angie to get the two babies changed and dressed and she chatted with her friend while Cait watched in amazement. "You do all that without even thinking about it, carrying on a complete conversation, diapering, goo-gooing at them, and keeping both of them amused with toys. I'm awed."

"Don't be silly. This part's easy. They could each use a bottle of juice," she said as she carried one baby on each hip. "Would you like to feed MaryLee?"

Cait was suddenly terrified. Feed babies? She'd played with her nieces and nephews, but they were older and could pretty much fend for themselves. She'd never actually dealt with a little one who wriggled and spit up. She looked down at her long fingernails. "I'm afraid of scratching her," she said, feeling panicky. "And what if I drop her? As you can see, I'm not too good with babies."

"You don't have to hold her if you don't want to," Angie said, putting the two now fussing children on a large mat on the floor, "but I thought you were considering having kids. Now's your chance to practice, and everything will go much faster with us double-teaming." She filled two small bottles with apple juice. "Want to give it a go? They're pretty indestructible, you know. I can give you a shirt to put over your clothes if you're afraid of the mess."

Cait looked down at her blue flowered blouse and navy slacks and shrugged. Here she was telling Angie to be brave and she was shaking like a leaf. Feeling totally out of her league, she wrapped a large, man-tailored shirt around her shoulders and took MaryLee from Angie. "She's heavy," Cait said as the baby settled in her arm.

"Watch your necklace!" Angie yelled as MaryLee grabbed for the strand of white summer beads that hung around Cait's neck. With Brandon on her hip, Angie rushed over, but Cait laughed as MaryLee put a fist full of beads in her mouth. "Don't worry. She can suck on the beads if she wants to."

She sat on the corner of the sofa while MaryLee slobbered on the beads and took the bottle from Angie. The baby was adorable, dressed in a pair of pink flowered overalls with a pink ruffled shirt. At eleven months, the twins were now quite self-sufficient. MaryLee grabbed the bottle and with only a little support from Cait, slurped down the contents. Cait beamed. "They're amazing."

It was Angie's turn to grin. "Yeah, they are, aren't they? And you're doing great with her."

It took several minutes and a bit of swearing to get the car seats firmly attached to the backseat of Cait's van, then they loaded the stroller into the cargo space and were off. "Okay, what's on the agenda?"

Angie reeled off a list of small errands, then said, "You know how you felt about taking MaryLee before? Sort of scared and a bit overwhelmed?"

"You noticed that, didn't you."

"Yeah. Actually you looked terrified, that deer-in-the-headlights stare. Well, that's how I feel a lot of the time. I feel small."

"That's all well and good, but I *did* take the baby and it worked out fine. Maybe there's a lesson there for you."

"Maybe."

Angie and Cait spent the next few hours driving from the cleaner's to the post office, from the drive-through at the bank to the drugstore. Eventually they stopped at the local mall and settled the twins in their stroller. Angie stopped at a baby store to pick up socks for the twins, then at a party store for a gift for one of Tony's nephews. Cait was amazed at the number of people who stopped to admire the babies and she felt a certain pride in being part of the little group. She sat with the stroller at a small table in the food court while Angie got them each a slice of pizza and a diet soda. When a woman with a cranky toddler stopped and asked about the babies, she answered the woman's questions as if the babies were hers.

When Angie returned, Cait wanted to reimburse her for lunch but Angie said, "This is to thank you for today. I've had such a wonderful time. It's not just getting all this stuff done, but having you keep me company has been so great."

"Yeah," Cait said, a huge grin spreading over her face. "It has, hasn't it."

They finished their day at the supermarket and made it back to Angie's just as the babies were ready to eat and go down for a late afternoon nap. Surprising herself, Cait offered to feed Brandon while Angie took care of MaryLee. She quickly got the hang of getting the food into the little boy's mouth, rather than on his cheeks and chin. Once the babies were down they quickly put the groceries away and Cait got ready to leave. "I've got to get going."

"It's been such a nice day," Angie said. "I can't thank you enough."

"Don't thank me," Cait said. "It's been a pleasure. I'll leave the car seats in the garage and maybe we can do this again next week?"

"I'd love to. Let's plan on it and I'll see you on Saturday."

"Will do."

As Cait walked back to her car, she thought about Angie's lack of self-confidence and thought she might be able to help. A trip to the hairdresser might be a good place to start and maybe they could pick up a few new clothes. Then they'd tackle the Jordanna problem. She stopped her racing mind. *Go slowly*, she told herself. *There's plenty of time.*

She didn't log onto the computer until the following afternoon and she was delighted to see that Hotguy344 was logged on. It was three in the afternoon in East Hudson, so Cait calculated that it was about eleven in Fairbanks. They set up their cameras and masturbated together to very satisfying orgasms.

She had become used to him calling her Cait and she'd been calling him Brett face to face. He asked subtle questions about where she lived but she carefully didn't tell him anything. She knew that he was thousands of miles away, but her discussion with her friends had made her extra wary so she carefully cleared the desk beside her computer of anything that he might see that could give him her address.

As long as she considered all the angles, she would enjoy him and not worry.

Chapter
18

Mid-September in East Hudson was a festive time. Always held on the third weekend in September, the East Hudson Grange Fair was a combination of an old-time country fair and amusement park. On the north side of the grange fairgrounds on the edge of town, tents were set up to show off and eventually judge everything from apple pies to pigs and chickens. As their annual fund-raiser, the local fire department hired a traveling carnival and had them set it up on the southern side. In between, food booths and games of chance dotted the field, which began as grass on the first night but by the end of the weekend wasn't much more than dirt with a few greenish-brown patches. The highlight of the annual fair was Saturday night's massive fireworks display.

To herald the fair, colorful posters were displayed on most store windows all over the county. Attendance was usually brisk and this September was no exception. The weather gods had smiled on the fair this year, so the town was blessed with above normal temperatures and cloudless skies during the day, and a full moon at night. A few of the largest maples were already tipped with flames of orange and deep red, heralding the beginning of fall.

Dan and Monica wandered the grounds arm in arm. They

both wore jeans, Dan's with a tan long-sleeved polo shirt. Since evenings were getting chilly, he carried a light brown windbreaker. Monica's black jeans were complemented by a red, white, and black plaid shirt and bright red sweater. This was their fifth date and the list of interests they shared had grown, as had the list of things about which they differed.

Their tastes were pretty similar on TV shows and movies, and they had agreed on several local restaurants, but they differed on many political issues, Dan a mild conservative and Monica a mild liberal. Their discussions about current events were heated but cerebral and kept them both on their toes. They did agree on tax cuts, but argued for an hour on the future of Social Security. "We're so different," Monica said after one particularly heated argument, "it's amazing that we get along so well."

"If we agreed on everything," Dan said with a wink, "one of us would be redundant."

Monica's laugh was genuine. Dan never lost his temper or let her get too angry about anything, and that allowed her to speak her mind. It was totally comfortable. When she was alone, however, she wondered whether she should just cut this off before it went too far. She knew that eventually he'd hurt her and the deeper in she got, the more it would devastate her. When they were together, however, she couldn't imagine not seeing him.

They hadn't made love yet and she was wondering whether she was totally misreading him. Maybe he liked her as a friend and nothing more. Maybe he was gay, using her as a shield against such accusations. Maybe he was asexual, just not interested in sex with anyone. None of those made any sense. She knew he was interested by the way he looked at her when he thought she wasn't looking. There was desire there, so why hadn't he acted on it?

Why hadn't she? She was no shy violet. In the past she'd asked many of her business associates whether they were interested in going back to the corporate apartment with her, so why was she so reluctant to ask Dan back to her town house? Yet she hadn't.

The hit of the fair that year was a gigantic Ferris wheel with thirty two-person gondolas. Dan bought tickets and they watched the wheel rotate and made idle conversation as they inched forward in the long line. They were at the front of the line as the previous ride ended, thus they were the first to be guided into an empty car. They sat and Dan draped his arm over her shoulders. "Are you warm enough?"

"Sure," Monica said. "You?"

"I'm great." He looked up at the stars, his grin boyish and irresistible.

She leaned over and kissed him and he kissed her back, his arms now tight around her. Finally, when they came up for air, they looked down and watched others loading into the gondolas. She couldn't hold the question back any longer. "Aren't you interested in sex?"

"What brought that on?"

"I've just been wondering. Either you're not interested in me that way or you have the most amazing self-restraint."

"Where you're concerned I've forced myself to have amazing self-restraint."

Puzzled, Monica asked, "Why?"

Dan leaned back, his arm still around her shoulders, and looked at her intently. "You have a very low opinion of men and I don't want to get lumped with all the guys you've known who fucked and ran."

"Why do you say I have a low opinion of men?"

"Come on, Monica, it's written all over you. I don't know what's poisoned you on my gender but it's pretty obvious you're soured on all males. I'm crazy about you and I'm doing everything I can to make you understand that I'm not like the men who've hurt you." When she took a breath to respond, he held up his hand to forestall her interruption. "Don't give me

the standard answer, and I'm not interested in playing shrink
as to why you feel that way. I want you. I want to make mad,
passionate love to you in every room of your town house and
mine, then start again, but I'm not willing to take the risk of
turning you off to me."

Monica was stunned, first that he wanted her that much,
and second that he was so perceptive. He was right, she did
have a low opinion of men. Her father's desertion and her
mother's venom had perpetuated that. In high school she'd
developed earlier than many of the other girls, and because of
her large bustline and outgoing manner, word got around that
she was easy. At first she'd been sick about it, but then she decided that, since she already had the reputation, she might as
well live up to it.

Boys, then college men, wanted sex and showed her a good
time to get it. She learned how to please and be pleased, and it
had stood her in good stead. Two of her professors gave her
better grades than she deserved because she decided that sexuality could be useful and had seen to it that they had a good
time when she went to their offices for extra help. In recent
years, she'd been rewarded at work for much the same reasons.

Now Bonnie was separated, Eve's boss was cheating on his
wife, and Cait suspected her husband of doing the same. Men
were all shits who thought with their cocks. Dan, however,
seemed to be another matter entirely. He was sweet, genuine,
and to the best of everything she knew, honest. "I'm surprised that you think I'm soured on all men."

"No, you're not," Dan said. "You're just amazed that I
know you so well on such a short acquaintance. Actually, it's
not short acquaintance at all. For me it's been a million years
of frustration and patience, and my body knows it."

Monica blushed. "You think you know me pretty well, don't
you?"

"Damn right." Dan grabbed a handful of her hair as the

gondola moved to the apex of the Ferris wheel to load yet another pair of riders. His mouth came down on hers in a de-
manding kiss. "You drive me crazy, woman." He grabbed her
hand and pressed it against his groin. "See what you do to
me?"

He was fully erect, throbbing against his slacks. She grinned,
took his hand, and placed it between her thighs. "I might say
the same to you." Leaving his hand where it was, she unzipped his fly and freed his engorged cock. He had velvety
soft skin over rock-hard flesh. She wrapped her fingers around
him and shifted so he could rub her and try to relieve the deep
need she too felt.

As the gondola shifted again, they fondled each other. "I'd
climb onto you right now," he said, his voice a harsh whisper,
"but this isn't the place."

Her pulse pounded and she couldn't catch her breath. She
knew that if she didn't satisfy her hunger she wouldn't be able
to function. "Do it for me right here."

Dan's grin was magic and he rubbed her, finding her clit
through her jeans. "Like this?" He turned so he shielded what
he was doing from prying eyes.

She leaned back. "Just like that. Oh God." It took only a
moment until she came, stuffing her fist into her mouth to
keep from screaming. Limp, she watched him tuck himself
back into his jeans and zip them. "I'm not wasting this up
here," he said. "Your place or mine?"

She giggled. "The way I feel right now, how about the backseat of your car?"

At that moment the wheel began its full rotations, and as
the wind blew her hair, she laughed from the joy of it. His
laugh was deeper and no less wonderful.

They both seemed to savor the knowledge that they were
going to make love later, so to her shock they actually stayed
and watched the fireworks, wrapped around each other, kissing deeply during each loud boom.

As her front door closed behind them, he leaned back against it and gathered her into his arms. "I'm torn between drawing out the incredible pleasure of knowing what we're going to do and the desire I'm feeling."

She pressed the length of her body against him, reveling in the feeling of her swollen breasts flattening against his chest. She cupped the back of his head and pressed her mouth against him. The kiss was deep, slow, and almost lazy, with an undercurrent of so much heat she felt she might melt. Might melt? She'd been melting ever since her intense orgasm in the gondola.

When he drew back and gazed into her eyes, obviously waiting once more for the signal that this was really going to happen, that she wanted it as much as he did, she bit his lower lip, then giggled and said, "Last one to the bedroom is a frustrated lover."

Instead of following her, he picked her up. Actually swept her off her feet the way Rhett had done to Scarlett in the famous scene. "Which way?" he growled.

She pointed toward the bedroom and he quickly carried her in and put her down in the center of her king-sized bed. When she began to unbutton her shirt, he stilled her hands. "I've waited a long time for this and although I'm in a hurry, I'm in no hurry." Realizing what he'd said, he laughed. "You know what I mean."

She did, and she was in the same mood. Softly, she said, "I know exactly how you feel."

"Then let me."

As he settled on the edge of the bed she dropped her hand to the mattress beside her. She watched his face as he slowly opened each button and stroked the soft flesh revealed. Suddenly she was glad she'd thought to wear the scarlet bra and panty set because it said what she wanted him to know. There was a sexual animal beneath her clothing and he would reap the rewards of uncovering it. As he ran his fingertips over the silky fabric of her bra, she moved her hips, using the tight crotch of her jeans to scratch the hungry itch between her legs.

"So hot," he purred. "I love what you're wearing."

"I love what you're doing," she responded.

He bent and pressed his mouth to her fabric-covered nipple, biting the swollen nub just hard enough that she squirmed with the heat of it. She tangled her fingers in his hair and held him close as he kneaded one breast and licked and nibbled the other. "You're making me crazy," she said, barely able to speak.

"Good," he said, his voice hoarse.

He slipped his hands beneath her back and unhooked her bra, baring her throbbing breasts. Again, he gazed with obvious admiration at her body, blowing on her skin, dampened by his mouth. Unable to bear another minute without his lips on hers, she again tangled her fingers in his hair and pulled his face to hers. The kiss was long and filled with their combined hunger. "You're a greedy woman," he said as he pulled his mouth away.

"I'm hungry for you," she said, pulling his shirt off over his head and rubbing her hard nipples against his lightly furred chest. She wanted to feel him, to taste him, to experience everything he was. Her mouth found his again and the kiss was filled with all their desires.

Eventually she tugged at the waistband of his jeans and he pulled them off along with his briefs. Beautifully naked, he crawled onto the bed. She gazed at his bare body. She'd been with so many men, some better developed than Dan, some with a bigger or longer cock, but never had she desired a man the way she wanted him now. Suddenly there were no other men, just him.

He quickly unfastened her jeans and dragged them down her legs. "I love those," he said, staring at her tiny, bright red bikinis. "It's like they're concealing yet inviting me to unwrap you."

She raised her hips in a silent invitation for him to completely undress her, and he did. When they were both naked, she expected him to mount her, but he surprised her as he did constantly. Although he was obviously ready to slide into her, he crawled between her legs and parted her thighs. She knew he was going to love her with his mouth, but she wasn't sure she wanted to wait to feel him fill her.

Then his tongue was flicking over her erect clitoris and she lost all conscious thought. He seemed to know exactly how much pressure, how fast, how to drive her upward inch by inch, mile by mile. She flew, higher and higher, until, when his finger slid inside of her, she came, her muscles clenching his hand. "Oh God, oh God," she screamed.

He barely stopped touching and licking her while he unrolled a condom over his rampant cock, then rammed it into her. She didn't know whether she came again or her orgasm merely continued, but she wrapped her legs around his waist and bucked with the explosions going off inside of her. Never had she been as oblivious to her partner's pleasure as she was at that moment, taking, luxuriating in the pleasure his body was giving her. His bellow as he came told her that whatever she'd been doing had pleasured him as much as herself.

Still imbedded within her, he dropped beside her and they dozed. They made love twice more before morning.

Late on a Wednesday morning toward the end of September, Eve was sitting at her desk when a small woman in a tailored suit approached her cubicle and smiled warmly. "Hello. You must be Eve."

Puzzled, Eve nodded, and the woman continued. "It's so nice to finally meet you. I'm Diana Kreuger, Mike's wife."

For a moment Eve was paralyzed. Mike's wife. Her Mike's wife. *Oh, God. She knows about us and she's come here to confront us. Oh, God.* She swallowed hard and having only paused a split second, said, "It's nice to meet you, too." They'd spoken on the phone from time to time when Diana was trying to locate her husband but here she was in the flesh. She was probably in her mid-thirties, maybe five feet two with a head full of short blond curls, hazel eyes, and a slightly sallow complexion. She wore a gray fall suit with a gold and gray print blouse and had put on only a little lipstick. She extended her hand and Eve shook it reflexively. It felt very strange to actually touch Mike's wife.

"Is he around? We're going to lunch and then a matinee. My folks are in town and looking after the kids so I'm actually a lady of leisure today. It feels really strange but wonderful."

Mike's wife. They were spending the afternoon together. The day before, she and Mike had been at their usual hotel. "He's in his office," Eve said, and pointed toward the side of the room. "You know where it is?"

"I hate to admit this but I've never been here before. Mike's worked here for four years and I've never gotten into the city to see this place." She looked around. "It's nice here."

Eve's brain was so frozen that she could barely put together a coherent sentence. "It's very comfortable." *For everyone right now but me.* She rose to show Mrs. Krueger to Mike's office but the woman waved Eve back. "That's okay. Don't get up. I'll find it."

As Eve watched Diana's back as she walked away, her eyes filled. Diana seemed like a nice enough woman, and from the glow on her face as she looked around, she wasn't someone who was staying with her husband merely for the sake of the kids. Had Mike been handing her that clichéd line all this time? Weeks ago when she told the girls about Mike, Monica had hit on it right away. No. Mike was wonderful and wouldn't lie to her. Diana must be a good actress, or a woman deluding herself.

Who exactly, Eve wondered, staring at her computer with her head down so she didn't have to look at Mike's wife, was deluding whom?

The following Tuesday, she lay beside Mike in their hotel room, both of them satiated. "I met your wife last week when she came to pick you up," Eve said.

"Yeah, she told me." Mike quickly propped himself on his elbow and stared down at her. "You didn't say anything, did you?"

Eve sat up. "Of course not. Did she say that I did?"

"No," he said, visibly relaxing. "I just wondered."

"I wouldn't do something like that. She seemed nice." Eve pulled the sheet up so it covered her naked breasts.

"Yeah," Mike said, reaching over and downing several swallows of soda. "She's okay."

"How old are your kids again?"

"Nine, six, and four."

"So you won't be able to think about a separation for several years."

Mike coughed, saying that he'd swallowed down the wrong pipe. When he caught his breath, he said, "Not for quite a while."

He was lying. How she knew she wasn't sure, but she knew, and it came as a revelation to her.

"Listen," Mike said, climbing out of bed, "I've got to run." He quickly dressed, and with a quick peck on her cheek, left.

What am I doing? And what about this new phone sex thing they were doing together? They were having erotic conversations every weekend, and although it helped to bridge the gap between their Tuesdays, she wondered how he'd come up with the idea out of the blue as he had. The tiny thought that had been nagging at her brain surfaced in a rush. Had he gotten the idea from another woman? Was he doing it with someone else, also not his wife? He'd been on a few out-of-town trips recently and hadn't taken her. Had he taken someone else?

Eve thought about a little snippet of the conversation she'd had with Monica over margaritas that wonderful evening two weeks before.

"If he were free, would you marry him?"

"In a minute."

"And have him cheat on you, too? He would, you know. Once a cheater . . ."

Monica's words had been echoing in her head ever since. Was she an idiot? Her eyes filled. He was her life. He was her love. They would be together eventually. Was that all a fantasy? Her eyes overflowed and tears trickled down her cheeks. *I'm some kind of idiot.*

Poor Diana. She's just like me, with no clue, just illusions. Or maybe she did know what he did in his spare time. No one could be as ignorant as she'd appeared. Maybe she knew there were others, but she was willing to accept it to keep her marriage together. Would Eve be willing to settle for weekly funches and not think about Mike's wife and the possibility of still another woman?

No! Yes! No! I don't know. She wept, then dried her eyes, washed her face in cold water, dressed, and headed back to the office. She'd think about this, maybe discuss it with her friends the following Saturday. Better still, they were getting together that Sunday night for girls' night out in addition to Saturday lunch. Things were more relaxed then, so that would be better. Saturdays were for small talk, Sunday evenings were for soul-searching.

She thought briefly about the other time she'd been made an idiot because she had such a low opinion of herself, then smothered the memories. That evening she ate an entire box of Godiva chocolates, watched both *Ghost* and *Pretty Woman*, then went to bed fantasizing about Patrick Swayze and Richard Gere fighting over her. As she drifted off, she wondered which one she hoped would win.

* * *

Thursday morning, after a particularly delightful day with Angie's twins, Cait met Logan over the breakfast table. She told him about the babies and her wonderful afternoon. She'd fed Brandon and actually changed his diaper for the first time, and it was a cinch. "That sounds great," Logan said, putting down his *New York Times*. "She sounds like a lovely woman."

"She is, and maybe we can do something about helping her out with a car."

"Sure," Logan said, "but if we buy one for her, even a used one, she won't accept it."

Cait sighed. He was right about that. "Maybe we can think of something." Before Logan could get back to his paper, she said, "There's something else. Spending time with those wonderful children made me think about us. Maybe we could try again."

As Cait watched, Logan's face became a mask. "I don't think so."

"Why not? There might be another doctor with other ideas. Several said that if we just stopped trying, good things might happen."

"I thought you didn't want to try anymore."

"I didn't then, but I've been thinking about it more and more lately, and yesterday was the icing on the cake. A baby would complete our family."

"I don't think so. I've gotten past that."

"I thought you wanted to give your folks their first grandson."

He leaned forward in his chair and rested his forearms on the table. There was a belligerence in his posture. "Not anymore."

"Why not, Logan?" Cait asked, totally shocked by his negative attitude. She'd thought he'd jump at the chance.

"I just don't, and that's that." He picked up his paper and buried himself in it, closing off the conversation.

Cait could see how adamant Logan was and backed off. Why

the complete about-face? she wondered. Stunned, she sat for a few minutes in total dismay. She'd been so wrong about his re-action, thinking that he'd be pleased that she wanted to try again. She could understand it if he'd been taken aback by her change of heart, but there was something more. He'd shut her down completely and that wasn't like him. Well, actually it was like him, but not on the subject of babies. He'd been so insistent until she'd finally ended it months before. What had changed? She knew he wasn't going to discuss it anymore today, so she got up from the table and headed for the shower. She had to give his strange new attitude more thought.

Chapter
19

Monica thought about Dan as she got out of her car in the parking lot of Huckleberry's the following Sunday evening for girls' night out. The fact that Dan's face jumped into her mind didn't surprise her, since he invaded her thoughts frequently, more frequently than she liked. She couldn't seem to keep him in proportion. Their relationship was about as hot as it could get, and despite all her efforts she was nuts about him. They laughed often, sharing what were quickly becoming family jokes. He was considerate and easy to get along with. And of course, the sex was wonderful, varied and intensely erotic. He loved to play, and although he didn't realize it, he was slowly teaching Monica to enjoy sex more and view it less as a means to an end.

She recalled their date the previous evening. He'd prepared dinner, and she found herself looking forward to it, since he was a quite respectable cook. She smiled as she remembered how inappropriate the word "respectable" was where Dan was concerned.

After putting her jacket away, she and Dan settled in the living room of his generously sized apartment. The first time she'd visited there she realized how much the eclectic room suited him and his varied interests. A pale tan, butter-soft leather sofa, a matching lounge chair, large maple coffee table, and a pair of roomy end tables sat on a brightly colored Navaho style carpet that added life to the room. An oversized TV hung on one wall while the others were filled with black and white prints of New York City street scenes. There were several large, brightly colored pots filled with corn plants and ferns to soften the otherwise exceptionally male room.

He put a Miles Davis CD on the player and opened a bottle of very good Merlot. She sipped the fine red wine slowly. "Dinner smells very good," she said to break the intense sexual tension that always existed when they were alone.

"I think it will be, but tonight's going to be a bit unusual."

"I'm always up for new things," she said, then felt heat rise in her face at her double entendre. When they were together everything seemed to have a sexual second meaning.

"I know," he said, leering at her playfully. "That's one of the things I love about you, and you'll get to prove it before the evening's over."

"Hmm," she said, sipping her wine to have something to do with her hands. "That sounds interesting." She was mildly aroused as she always was with him, but tonight she felt tense as well, holding herself tightly, not letting herself go totally, afraid she'd fall, and just keep falling, unable to save herself. Save herself? From what? From getting too involved with this wonderful man? God, why couldn't she shut off her brain and just let things roll? Why did she have to keep analyzing everything?

Even in yoga class on Saturday mornings she found her eyes straying toward him, and usually found him looking back. When their eyes locked, words became superfluous.

Dan put his wineglass on the table. "Let me set the ground rules for this evening. I've made several dishes, most finger foods—literally—so no utensils of any kind will be allowed. If one of us gets too messy, it's fingers and tongues."

The way he said "tongues" made her salivate, and she felt her nipples tighten. "Are you serious?"

"I sure am. Game?" he said with a deeply suggestive leer.

"Me?" Always. Why not admit it? "Always."

"Good," he said, rising. "Let me get the appetizers." When she tried to follow, he denied her access to the kitchen. "This is all mine."

Five minutes later he came into the living room and set the wooden tray he was holding on the coffee table. He'd made tiny hot dogs with a mustard-based dipping sauce and tiny pizzas with extra cheese. He'd also brought little serving bowls filled with olives, tiny pickles, and platter of assorted vegetables with a sour cream dip.

"That's quite a collection of goodies," Monica said.

"I slaved my fingers to the bone," he said teasingly. When she raised an eyebrow, he continued, "Okay, I will admit that most of this came out of my freezer and microwave. Remember the rules. No utensils."

Well, Monica thought, *this won't be too difficult to eat with my fingers*. For the next half hour they talked about trivialities, sipped wine, and munched appetizers. "Your fingers are a bit messy," Dan said after she'd eaten a miniature pizza. "Allow me."

He lifted her hand to his lips and put her index finger into his mouth. Warm and wet, his tongue made love to her hand. When she shivered, he moved on to the next finger. When he'd licked and sucked each one, he tongued her palm, swirling the tip over her skin until she couldn't keep her hips still. Then, with an infectious grin, he stood and went back into the kitchen. When she regained her senses, she called, "What can I do to help?"

"Nothing. Just sit there. We're eating in the living room tonight."

"There must be something I can do," she said, hoping he

could find something to keep her mind occupied with non-erotic images.

"Put another CD on. I'll just be a minute."

She washed her hands, messy despite his ministrations, and replaced the Miles Davis CD with an old Nat King Cole recording. As his mellow voice filled the apartment, Dan called, "Good choice. I see I've converted you."

"You certainly have. This is really good stuff." She settled back onto the sofa and kicked off her shoes. "I'm really grateful."

Dan came in from the kitchen with the same large tray, now filled with covered dishes. "I'm grateful to you for a lot of things." He put a plate in front of her and added one for him. "You were serious about this fingers thing," Monica said, realizing that there were no napkins or silverware.

"I was." He set a serving dish on the table and lifted the lid. One compartment of the three-sectioned platter was filled with small, Frenched lamb riblets, lightly breaded with crumbs and smelling of garlic, another with a mound of potatoes au gratin, and the third with tiny baby peas. "I remember that you liked lamb."

"I do, but how in the world are we going to eat this stuff?"

"We might have to wait until some of this cools, but I purposely kept most everything at a comfortable temperature." He sat beside her, picked up his plate, and served himself a lamb rib and a handful of peas, then scooped potatoes onto his plate with his fingers. "You'll probably want to serve yourself."

She'd never done anything like this. Her parents had been quite formal at the dinner table and good manners had been drummed into her from the cradle. Her father had even taught her how to eat chicken wings with a knife and fork before he left them. Her eyes flashed from her plate to the serving dish to Dan's eyes. "You've got to be kidding."

"You said you were up for new experiences," he said, his expression challenging, "but I can get forks if you insist." He licked the cheese and potatoes from his fingers with exaggerated motions of his tongue and almost dared her to join him.

Monica had never imagined that she'd eat gooey cheesy potatoes with her fingers. Her dinner companions usually took her to four-star restaurants where the serving staff stopped just short of chewing your food for you. Fingers? Maybe with sushi, but this? She huffed out a breath, then let her shoulders relax and giggled. Why the hell not? "You asked for it." She took a lamb chop and some peas, then dug her fingers into the potatoes and plopped a mound onto her plate. There was something sensual about the feel of mashed potatoes on her hand. Or was everything sensual when she was with Dan?

Once she got over her initial reluctance she ate with gusto, slurping cheese and garlic from her fingers and playfully sucking peas from the palm of her hand. It became a game—who would make the lewdest gesture with the food. "Remember the eating scene from *Tom Jones*, or the lobster in *Flashdance*?" she asked.

"That's where I got this idea. It seemed both decadent and erotic." He paused, then licked his lips. "It is. Both."

Getting more into the spirit, Monica took a finger full of potatoes and plopped it in his palm. Then she lifted his hand and with only the tip of her tongue, licked up the goo.

Aroused and giggling, they finally finished the main course and Dan quickly put all the plates on the tray and disappeared into the kitchen, leaving Monica to wash her hands, then change the CD again. Grinning widely, she found an old recording of Ella Fitzgerald singing Cole Porter and put it on to play.

Dan returned with dessert. "I should have known," Monica said, shaking her head. He had an ice cream scoop, a container of Jamoca Almond Fudge, her favorite flavor, a jar of chocolate sauce with a spoon inside, and an aerosol can of whipped cream. "This is so clichéd," she said, her eyes gleaming. "And so sexy." Her body was throbbing in expectation.

"Rules are that you serve with the utensils, but then hands—and other body parts—only."

He handed her the ice cream server and she dropped a scoop of ice cream into a bowl, spooned some fudge over the top, and handed it to him, then duplicated everything for herself. "As for the whipped cream, you're on your own."

"Yeah, I am." His expression was warm and tickled her in the pit of her stomach. She was falling in love with this man, she thought, throwing safety to the winds. Realizing how open she was leaving herself, she said a quick prayer. *Don't kick me. Please let this guy be the real thing.*

Carefully cleaning his fingers, Dan quickly lifted her sweater over her head, then unclipped her bra. He took a finger full of ice cream and coated one erect nipple, then took several minutes licking it off. The contrast between the cold ice cream and his hot mouth was devastating. She pulled off his shirt and rubbed fudge on his flat male nipples, then licked and sucked until he was moaning.

Over and over they coated each other's naked upper body with sweets, and licked and sucked it off. She wanted him badly, but she was also enjoying the torture. Finally she told him to remove his pants. When he was naked, she scooped fudge onto his hard, full erection, then slowly sucked his cock into her mouth.

"I don't want to make a mess all over your sofa," she said.

"To hell with mess, woman. You're driving me crazy."

Using every trick she'd ever learned, she excited him until she knew he was ready to come. Then she removed the rest of her clothes and rested against the arm of the sofa, offering herself to him. He didn't hesitate. Coating her folds with fudge, then spraying whipped cream on her pubic area, he took several long minutes delving and probing with his tongue to find every bit.

Eventually, neither of them could wait any longer. He guided her to the heavy glass coffee table in front of the sofa and when she'd knelt beside it, stretched her across it, face down, so her heated breasts pressed against the cool glass, her rear in the air. She'd indulged in anal sex, and for a moment, while he opened the ever-present foil package, she wondered whether that was what she wanted at that moment. She needn't have thought about it. He quickly slid his condom-covered cock into her waiting pussy, doggie style, holding her hips tightly so her buttocks pressed against him. For several moments, he remained still and she could feel the twitch of his erection, buried within her. Then he slowly withdrew and slid in again.

How did he have the self-control to draw out the pleasure this way? she wondered. God, he was a fabulous lover, and her body responded, heat flowing through her. She clenched her vaginal muscles, rhythmically squeezing his cock. "Shit," he cried, then came without moving. She continued to milk him until he quieted. Then he reached beneath her and rubbed her clit until she also climaxed, her thighs trembling, her fingers grasping the edge of the table. Panting and throbbing, they slowly returned to earth. Later, they showered together and made love again under the pounding spray.

Monica returned from her erotic memory and watched Cait's Honda pull into the parking space beside her Lexus. The Honda was followed almost immediately by Eve's battle-scarred Toyota. Monica couldn't suppress her grin. These were real heart-to-heart friends and it felt incredibly good to have them. It had only been two months since that first rainy morning but she felt as though she'd known the three of them for years.

Monica had been to her doctor the previous week and he'd commented on her decrease in blood pressure. Dan? Girls' night out? Whatever was responsible, she was glad of it. She waved to the other two, and as they walked toward Huckleberry's door, she turned at the sound of Angie's car entering the lot. They waited in the cooling October breeze until their foursome was complete, then, dressed alike, in jeans and simple shirts, each with a lightweight jacket or sweater for later, they linked arms and walked in.

Huckleberry's was unusually loud, with slightly rowdy Sunday Night Football fans filling the bar area, alternately cheering and moaning. Soon it would be the baseball playoffs that would be occupying the minds of all the local sports fans. Would the Yankees do it or disappoint again?

Ignoring that end of the restaurant, the four women were seated in a booth toward the rear of the other section, peering at the drink menu. "Those margaritas were wonderful last time," Cait said, closing the plastic-covered pages. "I'm going to do that again."

"I think I'll do something different," Angie said, gazing at the photo of a pink confection. "A strawberry daiquiri tonight, maybe. Tony was amazed when I came home a bit slozzed the last time we did this. I usually don't drink, but I was a bit tipsy and"—she colored and tried unsuccessfully to suppress a grin, —"well, if the truth were known, we made hot, hungry love like we haven't since before the twins were born. It was fabulous."

"Go, girl!" Monica said, raising her palm toward Angie for a slap. "And you didn't tell us until now?" Monica felt Angie's palm tap hers lightly, then Angie's face reddened still more. "Now you're really blushing. Was it that good?"

"Actually, it was wonderful," Angie said, head down. Then she slumped. "Too bad it hasn't lasted."

"We'll have to work on that," Cait said, leaning forward on her elbows. "Angie and I have been going out together once a week for almost a month. We call it shopping, and we do shop, but they're more therapy sessions for both of us. I think I'm hurt that you waited until tonight to admit to the occasional bout of good sex."

Head still lowered, Angie said, "It's so difficult to talk about. I come from a very closed-mouth family and I've never had friends like you three."

They all linked hands. "Yeah," Eve sighed. "Me, too."

"Three," Cait said, nodding.

"Four," Monica added.

"Okay, enough of this love fest. Let's get to the important stuff." Cait turned to the waitress who'd arrived at their table. "A margarita, a strawberry daiquiri, and . . . "

"I'll have a piña colada," Monica said. "Eve?"

"Give me a rum and coke. Two shots of rum, please."

"Let's have a plate of those irresistible nachos, too," Cait said.

"You're mean. Those are so bad for my cholesterol," Monica said.

"I know," Cait said with an evil grin. "Ain't I horrible?"

"Okay, new topic. I've got a question for you all tonight," Monica said, "and my own fabulous answer. What's the most unusual place you've ever made it?"

"Okay," Cait said. "No games. No answers from us. Spill yours."

"Dan and I finally did it." She paused, then when no one looked startled, she added, "You're not surprised."

"Nope," Cait said, looking quite proud of herself. "We all knew it was just a matter of time. I gather that you did it someplace weird, however."

"I guess I was the only one in doubt about having sex with Dan. Well, we started to make out at the top of the Ferris wheel at the Grange Fair."

"You're kidding," Angie said, her jaw literally dropping. "Tony and I took the babies, but they were asleep before the fireworks. I wanted to see their reactions but we went home early."

"At the top of the Ferris wheel?" Cait said, unwilling to let the story stop there.

Monica described her evening with Dan, leaving out only the most intimate details.

"Oh my God," Cait said, her grin wide, her hand reaching

out to shake Monica's. "That's so bizarre, and so romantic. You have to buy the first round."

Drinks arrived and the women took their first swallows, pleasure evident on all four faces. "So things are going well with you two, Monica," Angie said.

Monica set her drink down with a clunk. "Very well."

"What's he like when he's not doing yoga?"

"He's a very busy and successful man. He works for one of those Internet service companies and he's the guy who travels around fixing stuff. That's about all I know about what he does."

"What kinds of things do you do together, besides the obvious, of course?" Cait continued.

"It's really silly. A few weeks ago we went bowling. I haven't been bowling since high school but he insisted. He knows about my visit to the doctor that started this whole thing, and he says he's on a campaign to keep me relaxed and healthy."

"A very wise man. What else?"

"Last week we went to Yonkers Raceway. We had a really nice dinner at the restaurant that overlooks the track and I bet on the horses." She giggled. "He did everything scientifically, reading all the data about how the horses ran last time and in what kind of weather. I picked mine because of the name and I actually came out ahead." She winked. "He lost twenty dollars. He also taught me a word game called Boggle and we play a lot, sometimes for forfeits, but let's not dwell on that." She couldn't control her delicious discomfort. The forfeits were usually sexual in nature. "We just have fun together."

"It all sounds so perfect."

"It is, and it terrifies me."

"You can make the most fabulous things into such a problem," Angie said, shaking her head in wonder.

"I know. I can't help it. I'm frightened that he'll turn out to be like all other men." When three women took breaths to argue, she said, "Okay, not all men, but most. I'm scared that

I'll get hurt like my mom did when my dad left." She told them a quick version of her teen years. "Every time I think about getting deeply involved with Dan my stomach hurts. What if he splits like Jake?"

"You're right to be cautious, I suppose," Cait said. "If you don't try, you won't get hurt. But you won't know the joy of a great relationship, either. You know the old saying, nothing ventured . . ."

"Nothing gained," Monica finished. "I know. There's another aspect to this, too. It's obvious that I didn't come to Dan a virgin, but he doesn't know the extent of my exploits. You all know, work and all. Since we're sleeping together now I assume that he'll want us to be monogamous. I can't give up the freedom to be with whoever I need to be with. My business will suffer if I do."

"How do you know that?" Cait asked. "Maybe you're good at your job and the sex thing is just a fringe benefit for the guys involved. Maybe you'd have gotten everything you have without the casting couch."

"I doubt it. I'm good at what I do for the agency, but not that good."

"Maybe you're merely borrowing trouble?" Angie said. "Do you really think he'll feel that way?" When Monica shrugged, she continued, "Do you feel that way? Is he seeing anyone else?"

"No. At least, I don't think so. He seems really focused. On me."

"Is that a bad thing?" Angie said. "How do you feel about it?"

The waitress arrived with a plate of nachos, and to stall, Monica grabbed a tortilla chip and chewed slowly. After a swallow of her drink, she continued. "The whole thing scares me to death." Her shoulders slumped. "Men just aren't reliable. Things are so good now, but what about when someone else comes along? What guarantee do I have?"

"None," Cait said, "but there are no guarantees with anything in life. You could get hit by a bus tomorrow morning. Make the most of everything and every day. That's my motto, and if being with Dan is good today, suck the juice out of it, so to speak."

Giggles rippled across the table at her double entendre. Monica licked salsa from her fingers and thought about Dan. Maybe they were all right and she should just plunge ahead. "That's okay for you," Monica said. "You've got your on-line guy and Logan."

"I guess." Cait's face darkened. "Actually, my on-line guy worries me a bit. He's been hinting that he wants us to meet in person."

"That's not a very good idea," Angie said.

"I know that," Cait snapped, "and thank God he's in Fairbanks and I'm here." She turned to Angie. "Sorry I jumped down your throat. The whole thing makes the hair on the back of my neck prickle and as good as the sex is, part of me is sorry I started the whole thing."

"I don't wonder," Monica said. "If he's hinting at getting together, then maybe you should stop chatting with him. Keep your computer turned off."

"I know," Cait said, rubbing her thumbnail with her index finger, "but it's so good. It's the only sex I get these days."

"Then be really careful not to give him any information about where you live and stuff," Monica said. "How about telling Logan? He might be able to help calm you down."

Cait's mouth tightened and she said firmly, "Not a chance. Even though I don't think it's cheating, he wouldn't understand."

"Okay," Monica said. "Not an option. I can talk to Dan, if you like. He understands this stuff. That's what he does. Maybe he can help somehow."

"Don't tell him who you want the information for."

"Okay," Monica said. "I'll just say it's for a friend." She grabbed another chip.

"You say the on-line stuff is the only sex you get?" Angie said, obviously not letting that remark slip by.

"Yeah," she said sadly. "Logan's a non-event. It doesn't happen at all now."

"I'm sorry. I don't get much, but once in a while . . ." Angie blushed again.

"I have to admit that I miss him," Cait said with a sigh. "He's annoying at times, and very distant these days, but I do care about him. I feel there's a gigantic wall between us and I can't penetrate it. Last week I tried to talk to him about trying again to have a baby."

"I thought you didn't want to go the fertility route."

"I didn't, but I've been spending time with Angie's kids and it's given me the itch. I mentioned it to Logan last week and he snapped at me, positively cut me off. 'No kids. I just don't want to, and that's that.'"

"Didn't he want to give his parents a grandson?" Monica asked. "Why the sudden change of heart?"

"I've no clue."

Angie's voice lowered. "I hate to say this, but we're all pretty honest with each other. Could he be planning on leaving you? Kids would make that so much more complicated."

"I thought about that and it could be. I don't really know him right now so I can't figure it all out. He's positively schizophrenic. Sometimes he's easy to get along with and really seems to love me. At others . . . I just don't know anything anymore." She blinked several times, then said, "Let's change the subject."

Monica looked at Eve, who'd consumed her drink and not said a word. "Eve, you've been very quiet. Is something wrong?"

Chapter
20

E ve raised her head and fiddled with the straw from her drink. She'd been feeling depressed since the previous Wednesday. "Yeah, I guess there is." She paused as everyone turned to look at her. "I met Mike's wife last week at work and I can't get past it."

"Shit," Cait said.

Suddenly it all poured out. "I'd never met her until last Wednesday, when she came into the office to pick him up for lunch and a show. It felt awful." She held her hand up, her index finger and thumb about an inch apart. "I felt about this high. She's a very nice, kind of ordinary woman who seems oblivious to everything that's going on."

"Did you talk to him about it?" Angie asked.

"What is there to say? 'Oh, Mike, I met your wife. She's a nice woman and you're a shit for cheating on her.' No, and it's not about him anymore. It's about me. I have to decide what I'm going to do, and it confuses the hell out of me. I know I shouldn't want to be with a married man, but I still do." She folded and unfolded the straw. "Part of me thinks that I'm horrible for taking him away from his wife, but a voice in my head says that if he weren't with me he'd be with someone else, so why not stay with him. If I don't have Mike, what do I have?" She blinked several times, trying to keep tears from pooling in her eyes.

"You have yourself, and you have us," Angie said. "That's a pretty good start."

"I've been alone and lonely all my life. I don't want to start over." To have something to do with her hands, she dropped the mangled straw and fiddled with her napkin.

"Tony's got several unmarried cousins," Angie said with a weak smile. "I could have a dinner party."

Eve's voice was small and soft. "Thanks, but I'm not ready for that yet. First, I have to decide about my future with Mike." She crumpled the napkin and dropped it on the table.

"How do you think he'll take it if you tell him you don't want to see him again?" Monica asked.

"I don't know." Her hesitation lasted several long seconds. "If the truth were known, I suspect he's already got another girlfriend somewhere. I've become a convenient habit. Funch on Tuesdays."

Angie gasped. "You mean he's got three women with the hots for him? He must be quite something."

"He's really pretty ordinary, but in the beginning, he made me feel special and that was everything to me."

"He's just a man," Monica said, with a resigned sigh and a shake of her head. "Men will take what they can get."

"Don't do that!" Eve snapped, suddenly tired of Monica's persistent attitude about men and constant sniping. "I care about him, and by insulting him you insult me. Anyway, Mike may not be a particularly nice man, but that doesn't translate into your rule about all men."

Monica was obviously taken aback. "Okay," she said, quickly retreating. "I didn't mean anything about you personally, Eve. I'm sorry it came out that way."

Slightly mollified, Eve relaxed her shoulders. "Apology accepted. Sorry I yelled."

Cait jumped in. "Enough of your jaundiced view of the male gender, Monica. Eve, is there anything any of us can do to help?"

"I wish there were, but no, not really. It's my problem and I have to decide what to do about it. Let's change the subject." She huffed. "We seem to say that a lot."

"Yeah, we do," Cait said. "I guess we get into a lot of serious stuff. At least we're honest about the way we feel so we never have to guess where we stand. I think that's something really special." Everyone nodded in agreement. "Changing the subject right now is a good idea, however, and I know just the thing. I may be the only one, other than Angie, of course, who's focused on it, but I think it's time for a little celebration." She waved at the waitress. "Next Thursday is the twins' first birthday."

"It is? Already?" Monica said, her face lighting up. "Wow. Congratulations."

"Yeah," Eve joined her. "Happy birthday to both your wonderful babies."

"Their first birthday. They're surely not babies anymore," Angie said. "We're having Tony's family and mine over next Sunday for a party for the twins. I haven't seen Tony's folks since the wedding, and they're coming up from North Carolina and staying with one of his brothers." Suddenly the joy left her face. "If the truth be known, I'm not looking forward to all those judgmental relatives looking over my home and deciding whether or not I'm a good housewife and mother."

"They won't be doing that," Eve scoffed. "Will they?"

"A few of them will, I'm afraid. I love Tony's brothers and their wives, but Tony's mother thinks he was better off with Jordanna. His mother always says what a classy lady she was."

The waitress arrived with a small but heavily frosted chocolate cake with a pair of candles burning in the center. Several servers gathered around as everyone sang happy birthday to

Brandon and MaryLee. "Blow and wish," Cait said. To the others she added, "I brought this over this afternoon. There's always room for chocolate."

"You're really a peach," Eve said, then turned to a waitress. "Let's add a round of Irish coffees."

"Good idea," Monica chimed in.

Angie looked totally overwhelmed, but when Eve warned her that candle wax was dripping on the cake, she blew. "What did you wish for?" Eve asked.

"If I tell it won't come true, and anyway I don't know whether I get a wish on Brandon and MaryLee's cake."

"What would you have wished for?" Eve asked.

"For this coming weekend to be over and for all of the family to think I'm a good wife for Tony and mother for my babies."

"I'm sure they will, so just relax," Cait said.

"Is there anything any of us can do to help with the festivities?" Monica asked. "Blow up balloons or vacuum? I make a mean fruit punch."

With a small chuckle, Angie said, "We've got everything pretty much planned but I might make an emergency phone call if things get bad."

"You have all our numbers so phone away," Monica said. "We're all here for you."

"I know, and thanks. I'd invite you all, too . . . ."

"Next weekend is for family," Monica said. "Tonight is our celebration, for our little family right here."

"Yeah," everyone said.

The waitress had whisked the cake away and now returned with small slices on plates and steaming mugs of coffee, liberally laced with Irish whiskey. "I wish I had known," Monica said. "I'd have brought the twins gifts."

"Not a chance," Angie said. "They don't need more stuff and all the relatives will bring enough more to bury both the children. No gifts from you guys."

"Sorry," Cait said, handing her a small box. "Too late."

"You didn't."

"Oh, but I did. It will need some explaining, so open it and I'll fill you in." Angie opened the small box and pulled out a car key with remote starter attached.

"You didn't get her a car?" Monica asked, amazed.

Cait grinned and cupped her mug in her long fingers. "No, I didn't. Actually, I would have, Angie, but Logan and I talked about it and knew you wouldn't accept it. However, that is the key to our van. I talked this all over with him and we agreed. You can have the use of the van full-time unless we need it ourselves for some reason. He'll drive his little convertible and I've got my Honda."

Angie dropped the key onto the table and pushed it back toward Cait, shaking her head. "I can't take this."

"Of course you can and you will. It doesn't mean we'll stop visiting each week, but it's a genuine offer. What the hell do Logan and I need with three cars? Anyway, it's not for you. It's for the babies. A happy mother is better for both of them and now that they're within days of taking their first independent steps you'll need sanity more than ever."

"They're walking?" Monica cried.

"Almost. Cait, are you sure Logan agreed to this?" Angie was breathless.

"He was a lamb. Once he turned down the baby thing he was more than willing to let me have my way. When I told him about you and your twins being essentially carless, he suggested the loan of the van. It was actually his idea." She winked. "With a little prompting from me, of course. I've been telling him all about you, Angie, and the twins, and he knows I'm really stuck on all three of you."

"I don't want to take this if Logan's just doing it to placate you about not having a baby."

"Why not? Let him do something good for a change." There was a slightly unpleasant tone in Cait's voice.

"You're obviously really upset about the baby thing. I'm sorry if being with my kids has caused you such problems."

"Not at all, sweetie," Cait said, taking the key and pressing it into Angie's hand. "Logan's just weird these days. I don't have a clue what's up with him."

"You think something's going on? Maybe he knows about you and Hotguy." Then Monica's voice dropped. "Or there's another woman."

"Shut up, Monica," Cait said, her tone taking some of the sting out of her words. "You're very quick to believe the worst but I'm giving him the benefit of the doubt. I don't think there's another woman, and if he knew about Hotguy he would have said something straight out. He's gone a lot, but when he's around he's really pleasant to be with. He seems to be making quite an effort."

Monica tried to control her face so she didn't smirk. Eve saw the "Of course there's another woman. Men are all shits" look on Monica's face.

"I wonder what's up," Angie said, idly glancing around. "Damn," she hissed, then ducked her head. "What's she doing here?"

"Who?"

"Jordanna." She motioned with her head. "Just sitting down, over there."

The three women craned their necks and Eve saw a poised-looking woman with a long ebony French braid and deep blue eyes. She was dressed in a blue and white striped shirt and neatly pressed white slacks and was taking a seat across from an older couple. "That's Tony's ex?" Eve asked, sotto voce.

"The famous Jordanna who we all agreed to hate?" Cait added.

Angie nodded, then ducked her head and stared down at her cake. "I thought this was *my* place with *my* friends."

"She doesn't have anything to do with us," Cait assured her. "She's just another piece of furniture."

"Who's that with her?" Eve asked, trying not to stare. Jordanna was pretty much what she'd expected, classically good-looking but a little stiff and stuffy. Angie was so much warmer and more alive.

Angie took a peek. "Those are her parents, Martin and Pat, I think. I met them once several months ago. Tony, the babies, and I were in the mall and Jordanna came up to us, all sweetness and light. She introduced her parents and Tony seemed glad to see them. They mumbled a quick, slightly embarrassed hello in my direction, then pretty much ignored me while they made a big fuss over the babies. Jordanna made a point of saying that everyone missed Tony, but to her folks' credit, they both looked really uncomfortable."

"I'll bet," Eve said, still staring over at Jordanna's table. "Shall I go over there and spill a drink on her?"

Giggling, Angie said, "No. It's okay. It just startled me."

"It doesn't surprise me that she can hide her horns under all that hair," Eve quipped, "but I think it's amazing that her tail fits in those tight pants." The four women laughed. As Angie snuck another peek at Jordanna's table, Cait slapped her palm on the table, barely missing Angie's fingers. "None of that. Concentrate on us. We're much cuter anyway."

Angie looked at the other three. "You're much better than almost anyone. Thanks for being you."

"Cake," Eve said, forking a large piece into her mouth, to keep the conversation from getting too sticky, "and this wonderfully decadent coffee."

"I'm not much of a sweets person, so if you don't mind," Monica said, "I think I'll stick to the nachos."

Eve slid her hand across the table, caught Monica's plate, and eased it toward her. "Chocolate cake is the ultimate comfort food."

"Actually, the ultimate comfort food is mashed potatoes with lots of gravy," Cait said, "but this comes in a close second."

They spent the next several minutes in a heated debate

about the merits of various foods then moved on to other topics. Eventually, they got their check. Cait grabbed it and reached for her credit card. "Cait," Eve said, "if I can't pay my share it's going to get difficult for me to keep going out with you."

"That goes for me, too," Angie chimed in. "I don't want to feel like a charity case."

When Monica nodded, Cait surrendered the check to her, and Monica quickly did the appropriate calculations. The women put money on the little plastic tray and walked toward the door. "Angie," Cait said, "why don't I pick you up in the morning in the van, then we can install the car seats and you can drive me back to my place? If you want, we can go to the mall in between."

"I'd love to," Angie said with a wide grin. "I guess I'm supposed to protest some more about you lending the car to me, but it's so wonderful that I'm done with arguments. Wait until Tony hears that I'll finally stop whining about getting one of my own, at least for the moment."

The four women parted in the parking lot and Angie and Eve got in their cars and left. "Monica," Cait said as they crossed the lot, "will you talk to Dan about whether Hotguy can easily find me?"

"Sure. I'll call him when I get home, then call you."

"Call me on my cell. I don't want to take any chances that this will get back to Logan."

An hour later, Cait's cell phone rang. After a few pleasantries, Monica said, "Dan thinks that unless Hotguy's a real computer insider, finding out specific details about who you really are and where you live would be difficult. Don't give him any help, however. Dan said it's amazing what folks reveal, even when they're trying to be circumspect."

"I'll be careful, and thanks, Monica. You're a doll."

"No sweat. Just take care."

*　　*　　*

At home that evening, Eve sat in the living room, Minnie on her lap, *Titanic* playing soundlessly on the VCR, trying to get up the courage to tell Mike that she couldn't see him any more. This was silly. Even if she made the decision, she couldn't do anything about it until they were alone. She couldn't call him or talk to him in the office where someone might overhear. Well, if she could get some time alone with him, she'd do it tomorrow. If not, it would have to wait until Tuesday in the hotel. It wasn't the best place to do it but it would have to suffice.

She leaned back and turned on the sound so she could listen to Leonardo DiCaprio. As she scratched Minnie's belly, Maxie jumped onto the sofa and soon both cats were purring.

Tony was delighted at the idea of Angie using Cait's van. "You're sure she's really serious?"

"I'm sure," Angie said, feeling totally mellow. "She's such a wonderful woman."

"You'll have to keep the kids from making a mess in the backseat."

"I know. I'll keep up with it." They hugged and Angie felt lighter than she had in months. "It's so great. I feel so free." She kissed him deeply.

"Let's go into the bedroom and we'll see just how happy you are."

"Sounds good to me."

In the bedroom, Tony wrapped his arms around his wife and held her to him as he kissed her with so much passion that she forgot all the things that had been worrying her. The party, Jordanna, their lackluster sex life, all faded into the background. Even the joy that she was going to have a car at her disposal disappeared into the distance as his tongue invaded her mouth. She tasted him, so familiar, yet so sexy. She inhaled the scent of his after-shave, spicy and so, so, so Tony. God, she loved him.

It took only a few embraces for her blood to boil in a way that it hadn't in so long. Suddenly there were no twins, no long, predictable marriage, no quickies in the night. Now it was just the two of them, holding, touching, stroking. She held onto his biceps, strong and powerful from wielding a hammer and saw.

His fingers threaded through her hair and he held her head so he could deepen his kiss still more, while she went to work on the buttons of his shirt. Frustrated by her clumsy fingers, she pulled the tails from his jeans and found the skin of his back beneath. So smooth.

He started to unfasten her jeans, but she quickly stopped him, undoing buttons and zippers until they were both naked. Almost ravenous, they fell onto the bed and with little preamble, he was inside her. Although there had been little foreplay, this didn't feel like their usual quickie. Often she indulged him, enjoying the feel of him inside her, but not totally aroused herself. This time, she was as hot for him as she had been in a long time.

How perfectly he joined with her, how well he fit, how completely they complemented each other. They found each other's rhythm and rocked together, taking and giving simultaneously. When he reached between them to stroke her clit, she felt as if she were soaring, flying. She held him tightly and they moved together. Almost at the same moment they came, muffling their shouts against each other's mouth.

"Mustn't wake the babies," Tony said as he rolled off of her, laughing softly and yawning. He cuddled her against him and she kissed his chest. He usually fell asleep after they made love but this time it didn't bother her. She was totally satisfied.

"I love you so much," he purred, his speech slurred with sleep.

"I love you, baby," she said, meaning it deeply. Did having a car make that much difference or was it the end of a long year of parenting? Whatever, she made a silent vow to hold on to the feelings they had both enjoyed that evening.

"Good night," he mumbled, then drifted off, still holding her against him.

As she slipped away, too, Angie realized that Tony hadn't used a condom. Not a problem, she reasoned. She had just gotten over her period so she probably wasn't fertile anyway.

The entire Cariri family slept soundly through the night.

Chapter
21

The following morning, Cait drove her van to Angie's house and the two women hefted two car seats into the back. "Don't worry about any stuff the kids might do back here," Cait said, struggling with the latch on her side. "When you're done with the car I'll have it detailed, so let the twins be kids."

"I can't get over your generosity," Angie said, trying to jiggle the seat belt to be sure it was tight enough beneath Brandon's seat. "Tony was totally floored and sends his deep abiding love. That's a direct quote, mind you. Part of me keeps wanting to fight you and not take you up on your wonderful offer, but another, and I'll freely admit the louder part says, 'Yay. A car. Shut up and take it.'"

"I'm delighted that you listened to the right voice," Cait said, standing up and rubbing her lower back.

Once everything was in place, they put the twins into the van and Angie drove it to the mall. "Maneuvering this will take a bit of getting used to. It's so much bigger than our car. Until I master parking, I think I'll put it where there is lots of space."

"It took me a while, too, but eventually it will feel normal."

"God," Angie said as she pulled into the mall parking lot and aimed for a spot where there were no other cars around.

"Let's see what I can do with this boat." She tried to guide it between the parking space lines but when she opened the door to look out she discovered that she was straddling two spaces. "Parking this thing it like berthing a cruise liner."

"We're in no hurry," Cait said, remembering the time several years before when Logan had patiently helped her get used to driving this large vehicle. *He can be so great*, she thought. "Why don't you park and pull out a few times to get the feel of it?"

After fifteen minutes of maneuvering, Angie was feeling a bit more confident. With the twins, both dressed in denim baby overalls, MaryLee in a pink shirt, Brandon in navy, in their stroller, she and Cait entered the mall and went directly to the food court. "Real lunch today," Cait said, "in a real restaurant, in honor of the twins' birthday and the new car."

"You can't mean that," Angie said. She pointed to MaryLee and Brandon, comfortably gnawing on teething crackers, wet, chewed starch all over their hands and faces. "These two in a real restaurant?"

"I think I can cope. Come on, Mom, this is a celebration."

In Mimi's, a noisy restaurant with an entrance off the food court, Angie and Cait sat across from each other, a baby in a high chair on either side. The server quickly brought a small plate for each child, with a paper cup full of Cheerios and a package of crackers. "They're brilliant," Angie said, dropping three Cheerios on each of the children's trays. The two happily scooped up the cereal and stuffed the little circles into their mouths with gooey fists. "This is great. They really seem to understand kids here."

"That's why I thought of this place. I've been here several times and kids seem to be welcome and well cared for."

"You're brilliant," Angie said, suddenly getting choked up. "I really, really can't thank you enough for the car."

"Stop thanking me! It's getting tedious." Cait smiled, her tone deliberately soft. "Anyway, I want to talk to you about something else. I think it's time you graduated from being Mommy to human being status."

Angie cocked her head to one side. "I don't understand what you're getting at," she said, dropping several more Cheerios on Brandon's tray without really thinking about it.

"There's a beauty salon over there," Cait said, pointing to one end of the mall's upper level. "I think you should take time this afternoon to have your hair styled and maybe highlighted. You could have your nails done, as well."

"I don't think so," Angie said, handing two more Cheerios to a slightly slobbery MaryLee. "I'm fine the way I am."

"You are fine the way you are, but fine isn't good enough for my best friend. From what you hinted about at Huck's last night, you and Tony are on the right path. It's time for you to move along a bit further into the realm of sexual beings." As if she'd done it for years, Cait handed Brandon several more Cheerios, which he shoved into his mouth. Then he pounded his fist on the tray of the high chair. She was becoming pretty adept at this baby thing, Cait thought, not that visiting was anything like having her own, but it was as close as she was probably going to get.

"Tony doesn't care how I look. After all, we've known each other since high school."

"Ah, but you care. I saw the way you looked at Jordanna last evening and I heard you being envious of her appearance." Cait leaned forward, her forearms on the table and her eyes locked with Angie's. "You need this for *you*. The way you feel about yourself will become the way others see you. You're a pretty woman hiding behind all that hair. You've got a great body, probably from all that yoga, but who'd notice with the sloppy clothing you always wear?" Handing Brandon more cereal, she said, "Come out, Angie."

Angie looked down at her sweatshirt and loose-fitting jeans. "I'm comfortable, and with these two," she said, indicating the two babies, "there isn't time to be more than this."

"You have to make time. Believe me. It's important." Cait thought about Logan. Had she been letting things go so that they had nothing in common and no attraction anymore? No, this recent distance was all Logan's doing.

"Maybe, one day."

"You can't keep putting off things like this. Do it, babe."

"You mean right now? Today? After lunch?"

Rubbing her index fingernail with her thumb, Cait asked, "Do you have anything more pressing to do this afternoon? You could be beautiful before the party for the twins this weekend."

"What about the babies?" Angie said, obviously casting around for excuses.

"I'll push their stroller around the mall and suck up all the compliments."

"I'll think about it."

Without another word about the beauty parlor, the two women ordered sandwiches and sodas. Angie took containers of baby cereal and strained fruit from her diaper bag and the two women chatted as they fed the babies, Cait acting as if she'd done it for years. Then they talked about nothing specific as they ate their lunch, giving Brandon and MaryLee bread crusts to chew on, washed down with sippy cups of juice. When the meal was over, Cait didn't insist on picking up the check. Rather, she did the math and collected from Angie.

When they had the twins back in their stroller, they walked to Hair Today, and with Cait pushing at her back, Angie reluctantly went in. "Maybe they don't have anyone with time right now."

"I'm sure there's someone who can help us."

Cait told the hostess their requirements and she led Angie to a chair. "This is Marge," the hostess said confidently, "and she'll fix you right up. She's a whiz with new styles."

"Marge," Cait said, taking charge, "this is Angie and these two darlings are her twins."

"Aren't they the most adorable . . ." Marge, a thirtysome-thing blonde cooed as she squatted down to make silly faces at the twins. "How old are they?"

"They'll be a year on Thursday," Angie said, beaming as she did anytime anyone made a fuss over her children.

"Ah, I have not-all-fond memories of those days, and you have to deal with two of them. You've got to have arms ten feet long and quick reflexes to keep up with these two, I'll bet. Mine are six and four and I still feel like I need leashes for both of them." She whipped several pictures from the station's counter and showed off her children.

After the mandatory "What beautiful children" from both Cait and Angie, Marge asked, "Now, what can I do for you?"

"Angie wants a styling and maybe some highlights," Cait said, not letting Angie chicken out.

"Maybe a little shorter," Angie said, fingering her nonde-script, light brown hair, "but I don't think I want highlights."

"You really need them, love," Marge said, gazing at her in the large mirror that covered the wall of her station. "You hair would be so much livelier with a bit of color. Mine's just about your color underneath."

"Really? It looks so natural," Angie said, her eyes wide.

"It's supposed to, but this kind of coloring takes a few hours. How about just an auburn rinse for you?" She looked at Cait in the mirror. "It won't come out anything like that won-derful titian of your friend here, but it will add a little life."

"I don't know. There's not a lot of time until the twins' naps."

"I've got just the thing," Marge said, whipping a bottle from the countertop. "This shampoo will add just a little color. It will only take about an hour and that includes the styling."

"Great," Cait said, quickly pushing the stroller toward the door to the mall. "I'll be back then." She looked at her watch, then disappeared into the crowd.

* * *

After Cait left, Angie watched as Marge played with her hair and made suggestions for style and color. *Can I really do this? What will Tony think about me spending his hard-earned money on my looks?* Actually, if she were honest with herself, Tony would be delighted. He loved her and wanted her to be happy, and this, she had to admit, would make her happy. After all, Jordanna must spend mucho bucks on her looks.

Finally she and Marge agreed on a plan, then Marge spent the next hour washing, rinsing, and snipping. "I'm not going to make it too much shorter, merely give it some shape. With the little ones around, you'll probably still want to put it into a ponytail most of the time. It's still the easiest way to control it quickly," Marge said once the color was done.

After a final quick blow dry, Angie looked at herself in the mirror and beamed. She didn't look dramatically different, just like a well-retouched photo of her former self. "It does look wonderful and you're a miracle worker, Marge. I don't look very different, just better." She threaded her fingers in her hair and loved the silky feel. She'd always been afraid that if she colored it, her hair would look like straw.

"That's exactly what I was going for. A little life in the color and enough shape to the cut to bring out your eyes and long neck. I think I'm a genius, if I do say so myself."

"I couldn't agree more," Cait said, parking the stroller with the two sleeping babies behind the beautician's chair. She studied her friend in the mirror. "Angie, you look fabulous. Will it be difficult to maintain, Marge?"

"Not at all," Marge said. "I suggested a shampoo-in rinse she can use from time to time to keep life in the color and she'll only need to have it shaped every six weeks or so."

Angie stood up and after one last look in the mirror, bussed Marge on the cheek. "It's a miracle. I can't wait until Tony sees it."

Since the babies were asleep and would awaken if they put them in the car, Cait and Angie walked around the mall for another hour. Cait talked Angie into buying a lightweight pink sweater and a pair of tight-fitting mid-weight jeans. With her old clothing in a bag, they finally made their way to the car just as the twins were waking from their nap. Angie drove Cait home, then drove the van back to her house. She couldn't wait until Tony got home.

After Angie dropped her off, Cait wandered through the empty house, bored and restless. As usual, Logan was long gone, and wouldn't be home until late. She was reluctant to log onto her computer but she eventually gave in and clicked over to a new chat room. Watching insipid conversation scroll up her screen, she tapped her fingers on her desk. What would be the harm, she reasoned, in just seeing who was at Paul's Place? Before she met Hotguy344 she'd chatted with several men, both in open chats and privately, men who wanted to talk about sex. There were probably lots of places like Paul's, of course, but she was comfortable in this one. *These folks are my kind of people and Hotguy344 probably isn't even logged on.*

She clicked over, relieved, and she had to admit, also a little disappointed that Hotguy344 wasn't logged on. She stayed for a while, enjoying the conversation, right now about anal sex, but continually scanned the list of chatters. Finally she saw the name Hotguy344 appear. She reached for her mouse to log off, but then pulled her hand back. She shouldn't give him the ability to spoil her fun.

    Hotguy344: Hi, Loverlady. How's tricks today?
    Loverlady214: I'm fine.
    Hotguy344: Wanna go private? I'd love to <u>see</u> you.

He'd underlined that word and she flicked her gaze to her camera, peering at her from above her monitor. What was she to do? Her body was aroused and she needed release. She could masturbate alone, of course, but Hotguy could make her feel things she couldn't feel alone. What was the harm? She'd be really careful. Anyway, he was in Fairbanks.

Loverlady214: Sure

A few mouse clicks and a few lines of type and Hotguy's face appeared. "I can't get over how sexy you look," he said, now that they were able to see and hear each other.

She glanced down. She was still wearing the jeans and tailored shirt she'd been wearing for her day at the mall with Angie. Sexy? "I'm wearing jeans. How is that sexy?"

"You always look sexy and hot to me. Right now you're so tailored, but I know what goes on beneath those classy clothes. I'll bet that, if I had X-ray eyes I could see your nipples get hard and your pussy swell and twitch."

His smile was almost demonic, and Cait found it incredibly exciting. He was wearing only a pair of lightweight sweatpants and she could see his hairy chest heave with excitement. She glanced at his crotch and saw the large bulge. She knew his cock was large even when flaccid, but he was obviously very excited right now. *I do this to him*, she thought. *What a gas.* "You look really hot, too," she said. "I can see your big cock."

His smile showed his white teeth as he reached down and rubbed his palm over his erection. "This is for you, baby," he said. "Take your shirt and bra off. I want to see your tits."

His blunt words aroused her still more and she quickly pulled her clothes off. She knew she shouldn't be with him, but it was almost as though she couldn't help herself. She'd just be super-extra-careful. Her breasts were amazingly sensitive, the nipples swollen and tight until they were almost painful. "Rub them!" Hotguy snapped.

She swirled her palms over her nipples, loving the feel of both her breasts and her palms. "Now the pants!" he said.

Soon she was naked, her cheeks chilled by the leather of

her desk chair. "Spread your legs so I can see your pussy while you rub yourself."

She loved the pure power he exuded so she put her heels on the edge of the chair so the camera could get a full view of her crotch. "You, too," Cait said, her breathy voice barely audible. "I want to see you."

"You do, do you?" he said, still rubbing his cock through his sweatpants.

"Yes," she whispered.

"Tell me why?"

Why? "I like to look at you."

"You like to watch me jerk off, right?"

There was a slightly nasty edge to his voice. Strange. He was being a bit more abrasive than usual today. "Yes, and you like to do it while I watch."

He took a deep breath and let it out slowly. "I guess I do." He pulled down his pants and revealed his large erection. "This is for you," he said, wrapping his fingers around himself and stroking. "Now what have you got for me?"

Cait reached between her legs and massaged her clit. "This," she purred, relaxing now that he was backing off. She loved it when he dominated her, but there was a limit. Smiling, she reached into a small drawer in the computer desk and pulled out a small paper bag. Today she had a surprise for him. "I've got something for you," she said, pulling out a bright red vibrating dildo. "I bought this for us to share."

"Oh, baby," Hotguy said, his gaze flicking from her hand on her pussy to the large dildo. "That is so hot."

She twisted the knob at the base of the vibrator and rubbed it around her pussy. She could barely contain her orgasm, but she wanted to tease Hotguy for a little while. She inserted the tip of the dildo between her inner lips and gasped as it filled her, buzzing inside her body.

"Shit, baby, that's dynamite." His hand moved faster.

For a few moments, the two masturbated in silence, until Hotguy said, "I'm going to come. You ready to see me spurt?"

"Go for it, baby," she said. "I'm going to come, too." Cait felt the spasms fill her as she watched Hotguy's cock fill his hand with semen.

"Oh, Cait, you are truly the best."

Cait. The word brought a small part of her brain back to earth. She hated it that he knew her name, but the afterglow of her orgasm felt too good to ruin with worries so she forced her negative thoughts from her mind. "You are, too," she said, meaning every word. Logan, even at his best, had never made her feel the way Hotguy did.

"That was quite a trip," he said. "By the way, I've been wondering, are you a Valentine's baby?"

"Valentine's? Why would you think that?"

"The two-fourteen beside your name. Loverlady214. I thought it might be your birthday."

"Nope. Just a number." Actually it was her house number but she didn't want to tell Hotguy that. She was being careful, just like she promised herself she would be. She idly glanced around Hotguy's room as he said, "You know I might be visiting your part of the world to see my cousin sometime soon. Maybe we could get together."

"I don't think so."

"Why not? We could have some real fun together. After all, we're pretty compatible."

"Let's just keep it on the screen, okay?"

"I'd really like to be with you for real. It wouldn't have to be at your place. We could get a motel room or something."

"No. I'm sorry but I'm not interested in seeing you in person. This is exactly what I want. Okay?"

She could see his shoulders slump. "You're saying I'm not good enough to be with?"

"I'm married and very well-known around town here. There's no way I could do anything so dangerous. I've got to run now."

"A quick cyber-fuck and then you run off?"

"I have to. My husband will be home soon." He wasn't due until midevening, but Cait was starting to feel very uncomfortable.

"I hate that we have to cut this off so quickly," Hotguy said, a lewd expression on his face. "I'll bet you're good for several more orgasms."

"See you sometime soon." No, she wouldn't. She'd never see him again. Too bad, but she couldn't risk it. She knew that now. Cait quickly signed off, shivering slightly. Seeing him had been a really bad idea and she vowed she wouldn't do it again. It took several minutes for her heartbeat to return to normal, both from the sex and the nervousness, but slowly her body calmed.

She wandered into the bathroom to wash the dildo, then put it back in its usual hiding place in her lingerie drawer. Okay. She had to admit to herself that she'd put it in the computer desk hoping she'd get to play with Hotguy344. It was like some kind of addiction but she vowed that she would do without. Maybe she'd find someone else on-line. That was a good idea. She'd find another erotic chat room and hook up with someone else. It certainly didn't have to be Hotguy.

As she dried the dildo, a picture of Hotguy's room flashed through her brain. It looked like a bedroom, his bedroom. Too bad she'd never see it again. No, not too bad. It was a good thing. He was too complicated and dangerous. Why, she wondered, wasn't he at work? She kept forgetting that there were four hours' difference between New York and Fairbanks. It was only one-thirty there and Hotguy worked nights. Then her brain flashed on the clock beside his bed. It had said five-thirty. She'd seen it but hadn't focused on it until that moment. Five-thirty. That was strange. Why would he have a clock set to her time zone? Unless it was his time zone, too.

Fairbanks? He said he lived there, but what proof did she have that he actually did? Was that a lie? Was he here in the eastern time zone? Shit. Her entire body trembled. No. It couldn't be. He was four time zones away. Wasn't he?

In New Jersey, Nick signed off the chat site and brought up the phone directory for Westchester County, New York. He had made Cait uncomfortable today and he had the feeling that he wouldn't be able to meet her on-line any more. Well, that would be all right. He'd do things his way.

He knew she lived north of New York City, and since it was obvious from the fancy room he could see behind Cait that her husband earned big bucks, he probably commuted. A few clicks and he was on a site where he could access the local phone book. He'd tried this before, but Johnson was such a common name that hunting for her address had done him little good, so now he made a few assumptions. He decided to try 214 as her house number. Many people had to add numbers to their screen names since most of the plain ones, like Loverlady by itself, were already taken. The easiest numbers to remember were birth dates or addresses, and 214 wasn't her birthday.

He clicked several times and typed in what he knew. Sure enough, there was a Logan Johnson at 214 Sheraton in East Hudson, New York. He found some official stuff about the town, then accessed the local paper and flipped through several issues on-line. He found a picture of Caitlin and Logan Johnson at some local fund-raiser several months earlier. It was her.

Gotcha, Cait Johnson of Sheraton Avenue, East Hudson, New York. He clicked on an icon on his computer's desktop, and with a few more clicks, the scene he and Cait had just lived replayed on his screen. He zoomed in, and while he watched her beautiful pussy fill the screen, he rubbed his already erect cock until he came again. Now that he knew who and where, it was just a matter of time before they got together, up close and personal, as they said on TV. Until then he would relive their last two meetings over and over again.

Chapter
22

It finally felt like fall in East Hudson. The day was more typical of November than early October: winds gusting at over thirty miles per hour, temperatures in the low fifties and rain for a sixth straight day. Just before noon, four women dashed from the 3Cs to the diner and shaking off like wet dogs, slid into their normal booth. "God, I hate this. We had such beautiful weather until last Monday, then whammo." Monica made a rude noise and motioned to the rivers of rain cascading down the window. "Even my trusty umbrella doesn't help when it's this windy."

"I'm starting to grow green mold," Cait said, "and to add insult to injury, instead of drought, the radio's now screaming about flooding. I don't think we can ever win."

"I know that diner coffee has become our personal taboo but today I need my hot, brown liquid," Monica said, and the others nodded sagely. When the waitress arrived, they each ordered a sandwich and coffee.

"Okay, first order of business. Angie, tell us about the new you," Monica said.

Angie told the other two about her day with Cait. "So what happened when Tony saw you?" Cait asked. "I'm dying of curiosity."

"He was floored," Angie said, playing with a strand of reddish brown hair. "For several beats he stared at me, then said, 'What happened?' I told him and he stood and applauded."

"He really did that?" Cait said, her grin wide and triumphant.

"He did. He said he's been wanting me to do something with myself for a long time but he was reluctant to say anything."

"Why?"

"He was afraid he'd make me feel like he'd insulted me. He never wanted to make me feel less than I am, but he's wanted me to spruce myself up for a while."

Cait looked at her. "I see you're wearing another new shirt."

"Actually it's not new. This"—she smoothed the collar of a soft navy and white striped cotton blouse with a navy tank top underneath—"was in the back of my closet. Tony actually went through all my stuff with me and pulled out several things that I'd stopped wearing." She grinned ruefully. "This dates from before the twins were born."

"Well, I'm proud of you both," Cait said. "So tell us, when he saw the new you, did he jump your bones?"

Monica could see the flush on Angie's face. Over the months the women had been getting together, Angie had gotten more used to blunt conversation but it still made her face redden. "Yeah," Angie said. "It was like I was a new me."

As the sandwiches and coffee arrived, the other three women clapped softly. "Bravo, Angie," Cait said.

"Way to go, girl," Eve chimed in. "Are you all set for the party tomorrow?"

"Strangely enough, I am," Angie said, warming her chilled hands on her coffee cup. "The house is as clean as it's going to get and I've got enough food and drinks to feed a small army. If the weather cooperates, Tony's parents fly in early this afternoon and the festivities begin with a pre-party party tonight at Frank and Linda's."

"I'll bet they'll all be astonished with the new you," Eve said.

"I hope so," Angie said, with an irrepressible grin, then her face sobered. "There's been a scary incident since I last saw you," she continued, her voice much more serious. "There was a shooting at Tony's school."

The three women put down their food and leaned forward. "He's okay, right?"

"Yeah," Angie said. "He's fine. It was in another part of the building."

"Oh, shit. I think I saw it on the news on TV," Monica said. "I had no idea that was Tony's school. They said it was some gang war thing?"

"Always," Angie answered. "This was some gang kid whose girlfriend was supposedly fooling around with some guy from another gang. No one knows how he got the gun into the building through the metal detectors, but he did. Shot the other guy in the belly. One kid's in intensive care and the other's in jail." Her head shook slowly. "I just don't get it, and it totally freaks me out. Tony said cops were climbing all over the building but they still don't know how the gun got in or where it got to after the kid shot up the place."

"Shit. That's really scary," Monica said.

"He's just a high school teacher but right now I feel like a cop's wife, worrying whether my husband is going to come home from work at the end of the day," Angie said with a shudder. "He's more determined than ever to get out of that school, but he's got nothing lined up. Frankly," she said, taking a large swallow of her coffee, "I can't wait. I would love him to quit and work with his brothers until he finds another teaching job but he keeps talking about his pension and benefits. With a family, it's doubly difficult to move around. I think the powers that be count on that. He's been trying to get a transfer, at least, to a school in a better neighborhood, but he's so good with these tough kids that they want to keep him right where he is."

Monica could tell how upset Angie was by the length of her diatribe. Seldom before had she talked about her personal life in such detail. "Is there anything any one of us can do to help Tony with his job?"

"I wish there were," Angie said, "but it's something that we'll have to live through. I tell myself that the chances of something like that happening again are miniscule, but still . . ."

"We're here for you, babe. We all are. Moving right along," Monica said, deliberately changing the subject, "I got wind of some good news this week."

"Tell!"

"It seems I'm up for partner at Conroy & Bates."

"That's fabulous. Congratulations," Cait said.

"It will mean more work but lots more money, too. It's not only a piece of my action, but everyone else's as well." She had long since realized that she could be happy about her six-figure salary without making her friends envious. Grinning, she continued. "It would take my annual income quite a bit higher into the six figures."

"That's wonderful," Angie said. "I can't even think in those numbers."

"What about your vow to relax a little? Remember your doctor's words?"

"I do, but I can do it. I won't stop my yoga and lunches with you ladies. I'll just work harder during the days."

"How does Dan feel about it? Would it mean more time in the city and less for him?"

"I don't know what it would mean, but I haven't really had a chance to tell him yet. I am a little worried about how he'll take it. I'd be making more than he does."

"Do you think he'd mind the salary differential? Is he that ego involved, that shallow?" Cait asked.

"No," Monica said as she picked up her sandwich, then put

it down again. "He's not that way. I think he'd be happy for me." Her voice lowered. "I think he really cares."

"There's something more bothering you, though," Cait said.

"Yeah. I'm worried about his reaction if he finds out how I get business, how I entertain clients."

"You mean your outside activities?" Eve said.

"Let's put our cards on the table here," Monica said, leaning on her elbows and staring intently at the other three. "I'm a whore. Okay, it's for a good cause, my business, but if we were to call it what it is, it's prostitution. I sell myself."

"Don't say it like that," Angie snapped. "You're doing what you need to do in a very tough business. That doesn't make you a whore."

"That's putting a nice spin on it, Angie," Monica said, "but whatever you want to call it, it embarrasses the hell out of me where Dan's concerned. I don't want to tell him why I don't come home many evenings. I don't think he'd view it as 'doing what I had to do,' as you put it."

"Maybe he won't find out," Eve said.

"Maybe he won't, but I'm still lying, even if it's only a sin of omission. I don't have the courage to talk to him about it, though. I want things to go on the way they are, light, close, but not too close."

"So keep it that way," Cait said. "Be happy together. Tell him about the partnership and have a really hot celebration. You don't have to do anything more for the moment."

Be happy together. Could she? Could they? Her relationship with Dan was getting more serious by the day and she thought Dan felt it, too. Could they do this? She wanted both, Dan and the partnership. If she had to choose, which way would she go? In the past, becoming partner was everything she'd ever wanted but now Dan had become terribly important. "Yeah. That might work, at least for the moment."

"Where was he this morning?" Angie asked. "I missed gazing fondly at his buns."

Monica had missed him, too. "He got back from California late last night and he's sleeping in this morning."

"At your house?" Cait asked with raised eyebrows.

Monica couldn't suppress her grin. "Yes, at my house."

"Was it good last night?" Cait continued.

"Enough third degree, and yes, it was good. It always is. Moving on to other topics, Cait, what's up with Hotguy?"

Cait quickly sobered. "I've decided to cut it all off completely."

"That sounds like a good idea," Eve continued. "At least he doesn't know where you live or anything." When Cait didn't respond, Eve said, "Does he?"

Cait shuddered. "I think he might know more than I'm happy with."

"Even if he knows, he's in Alaska so what's the harm?" Angie asked.

Cait took a long swallow of her coffee and sensing she had more to say, the others remained silent. "I'm not sure he is in Fairbanks," Cait said as she set her cup down. "While we were playing early this week, I saw a clock on his table. It was set to our time. Alaska's four hours earlier."

Eve's expression tightened. "You think he was lying about where he is?"

"He might have been. I've been thinking about it and what better way to ease someone's mind than to say you're so far away. He might have just been suckering me along."

"That's pretty scary," Angie said. "How much does he know about you?"

Cait hung her head. "If I were being honest, I don't know what I might have let slip. If he's computer savvy he might be able to find out where I am." She slugged down another long swallow of coffee.

"Do you think he'd really want to see you in person?" Monica asked. "After all, I assume you made it very clear that this was an Internet thing only."

"I did, several times. Why would he want to find me if he knows that I don't want to have anything to do with him?"

"You're probably right and that's probably that," Monica said.

"I hope so, but I wish I could be sure."

The others murmured their agreement. After several minutes of idle chat, Cait asked, "Eve, did you decide what to do about Mike?"

"What I decided and what I did are, unfortunately, two different things. I was determined to tell him that I didn't want to see him again, but I couldn't do it where someone might hear. I waited until we were alone, in our hotel room Tuesday at lunchtime."

"Bad idea."

"I know, but I couldn't think of anywhere else."

"The inevitable happened, I assume from your expression," Angie said. "You didn't tell him."

"I didn't. I tried, but he looked at me and . . ."

On her way to the hotel she'd picked up sandwiches and drinks as she always did, and was sitting on the room's only chair when Mike used a card key and opened the door. "God, Eve, I've been so hungry for you since the last time we were here. You've been difficult to get ahold of."

"I'm sorry, Mike," Eve said. "I've been busy."

"I understand but I got some time Sunday afternoon to call and I thought we could play. I got your answering machine."

She had heard the phone and since not too many people called her over the weekend, she had let the machine pick up. "Hi, baby, it's me." Mike's voice had echoed through the apartment. "It's Sunday at about two-thirty and I'm parked in the elementary school parking lot, eager to talk to you. If you're there, pick up." There was a pause, then the voice continued, "Well, I guess you're not there. I'll try you on your cell. See you Monday in the office, and Tuesday in our usual place."

"I was out," Eve had said, shifting in the motel chair. "Sorry I missed your call."

"I tried your cell phone but I got a stupid message," he said, sounding petulant.

"I guess I forgot to turn it on."

"Well, we're here now," Mike said, taking her hands and guiding her to her feet. "I'm not really hungry. For food, that is."

"Mike, I've got to talk to you," Eve said, feeling the warmth of his hands against hers.

"Can't it wait?" Mike said, placing her palm against his erection. "I want you very much."

"I need to talk to you now."

Mike kissed her deeply, gently massaging the back of her neck, making purring sounds against her lips. He buried his face in her neck and whispered, "Later," as he nibbled at her ear.

"But . . ."

He unbuttoned her blouse and slid it down her arms, then kissed his way from her throat to her cleavage. "No buts."

She was lost. She wanted him. Why should she deny herself? If it wasn't her it would be someone else. Why should she make the sacrifice? She enfolded him in her arms, and later, when his cock was moving deep between her breasts, she kissed the head as it approached her mouth. She stomped on the little voice that whispered about his wife.

When Monica started to say something, Angie stopped her. "I understand," Angie said. "I think we all do. You have to do what you need to do to make you happy. Everyone has his or her own path and whatever yours is, we're with you."

Monica sighed deeply. Angie was right. What right did she have to judge anyone else's way of doing things? How would Dan judge her relationships with clients to get more lucrative business for C & B? "Angie's right, Eve. Do what makes you happy and we'll give you as much support as you want."

"That means a lot coming from you," Eve said to her. "You've always been my worst critic where Mike's concerned."

"I'm sorry if I've seemed judgmental. Coming from someone who doesn't have the courage to tell Dan about my life, how in the world can I say anything about you and Mike?"

"We all are who we are, no more and no less," Angie said. "The wonderful part of our group is that we can freely be our real selves. I don't mean to say that we'll support each other in everything. We all have our own opinions on everything, and we don't hesitate to voice them, but it's because we care."

"Amen to that," all four voices said together as they joined hands.

Chapter
23

The ensuing week sped by and again the following Saturday the four women met for lunch after yoga class. As soon as they were seated, Eve asked, "How did the twins' birthday party go?" Cait couldn't help noticing that Angie sat up a bit straighter and she hoped that she'd had something to do with Angie's newfound confidence. Although Angie had pulled her hair back into its normal ponytail, wisps of bangs softened her face. She also wore a bit of light lipstick.

"It was a total success." With a wide smile, she whipped out about a dozen pictures, three of cake-covered babies being hovered over by adoring relatives. As the women raved over the twins, Angie related all the details of the celebration.

"What about you?" Monica asked. "You look just great in these photos. What did your family say about the new you?"

"No one commented on my new look directly but several women said how healthy I seemed. 'It must be finally getting out from under babyhood,' one woman said. I guess the changes are subtle enough that people think I just look better, especially those who don't see me that often."

"How about Tony's parents?"

Angie beamed. "They were really nice. They fussed over the twins so much that I barely saw my babies all weekend.

They took them shopping and I think they bought out Baby Gap. I can't imagine there was anything left in their size when Barry and Marie got finished. Tony and I actually got some alone time together." She sounded really up.

"Sounds like things are going well with you and Tony," Eve said.

"They are. Cait," Angie said, turning toward her friend, "having the van has made a tremendous difference. I don't have to bug Tony about errands over the weekends, and because I've been easier to get along with, he's been taking more initiative with the kids. He takes them out Sunday mornings by himself. It might only be for an hour and I think he just drives around, but it's the thought and effort that count. An hour of peace and quiet for me is an amazing stimulant for both of us." She leered when she said the word "stimulant."

"You mean sex is good?" Eve said.

"Well, it's better, anyway." Angie half-stood at her end of the booth and reached over and grasped Cait's shoulders. "I can't thank you enough." Angie kissed her friend on both cheeks.

"You don't have to," Cait said, incredibly gratified by Angie's thanks. She vowed that she and her friend would still get together once a week to go to the mall with the babies. It had become the one bright spot in her life and she wouldn't let it go, not when the rest of her life stank. Logan was more distant than ever and she hadn't been getting much sleep. She'd begun to have nightmares about Hotguy. It had started several days before.

In her first dream she was walking down a sidewalk in a residential area of a town she'd never been in before. Although the sun was shining brightly, the gigantic overhanging trees made the street dark and foreboding. A black car with opaque windows was parked across from what she knew was her house, although it looked nothing like her real home on Sheraton Drive. There was something or someone menacing in that car.

She couldn't see what, but she knew that whatever it was intended to hurt her. If she could only get into her house, she would be safe from the fear that filled her, so she ran.

Then she was home, in her room, in her bed. She didn't know how she got there but she was safe now. Or was she? It was as if she were watching herself there in her bed in a movie, knowing something dreadful was going to happen and powerless to stop it. For several minutes she didn't hear a noise in the house, then suddenly there was the slow, rhythmic sound of footsteps on the stairs, and a shape appeared in the doorway of her darkened room. Hadn't she closed and locked that door?

He was beside her, looming over the bed where she lay, clutching the blankets to her chin, trying to cover herself. She wanted to scream but no sound came out. She lay, shivering, knowing that evil things were going to happen, things she wouldn't be able to prevent. She couldn't make out the intruder's face, but in a deep, gravelly voice he said, "Hi, Cait. Ready to be my Loverlady?" Hotguy. She'd known it was him and yet hearing him sent tremors though her.

Then she was naked, uncovered, hands and ankles tied to the bed, open to him and completely vulnerable. She pulled at the bonds but they held her firmly. "You and I both know you want this," he said, his voice exactly like his voice on her computer. "You want it rough and hard." His laugh was deep, evil, as if he were enjoying her struggles. "Try the restraints, Loverlady. Test the extent of my power. You'll find out quickly enough that there's no limit to my control over you."

He was right and she knew it. He could do anything. He found the dildo she'd used on camera in her drawer and without hesitation shoved it into her body. It slid in easily. "See how wet you are? You're hot for your Hotguy. I've always known that you'd like it like this."

He pulled the dildo out, then thrust it in more deeply. She wanted to pull her knees together, stop the onslaught, but she was helpless. Over and over he fucked her with the plastic phallus, and to her chagrin she found the pleasure increasing. Her hips were soon moving with the rhythm of his plunges. Eyes closed, she tried to convince herself that she hated what he was doing but to no avail. She tried to scream but couldn't.

She was humiliated by the erotic joy she was taking from the man's violation.

Suddenly her eyes popped open and she sat up. She was in her own bed, Logan snoring lightly beside her. She was panting as if she'd run several miles and her heart was pounding in her ears. She was totally aroused.

Knees trembling, she stumbled to the bathroom and in the dark, sat on the toilet and reached between her legs, rubbing her swollen clit until, within seconds, she came with small whimpers and moans of pleasure.

The following night she had a similar dream, but in that one Logan tried to stop the man and was severely beaten for his efforts.

Since then she'd had nightmares almost every night, simultaneously terrifying and exciting. What kind of woman was she? She wasn't the kind of person who dreamed of rape, but the man who came to her in her dreams and assaulted her with her own vibrator inflamed her more each night. She was hardly sleeping and it was starting to show on her face.

"Earth to Cait. Where did you go?" Monica said, staring at her. "You were a million miles away for a few minutes."

"Sorry. I guess I fuzzed out," Cait responded. "I'm not sleeping well and I guess it caught up with my brain." As close as the three other women were to her, she had no intention of telling them about her nightmares or about her worry that Hotguy might want to do something really evil to her.

"I'm so sorry," Monica said. "Something wrong?"

Cait sighed. She wanted to tell the women but what could she say? It was all so bizarre and if she were honest, scary. Maybe Hotguy was right. She liked it rough and he'd sensed that about her right away. Something was very wrong with her. "I'm okay. A little stomach upset, that's all."

"You do look a little under the weather," Monica said. "I hope you feel better."

"I'm sure it's only a twenty-four-hour thing."

"How's your sister, Monica? Is she back with her husband or what?" Angie asked.

"According to Bonnie, Jake wants to come back but she doesn't think she wants him. He's moved to a hotel. Bimbette didn't work out, I guess. He says it was just a totally stupid midlife thing, but midlife crisis or no midlife crisis, it's not easy to repair the damage that's been done."

"Does Bonnie want to fix it?"

"I don't really know. She vacillates from moment to moment. She loves the guy very much, always has. They met in high school and have pretty much been together ever since. It's hard for her to adjust to not having him around, but he's been a real shit and I'm not sure she can forgive him, or even wants to try."

"I hear you, Monica," Eve said. "Jake was a beast."

"I don't know about that," Monica said. "It's her decision, of course, but maybe it would be best if Bonnie took him back. I gather he's willing to do anything."

"You're kidding," Eve said, her eyes wide. "That's the first time you've said anything positive about any man except Dan."

Monica slumped in her seat. "I know, and I realize that I've let my mother's jaundiced attitude push me into ways of thinking that might not be all true."

"Hallelujah," Angie said in a loud singsong voice. "Monica has seen the light. Men aren't all shits."

Over Angie and Eve's laughter Monica said, "Okay, lay off. I know I've been a bit one-tracked on this, but I'm willing to admit that I might have been wrong."

"Dan's gotten to you, eh?"

Monica flushed. "Maybe. He's such a good man and a real straight arrow. He wouldn't cheat. If he wanted to date someone else he'd tell me that he was doing it. There's not a deceitful bone in his body."

"That's an amazing statement," Eve said, "especially coming from you."

"I know," she said. "Dan says hello to everyone, by the way."

"Have you told him about the impending partnership?" Eve asked.

"Yes, and he was thrilled. I haven't told him what I do to keep clients happy, though, but nothing's been necessary in that department since I've been dating Dan. Maybe it will all work out and I'll never have to tell him anything."

"That would be fortunate. What will you do if you want to make love to a client?" Eve asked.

"I don't know. I just don't know."

While the other women talked, Cait's mind returned to her dreams. There was a menacing car in every one. Did that mean anything? As she dwelt on it, she realized that she'd seen a car like the one in her dream cruising her neighborhood several times over the past week. Could that have been Hotguy? Could that have lodged in her subconscious and caused this spate of nightmares? What if he were after her because he thought she really wanted to be raped?

She didn't want to be raped, not by some guy off the street, or off the 'Net. Not by Hotguy. Okay, she had fantasies about control, but from what she read recently on the Web, that was pretty common. Lots of women wanted to be dominated by their lovers, told what to do so they didn't have to worry about doing things wrong. Actually, Cait thought, it would be freeing not to have to wonder exactly what a man wanted. She'd know because he'd tell her, or order her, or have her tied down so she'd have to submit to what he wanted to do. That didn't make her a pervert, though, and she certainly didn't want to be raped by some guy she didn't know or trust, no matter what Hotguy said. And no matter that she woke up so hot that she had to masturbate, it was an erotic fantasy and nothing more.

Luckily Cait was on the outside of the booth this week so she stood and gathered her jacket. "Listen, guys, I'm really feeling lousy so I think I'm going to head home."

"Sure, babe," Monica said. "Are you okay to drive home?"

"Of course. I'm sure that with a good night's sleep I'll feel fine." A good night's sleep would be a blessing.

Monica watched Cait leave, then turned to the rest of the group. "I'm worried about her," she said. "She seemed really preoccupied all morning."

"I noticed several times that she was not with the class," Angie said. "I wonder whether something else is going on, or maybe something's wrong with Logan."

"Or Hotguy," Eve said. "Maybe Logan found out, or maybe Hotguy wasn't content to find someone else to play with."

"What could he do about it?" Angie asked. "He doesn't know who Cait is, right? What trouble could he make?"

"I don't have the foggiest idea," Eve said, "but it all makes you wonder."

"Yeah, it does." Monica paused, then looked at Eve. "How's Mike?"

"He's fine," Eve said with a sigh. "I keep meaning to break it off, but it just doesn't happen. He says funch on Tuesday and I'm there. It's terrible. I feel like some weak-livered little mouse being led around by a cat. It's not the cat's fault. I'm letting myself be led. I'm stuck like a fly on flypaper."

"You're only as stuck as you think you are," Angie said, "but I don't want you to think that we're all bugging you about this. We love you and don't want to see you hurt, that's all."

"One day the moment will come when I can't deal with it all anymore and I'll blurt it out. Until then, I'll roll with it."

Chapter

24

The call came to Angie's house at two o'clock the following Wednesday. The twins were napping and having just finished stuffing the dishwasher, she was trying to decide what to make for dinner. "Mrs. Cariri?" an unfamiliar voice said when she picked up the receiver.

"Yes. Who is this?"

"Is your husband Anthony Cariri who teaches English at Bronx Technical High School?"

Suddenly Angie was terrified. Something had happened to Tony. "Yes," she said, trying to control her rising panic. "He's my husband. Is something wrong with him?"

"My name is Hector Martinez and I'm the principal at your husband's school. I'm sorry to tell you that there's been a shooting in his classroom. He's being sent to the Bronx Borough Trauma Center by ambulance. I don't know much about his condition, but I do know that he was conscious and talking to the police officers when he was loaded into the ambulance."

"What happened to him?" She was barely able to get the words out.

"He was shot by a student."

Oh my God, shot! "Shot? Like the shooting a few weeks ago?" She pictured Tony's beautiful body covered with blood.

"Yes. I'm so sorry. He was in the wrong place at the wrong time and got hit with a stray bullet. Again, I'm so sorry."

Angie felt like her heart had stopped. "Tell me where the hospital is?"

In a fog, Angie reached for a piece of paper and wrote down the address and directions. "I'll be there as soon as I can."

"Take your time," the man said, "and be careful on the road. It's really pouring out. I'm sure he'll be in the emergency room for some time and it's important that you not get into an accident driving down there. And take care of those twins of yours." The man's voice brightened. "Tony talks about them all the time."

"Yes. Right." In a total panic, she hung up and dialed Cait's number. When her friend answered, she told her exactly what Mr. Martinez had told her.

"I'll be right over," Cait said. "Don't go anywhere. I'll drive you down to the city. Can you call one of your sisters-in-law to take the twins?"

Angie was so scrambled that she'd forgotten that Tony had brothers. Actually she'd almost forgotten about the twins. "Yes, of course. I'll have to let them know. Of course. Someone will take the babies."

"Tell me the name of the hospital and I'll call from my cell in the car and see what I can learn about Tony's condition. I'll be over in ten minutes."

By the time Cait arrived, two women whom Cait assumed were Tony's sisters-in-law were already at Angie's house, getting the babies organized. "Diaper bag," one bulky lady said.

"In the van." Angie handed the woman the keys. "Their car seats are in there, too, but you can't take the van. It's not mine."

"Hi," Cait said, interrupting the chaos, "I'm Cait Johnson

and it's my van. Take it, by all means. It will be easier with the two car seats already set up inside."

The bulky woman extended her hand. "I've heard a lot about you from both Angie and Tony and it's nice to finally meet you. I wish it were under better circumstances. I'm Linda, Tony's brother Frank's wife, and this," she said, pointing to a tiny, dark-haired, dark-eyed woman, "is Sandra, Paul's wife. We'll take good care of the babies and Tony's brothers will meet you at the hospital. Cait, I don't think Angie's up to it, so we're depending on you to keep in touch." They exchanged phone numbers as Cait whisked Angie out of the house and into her Honda.

"I called the hospital," Cait said as the two women buckled their seat belts, "but I couldn't get any information. I even lied and said I was Tony's sister but it didn't help. They're about as close-lipped as the FBI."

"Thanks, Cait," Angie said, her face white, her voice strained. "Let's just get there."

"Done." Cait capably maneuvered down the rainy parkways and using her car's GPS system, found the hospital and parked in the gated parking structure. The two women hustled through the main entrance and followed the signs to the emergency department.

The waiting room was chaotic, filled with people needing attention: several crying babies, two bandaged young men, a couple having a screaming fight, with a security guard trying to calm them both down, and several older couples, holding hands and looking totally lost. The entire area was presided over by a nurse who looked like she'd spent several tours of duty in the military, with a rigidly straight back, a grim expression, and rimless glasses. "Yes?" she said when they reached the front of the line snaking up to her desk.

"We're here to see Anthony Cariri," Cait said when Angie seemed too cowed to say anything.

"And you are?"

"This is Angie Cariri, his wife."

"I don't understand" the woman said, looking slightly puzzled. "I sent Mrs. Cariri in to see him a few minutes ago." The woman looked down her large nose at a stack of file folders on her desk.

"That's not possible," Angie said, bewildered. "I'm here and his sisters-in-law are in East Hudson. We're the only Mrs. Cariris there are."

"I'm sorry but you'll just have to wait. I don't have time to straighten out who's married to whom."

"This is his wife!" Cait snapped. "Want to see her driver's license?"

"That won't be necessary. Take a seat and when Mrs. Carirri comes out, we'll get this all settled."

Angie was too confused to make any sense out of what was happening. "Can you tell me how my husband is?"

The woman sat up even straighter and leaned forward. "Mr. Cariri's condition can only be given to a family member. Maybe his wife will fill you in when she comes out."

Angie took out her driver's license to show to the "guard dog" but the nurse had already turned her attention to the next person in line, a gaunt woman with a two-year-old on her hip. "One more thing," Cait said, using her most authoritative tone. "What did 'Mrs. Cariri' look like?"

"She had a long black braid down her back and blue eyes. Satisfied?" she snarled.

"Jordanna," Angie and Cait said in unison. "She's his ex-wife," Angie said to the nurse.

"I didn't ask about divorce papers. She said she was his wife so I let her in. You'll still have to wait." Again she shifted her attention to the woman with the baby. Angry and frustrated, Angie and Cait made their way across to the waiting room.

"Sit here and don't move," Cait said, walking back toward the emergency department door as if she owned the hospital.

For several minutes Angie sat in the room, listening to whining children and whispering adults, totally numb. Tony. Shot. How? What had happened? Was Tony badly hurt? She had to get in to see him, touch him. Angie had confidence that Cait would make that happen, but how quickly? She had to know now. Why wasn't she in there? What the hell right did Jordanna have to usurp her position as Tony's wife? How did she find out so quickly about the shooting?

All these questions were whirling in her mind when she saw Cait approach, grab her by the arm, and hustle her to the other side of the area from the watchdog nurse, toward the emergency department door. "It's through here and he seems not to be too badly hurt. Look like you belong and you won't be challenged." Cait pushed her hand into the small of Angie's back and shoved her forward. They entered the emergency department without being stopped and squeezed through the curtains into Tony's cubicle.

His left shoulder was heavily bandaged but other than the white gauze and his slightly pale skin, he looked okay. Jordanna stood beside his bed. "Angie, you're here," Tony said, extending his unbandaged arm. "Jordanna looked a few minutes ago and said you weren't here yet."

Angie leaned over and kissed her husband then looked him over to assure herself that he was in one piece. Then she turned to Jordanna and something snapped. "Get out."

"Excuse me?"

"Get out of here! Go home. Tony's my husband, not yours. How dare you tell the people out front that he was your husband!" She turned to Tony, now relieved that he seemed all right and so furious with Jordanna that she could barely speak a coherent sentence. "How the hell did you find out he was here?"

"My name was still on some of the papers at school as his emergency contact. The vice principal called me, and of course I rushed right over from work by subway."

"You were called by mistake and you should have known that. Get out!"

"You told them out front that you were my wife?" Tony said, staring at Jordanna, totally confused.

Looking like the aggrieved party, Jordanna whined, "I wanted to get in to see you and they told me that only family members could be here. I am your wife, after all."

"Ex-wife," Angie hissed. "Get out of here right now. I couldn't get in here because of you and your convenient lie." Everything she'd held inside for so long came flooding out of her mouth. "I've tried to be nice. I never argued with Tony when he volunteered to fix all the things that went wrong in your house, but that's over. I've always believed that exes should get along, so I swallowed my hurt and smiled when Tony made plans with you. This is the end of that as far as I'm concerned."

Her lower lip slightly stuck out, Jordanna said, "Tony's a big boy and if he wants to see me, he will." Her voice was almost a whine.

Cait grabbed Jordanna by the shoulders and turned her toward the exit, but Jordanna twisted out of her grip. Ignoring Jordanna, Tony turned to Angie. "You mean you were upset that I went to help Jordanna out? It was all perfectly innocent."

"God," Cait muttered, "you're such a jerk. It was innocent for you but I suspect that your darling ex-wife knew that she was causing trouble." Jordanna tried to look guiltless but she couldn't keep the small smirk from her lips.

"I was jealous," Angie said, tears streaming down her cheeks, "and I'll admit it. She's so much more than I am and it makes me crazy, but I believed that it was important that you and she have a good relationship so I bit my lip and tried to be a good sport. Right now, I've no idea why."

Tony looked totally nonplussed but when he remained silent, Angie said, "I think it's time for you to make some

choices, Tony. I never intended to be a problem, but I think
it's time you spent time with me and the twins rather than
with your ex-wife. We miss you when you're gone."

"Really, Angie," Jordanna said, "be serious. Do you think
he'd rather spend time with you and those twins of yours than
with me?"

Tony took a deep breath, winced, and grabbed his shoulder,
then said through gritted teeth, "Jordanna, shut up! Angie,"
he said, turning toward his wife, "I never realized. I'm really
sorry. I felt needed and flattered by Jordanna's attention but
that's all. Really. Cait's right. I have been a jerk. I really never
realized how you felt and I didn't see how much Jordanna was
hurting you. I guess there's a lot we have to talk about. Never
forget this, Angie. I love you totally, and no one else. Jordanna's
my past, you're my present and my future."

"Oh, Tony," Jordanna said, straightening her spine, "don't
be silly. We have such nice times together. You're important to
me."

"Jordanna," Tony said, "get out. Angie's right. She and the
babies have first call on my time and my love. Just get the hell
out."

Jordanna turned, seemingly in shock, and it was difficult for
Angie not to feel some triumph. Trying not to gloat she said,
"Someone will keep you informed about Tony's condition but
he seems just fine to me right now."

Cait found Jordanna's coat on a side chair, handed it to her,
and guided her toward the break in the curtains surrounding
Tony's stretcher. "Nice almost meeting you," she said. Behind
Jordanna's back, she gave Angie a thumbs-up sign. "I'll wait
outside."

When Angie and Tony were alone, she held him and kissed
him deeply. "I was so scared," she said.

"I know, and I wanted to call you to let you know I was
okay, but my cell phone is in my locker at school and I couldn't
get hold of a phone here."

"What happened?"

Tony explained that the same gun that had been smuggled in the previous week had appeared again in the hand of another gang member, attempting to shoot another member of the rival gang. Tony had accidentally gotten in the way and a bullet had traveled through his shoulder. "It's only a flesh wound." His grin was irresistible. "I've heard that in so many TV cop shows and I always thought that meant it was minor. Well, it hurts like hell." He wrapped his good arm around Angie's waist and squeezed. "I'll need lots of care when we get home."

"Are they going to let you go home today?"

"Seems so. They've already patched me up pretty good so I'm just waiting for discharge instructions. I have to see my regular doctor sometime soon to have the stitches attended to, but other than that I'm really okay. I'm on light duty for a week or so."

Angie buried her face in Tony's hair and finally let the tears flow.

An hour later, when Tony finally walked out of the emergency room, both his brothers, Cait, Monica, and Eve were all waiting. Hugs were exchanged and introductions made. Finally everyone made their way to the exit. "Angie," Frank said, "Linda and I will keep the twins tonight. You guys go home and hold each other like I know you need to."

"We're here, too, in case you need anything," Monica said.

"I'll drive you guys home," Cait said. "If you want, we can drive past the school and pick up your car."

They settled on arrangements and eventually Angie and Tony were together, alone at home, sharing a pizza. "I love you, you know," Tony said, a slice of pepperoni between his teeth. "Very much. I'm so sorry about Jordanna. I was blind and a dope."

"I should have let you know how I felt long ago. Swallowing all this was dumb on my part, too."

"Let's start this thing all over, and this time, it's just us in this marriage. Right?"

"Don't forget the twins."

"How could I forget the twins?"

Later that night Tony and Angie climbed into bed. Tony had declined to take the pain medication the doctor had prescribed and had only taken two over-the-counter pills. He lay propped on several pillows, watching the end of the TV news. His shooting had been one of the first local stories and he watched in fascination as his students told interviewers what a great teacher he was. "I'm amazed," he said to Angie, who lay beside him, "to hear what they think. Of course, most of it is for the benefit of the TV cameras but I must mean something to them, don't you think?"

"Of course you do. You're a great teacher and your students really like and respect you."

"Makes me feel like hot shit." Tony wrapped his good arm around his wife's shoulders.

"How do you feel?" Angie said, her palms sweeping over his chest and belly.

"Is that a leading question?" Tony asked.

"It's leading wherever you want it to." Her hands stroked his good shoulder, then down his arm until she could link fingers with him.

"I'm not good for much," Tony reluctantly admitted. "When I move it still hurts like hell."

To Tony's amazement, Angie said, "I could do all the work." Angie had never been the aggressor, and here she was all but propositioning him, but she wanted him badly. He merely raised an eyebrow as Angie's fingers slid to his belly, then down to his growing erection. "God, Angie, what are you doing?"

Angie pulled her hand back as if she'd been burned. "I'm sorry. I just . . ."

"Don't apologize. It's wonderful." He used his good hand

to guide her back to his cock. "Touch me. It's the best medicine there is."

"Are you sure?" she said, suddenly unsure of herself again.

"Baby, I'm more than sure. I love the feel of your hands on me." He stretched his good arm across the bed. "Have your wicked way with me, woman. I insist."

Grinning, Angie began to explore her husband's body. She touched, petted, and stroked until he was ready for her. Tony handed her a condom and she capably unwrapped and unrolled it. Then she straddled his hips and slowly lowered herself onto him. For several moments she just sat and watched Tony revel in the feeling of her slippery pussy surrounding his engorged cock. When she started to move, he clenched his muscles to try to keep from coming, but it was no use. He was well past the point of no return, and with a long, low moan, he came.

Later Angie lay beside him again. Drowsily he said, "You didn't come."

"I got my pleasure from you. Now go to sleep."

Grinning, he turned and wrapped his good arm around her waist. "Bossy woman." Then he was asleep.

Chapter
25

"Monica, we need to talk." Harrison Conroy, the now semi-retired senior partner, closed Monica's office door behind him, then settled into one of her office chairs. It was several days after Tony's shooting, and according to her phone call with Angie the preceding day, he was recovering quickly. "How are you doing?"

"I'm fine," Monica said, totally puzzled by his unexpected visit. Although he'd cut back his hours at the firm to one or two afternoons a week several years before, as senior account executive she met with him occasionally to go over details of account relationships and presentations, discuss prospective opportunities, and go over billing issues. Those meetings had always been either in his office or in the conference room, however. Rank had its privileges. He seldom arrived in her office, especially unannounced. "What can I do for you, Mr. Conroy?"

Who sat down first was always an issue, so now that he'd seated himself in one of her two leather-upholstered side chairs, she settled in her buttery soft black leather chair behind her granite-topped desk in front of the wall of windows. The office was set up to impress potential clients, so in addition to her kick-ass desk—as she often called it—and side chairs, there was a deep burgundy seating group around a walnut coffee table, covered with magazines. Prominently displayed on her walls were matted and framed layouts of some of her more successful campaigns. A fully stocked bar was cleverly hidden behind the false front of one of the shelves in her wall unit and a small refrigerator in the corner held ice, soft drinks, and bottled water.

"Harrison. It's Harrison, or even Harry. We're better friends than that, Monica. I shouldn't be Mr. Conroy to you, especially in private."

They weren't friends at all and she'd never been invited to call him by his first name before, but Monica let that go. She'd always thought of the "Mr. Conroy, Monica" name thing as a hierarchy issue. He could call her by her first name but she was expected to address him by his surname. Maybe there was a gender component, too. After all, this was a man's world, or at least a man's company. "Okay, Harrison." Harry sounded too diminutive for such an overpowering man. "What did you want to talk to me about?"

"Interesting question, Monica." He cleared his throat and balanced one ankle on the other knee. His tasseled black loafers gleamed with fresh polish. She looked at him seriously for a moment. He was in his mid-sixties, very attractive, with wings of silver in his chestnut brown hair and deep creases around his intense gray eyes. His light blue shirt was heavily starched and serious diamond cuff links twinkled on gleaming white cuffs. His carefully pressed slacks draped neatly over his legs. He steepled his fingers. "I'm sure you've figured out that you're up for a partnership."

"I don't know how to answer that, Harrison, so I'll be honest. It's supposed to be a secret but nothing's truly secret in this office. Yes, I know and I'm very excited about the prospect of joining you."

"You know that I will make the decision. Of course, it's up to all the partners, but they will pretty much do as I say."

When Monica remained silent, unsure of where this conversation was leading, he continued, "I've been talking to a few of your clients and I've caught inferences that you will do special things for some of your best."

What was he leading up to, she wondered. Was he upset that she did sexual favors for a few of the biggies? A few of the not-so-biggies, too? She found it difficult to believe that he'd care how she kept her billing up, since it added to the firm's bottom line. She still said nothing. Let him explain himself.

"I just got to wondering how much you want this partnership." He let the sentence hang in the air.

Shit. Monica couldn't believe he meant what he was implying. The guy was pulling out the casting couch. *Fuck him and get the partnership. Don't and you can kiss it good-bye.* He said nothing more, just uncrossed his legs and stood up. "Stop by my office anytime and let me know how you feel about this." Without another word he crossed the thick carpeting and closed the door behind himself.

How much did she want the partnership? It was really important to her—more money, more prestige in the industry. She'd be the only female partner of Conroy & Bates, quite a coup for someone who had worked her way up through the ranks. Her face would be on the cover of *Advertising Age,* maybe even a mainstream magazine like *Time* or *Newsweek.* What would she be willing to do to get it? She rubbed her jaw in front of her ears, the first place she always felt tension.

In the past she wouldn't have hesitated for a moment. She might have even suggested it herself. But now? Since she'd been with Dan she hadn't wanted to be with anyone else. Shit!

She could scream sexual harassment, and that was certainly what Mr. Conroy—she couldn't call him Harrison—meant by his comment, but it wouldn't float. She had no real proof of anything threatening and he'd merely deny that he meant anything untoward by his comments. She could wear a wire as they did in the TV crime shows, but what good would it do?

C & B would toss her out on her ear, whistle-blower laws or not, and her name would be mud in the business, even if she were right.

What would Dan think? She could just not tell him, of course, sleep with Harrison, and be done with it, but that would be cheating. What would she do?

She'd think about it, and for several hours she thought about little else.

"Monica Beaumont," she said into her phone at work later that afternoon.

"Hi, Monica, it's Eve."

Monica unhooked her earring and cradled the cordless phone against her ear as she crossed her office and closed the door. "Hi, Eve." Strange. Eve had never called her at work before. They'd chatted occasionally in the evening but this was a first. "What's up?"

"I've got a little problem."

From the tone of Eve's voice, Monica suspected that it was more than just a *little* problem. "What can I help you with?" she asked, settling behind her desk and swinging her chair around so she could look out over the Hudson.

"You seem to be pretty knowledgeable about doctors."

"Not much more than you are, I'm afraid."

"You had a cardiologist. I remember you talking about your visit with him and your need to relax. How did you find him? Or is it a her?"

"It's a him, and my internist recommended him. I looked him up on the Web and was satisfied with his background, so I made an appointment. Have you got heart problems?" Eve had never struck her as a high-stress person so why would she need a cardiologist at her age?

"It's not that," Eve said, a catch in her voice. "I went to my gynecologist this morning."

Monica interrupted. "You're not pregnant?"

She could hear Eve's chuckle. "No. That's not it. Somehow

I wish it were. Pregnancy would be simpler. The doctor found a lump in my right breast."

"Shit." Monica swallowed hard. She tried to calm her racing heartbeat with the thought that not all lumps were cancer.

"Yeah. Don't tell Angie or Cait. Not yet. Everyone's so happy that Tony's fine now and everything." As an incentive not to sue the New York City schools, he'd been offered a desk job in the administration building until a job opened up in a better school. The union was also talking about a lawsuit because of the lack of protection for its teachers. "I need to know whether the oncologist my guy recommended is any good."

"I can certainly look him up on the Web for you," Monica said, her hands shaking. "Then, when you decide on someone, we can go together."

"That's not necessary, Monica. I'll go by myself." She heard Eve's voice crack.

Monica's jaw tightened. "What part of 'we'll go together' didn't you understand?" Monica listened as Eve wept, then said softly, "It's okay, Eve. It's probably nothing. Something benign. A fatty cyst or something. One of the women at work had a lump that turned out to be nothing. Odds are—"

"It's okay, Monica. You can stop with the pep talk. My doctor told me that the odds of it being something terrible are small, especially at my age with my lack of family history, but it's difficult to hear about anything that might be cancer, however minuscule the chances. Help me find someone, will you? In the city, maybe, since we're both down here every day."

"Of course. Let me do a bit of research and I'll call you back." Monica took Eve's cell phone number and spent the next hour bouncing from one Web site to another, amassing data on breast cancer and oncologists. When she called Eve back, she rattled off statistics, then mentioned the names of three well-respected specialists.

"The second one you mentioned," Eve said, "is the one my doctor referred me to so that seems good enough for me."

Respecting Eve's wishes, they didn't discuss her problems
the next day at lunch with Cait. It had only been five days
since the shooting, and since Tony couldn't really lift much
with his sore arm, especially a wriggling baby, Angie had dashed
home right after class. The other three had met for lunch, feeling incomplete. They had each talked to Angie on the phone
and knew that Tony was doing very well and preparing to go
back to the city in a week or so. He hadn't yet decided whether
he'd go back to teaching or take the desk job the administration had offered. They marveled at the fall colors, now at their
peak in Westchester County, shared some gossip about a
celebrity, but the group felt alien without Angie. Monica told
the other two that Bonnie was adjusting to life without Jake
and the kids were settled in at school. Jake was still talking
about moving back in but Bonnie was still not sure what she
wanted to do. He was, thankfully, visiting with the children
several times a week. Eve was noticeably silent, but told Cait
that it was just some problem at work so she wouldn't get too
curious.

The following week Monica sat in the waiting room while
Eve talked to the cancer specialist, trying too read the latest
issue of *Newsweek*. Frightened was far too small a word for what
she was feeling. Her palms were sweaty, her heartbeat rapid.
What if the news was really bad?

She'd gotten Eve's permission to tell Dan and he'd been
completely supportive. "You know I'm there for both of you."

"I know, Dan. I'm just so scared." She held him closer. "It
really puts everything in perspective. You're what's important
to me. Not my job, not anything else. You and my three good
friends and my family head the list, then everything else
comes lots farther down."

"I love you, you know." Dan had said it before but never in
the serious tone he was using today. "I've said it lightly a few
times, and when I did, you've always shied away from the subject. Now I'm saying it for real. We've only known each other

a few months, but when something's right, it just is, and I've known it for a while."

She took a breath but he put his finger across her lips. "Don't say anything. Think about it for a while. Let it percolate through your brain and see what you think later."

"Dan, I don't have to let it percolate, as you put it. I love you."

"With one of your best friends in trouble the way she is, and just after Tony's shooting, this isn't the moment to make lasting pledges," he said. "Relax and let's see where this all leads. I merely wanted you to know how I feel."

Now, sitting, waiting, she knew that she really did love Dan. He was right, of course, not to let this really emotional experience with Eve color her thinking, so she wouldn't tell him anything more about the way she felt, nor would she do anything differently, but she knew. It wouldn't change. Should she tell him that she was giving up the clients she'd entertained? She thought about Mr. Conroy and knew she wouldn't consider his proposition. She had to tell him that, but not right now.

Eve emerged through a wide wooden door, pulled her coat off a hook, and whispered to the receptionist. Then she motioned to Monica and they left the office. "So?"

"I have some tests scheduled next week. The doctor examined me and told me that he couldn't tell much from an exam and the X-ray and sonogram I brought from my regular doctor. It would have been nice to know when this thing started to grow but I don't do a self exam as often as I should." She smiled ruefully. "Read for that, never. So the only indication we have is that my gynecologist didn't find anything a year ago."

"What kinds of tests are they going to do?"

"The main one is something called a needle biopsy and it will show whether it's benign or not."

There was a catch in her voice and Monica noticed that

she'd never actually said *cancer*. She remembered her terror when her cardiologist had first used the word *coronary*. She'd be with Eve every step of the way, no matter what. "When are the tests, and where?"

Eve named a hospital, then told her the tests were scheduled for the end of the following week. "I wanted to do everything as quickly as I could but she said a week, or even a month, wouldn't make a difference. It probably doesn't make a difference to her, but to me, it seems like an eternity. Unfortunately, next Friday was the first appointment I could get with the radiologist she wanted me to see, so I wait."

"Are you going to tell Angie and Cait? We have girls' night out this Sunday."

"What can I tell them, when I don't know anything myself? Within a week I'll know more." She paused, deep in thought, then said with a sigh, "There's more to this than even you know so I probably will tell them. I need help with several decisions and you and Angie and Cait are just the women who can give me guidance."

The following Sunday was Halloween, so driving through East Hudson had been an adventure for Monica, with children of all ages wandering the streets, dressed in all manner of costumes. Heedless of the fact that in their dark clothing they were almost invisible, they tramped up and down front walks, occasionally waving flashlights and lugging gigantic bags of loot. Although she drove through side streets at about fifteen miles per hour, Monica barely missed several children who recklessly darted out between cars.

The four women gathered in their familiar booth in Huckleberry's. Several of the customers, and all of the wait staff, were in costume, and the women smiled as they surveyed their surroundings. "What a zoo," Cait said as their order for three piña coladas, a Diet Coke for Angie, and nachos was taken by a waiter dressed as a gypsy dancer. Once she was gone, Cait continued, "I'm so glad Tony's doing so well."

"Actually, he's fine," Angie said. "Except for a really nasty scar on his shoulder, he's back to where he was before the 'happening.' That's what we've been calling it since the word shooting makes me cringe."

"I'm so glad the shooter wasn't one of his students," Monica said. The four women had been keeping in touch by phone and had seen each other briefly during the yoga class but it was especially good to be able to meet again, face to face, and further reassure each other about Tony's physical and mental health.

Monica noticed a new glow on Angie's face as she answered, "No, it wasn't. Tony said that most of his kids, as he calls them—even though several of them tower over him—have e-mailed him and begged him to come back. A few of the letters were slightly illiterate, but all of them were genuinely touching. He's thinking of going back to his old classroom. That frightened me at first, but I think it's what he really wants."

"Is he going to sue?" Cait asked.

"We must have gotten a hundred calls, letters, and e-mails from lawyers who want to take his case, and the union is involved. I don't know what he's going to do since there were no out-of-pocket expenses. The lawyers all point out that lax security and ineffective police work finding the gun after the previous shooting were responsible for what happened, but Tony keeps saying, 'Shit happens and they can't protect us from everything and maintain an atmosphere where any learning goes on.' The system might offer a settlement anyway, in addition to the desk job, if he takes it. It would be nice to have something in the bank for the twins' education," she said, fiddling with her napkin, "but I can't help but agree with Tony. Shit happens."

"Did they find the gun?" Monica asked.

"Oh, yeah. They didn't have to look for it this time. Several of the kids in Tony's class tackled the shooter and stomped on him until the school security officers arrived."

"They have security officers?" Eve looked truly shocked.

"It's a really tough school, which I didn't realize until Tony told me all about it in the hospital."

"Still, he wants to go back."

"He's seriously thinking about it. He really loves the kids and thinks he's making a difference. He teaches them about books and filling out job applications, along with deceptive advertising and taking some responsibility for what politicians do. From the passion with which he talks, I think he probably does get to some of them."

Their drinks and chips arrived, served by a waitress dressed as a vampire. They took deep swallows, then Eve asked, "What about Jordanna? I still can't believe what she did."

"I think Tony's through with her. He couldn't believe that she'd said she was his wife and was doubly furious that I couldn't get in because of it. She pled innocent, but I think she knew. Cait was a tiger."

Cait chewed a chip. "I think Tony understands what's been going on. I gather things are pretty good between you."

"Very good. Except the twins are cutting molars. Some things never change." They all laughed.

Monica looked at Eve but she remained silent. When Eve was ready, if she was that evening at all, she'd tell Angie and Cait about the lump. "How's Dan, and is there any news about the partnership?" Eve said, turning the conversation in a different direction.

"Another knotty problem," Monica said slowly. With all the terror about Eve's lump, she hadn't shared this part of her job difficulties with anyone. Her problems seemed so small. She related her conversation with Harrison Conroy. "I know exactly what he wants, and every time I think I've decided to kick him in the nuts, a little voice chides me and talks about how great the partnership would be. After all, I'm not getting any younger."

Cait made a rude noise. "What does Dan think?"

"I haven't told him about my 'extra-curricular activities' or my conversation with Mr. Conroy. He says he loves me, but I'm still not sure he's ready to hear all about me and my job."

"He actually used the 'L' word?" Angie asked.

"He did, and I think I feel the same way about him."

"You've been putting this off for a long time, Monica," Cait said. "Don't you trust Dan to stick around if you tell him?"

Monica was silent for several moments. "I hadn't thought about it that way but you're probably right. I don't trust him not to run out if things get difficult, even with the 'L' word . . ."

"It's time to fish or cut bait," Eve said, a purposeful tone in her voice. "For all of us."

"All of us?" Cait said, her head snapping around to face Eve. "What the hell does that mean?"

Monica reached out and took Eve's hand. "I've been to a doctor and had tests," Eve said. "I have a lump in my right breast."

There was silence for a heartbeat, then Angie said, "Of course, it's benign."

"We don't know yet. The tests next week should tell us that, so I have to wait. Patience isn't something I'm good at."

"Oh, God, Eve, I'm so sorry," Angie said. "How long have you known?"

"Less than two weeks but it seems like months."

"You didn't tell us," Angie said, looking slightly hurt.

"Oh, Angie, you had enough on your mind. I didn't tell anyone but Monica and I only told her because I needed her help finding a doctor."

"Can one of us go with you?" Cait asked, reaching out to hold Eve's hand.

"Monica's been a gem. She went with me to the oncologist

and she'll keep me company next week, as well. It's already planned." She gripped Cait's hand. "Thanks so much for the offer, Cait. I have no doubt that you'd be there for me if I needed you."

"I'm glad you were there for her, Monica," Angie said. "I'm just frustrated that I can't do anything."

"Me, too," Cait said. "I want to help in some way."

"You do help, just by being here for me."

Monica watched Eve's efforts not to cry. "I'm sorry that I couldn't tell you guys," she said, "but this was Eve's story to tell."

"Of course," Cait said. "We understand. Sometimes there are things that are private."

"Private. Yeah. There's something else," Eve said, cradling her glass in her hands, "something that I haven't told anyone. Facing my own mortality, I've been thinking about someone from my past." She fiddled with her straw, then took a long drink of her piña colada.

"You don't have to tell us anything, if it makes you so uncomfortable," Monica said. "We all have secrets."

"I hate keeping secrets," Eve said, "but this one's been deep in my gut for almost sixteen years." She paused, then said quickly, "I have a daughter."

There was dead silence around the table so she continued. "I was in high school and there was a guy. It was brief, but I found myself pregnant. To make a long and, I guess, irrelevant story short, I left the area and had the baby. It was a little girl and I gave her up for adoption."

Again Eve took a swallow, then set her glass down in front of her with a slight clatter. "It was an open adoption so I know the family who took Brittany." Her smile was distant and wan. "I named her that even before she was born. I'd always loved that name and the new family agreed to keep it. They also agreed to tell her that she was adopted, but say that they didn't know anything about her birth mother. Otherwise, I left everything to them."

"Do they live around here?"

"In Mount Kisco. I've never visited or even driven past the house, but I know the address. I asked that they keep me informed if they moved, but they've been in the same house since the year after they adopted my daughter. They are really nice people and they drop me a card from time to time with school pictures and such." She took a long, slow breath. "My daughter. I haven't said those words out loud in more than fifteen years."

"Are you thinking about seeing her now?" Monica asked. She couldn't imagine how Eve was feeling. To have a child and not have seen her for all those years. It was probably for the best for Brittany, but it must have caused Eve so much pain.

"Every doctor I've seen recently asked me about my family history and of course, I was able to tell them everything I knew. I've denied Brittany that and maybe a lot more. I think I do want to see her. When you look your future, whatever it holds, in the face, lots of things get clearer." Again she paused, then added, "I told Mike good-bye."

"Good for you. How did he take it?" Cait asked.

"He was upset, but what could he say? He said that he hoped I'd change my mind, that he'd miss me—he even went so far as to say he loved me. He didn't really mean it, it was just something he said to try to get me to stay. It's going to be awkward working with him, but I'll get over that and I don't care whether he does or not."

"More important things seem to put others in perspective," Angie said, obviously thinking of Tony's shooting.

"Yeah, they do," Eve said. "I have no idea what I'd say to Brittany, but I think I have to try. I owe us both that."

When the three other women lapsed into silence, Angie

took a deep breath and said, "I wasn't going to say anything this early but I think we all need some good news. At least I think it's good news." She sipped her coffee. "About a month ago, Tony and I did a dumb thing and had sex without protection."

"You're not!" Cait said, and Monica suddenly realized the reason for Angie's Diet Coke.

"I am. I took one of those pregnancy tests yesterday."

The three other women squealed in delight. Monica watched Eve's face to see whether a new baby would make her even sadder about giving her daughter away, but she saw nothing but joy on her friend's face. "That news makes everything else a little less scary," Eve said. "Thanks for sharing it. I've only just begun to realize what a special thing a baby is." As Eve reached over and hugged Angie, Monica realized that the deep friendship that she and these three other wonderful, totally different women shared was one of the best partnerships that life had to offer. Maybe she and Dan could become another such partnership. They were good friends and great lovers. What more was there?

She slid out of the booth and wrapped her arms around Angie, letting all the love she felt for her show. "Ladies," she said to the occupants of their booth, "I think I'm going home and calling Dan. We've got a lot of talking to do."

The other three raised their glasses. "Here's to all our changes. May everything go the way we all want."

Monica grabbed her glass and drank deeply. "Amen to that." Then she hastened out of the restaurant.

Chapter
26

As Cait left Huckleberry's and bade good night to the other women, she thought about tonight's news. Eve might have cancer, and had a child. Tony was almost completely recovered and Angie was pregnant again. My God, so much was happening. Children were at the center of so much. Children made everything different. Maybe she'd talk to Logan again.

As she climbed into her cold car she shivered, pulled her heavy jacket around her, and looked carefully around the parking lot for the dark, late-model sedan she'd seen cruising her neighborhood several times in the past week. Why hadn't she shared her fears with her friends? She hadn't wanted to frighten them the way she was frightened, probably for nothing. What were the odds that he'd found her, that he even had the desire to pursue her? She was imagining things. Wasn't she?

It was also difficult to admit to anyone that she'd been so stupid. She'd all but told Hotguy her full name and where she lived. What an idiot she'd been. Hot chatting wasn't inherently dangerous as long as you were wary. She hadn't been.

She drove home slowly and carefully, Johnny Cash pounding through her car's speakers but not cutting the edge of fear that seemed to pervade everything she did these days. She'd snapped at Logan the one time he'd come home at a reasonable hour that week. Even surfing the 'Net hadn't helped. Between her nightmares and her constantly shaking hands, she could barely function. Her friends had noticed it, but even when asked, she denied the truth.

Fortunately the number of young children on the streets had dwindled to a few small bunches. She passed a few cars covered with flour and eggs and one tree in the neighborhood that had been festooned with toilet paper. Shaving cream had been sprayed liberally on several mailboxes. A few teens still hung out in groups here and there, dressed in outlandish get-ups, smoking and howling at passing cars. Thankfully Halloween was waning for another year.

She drove down Sheraton and eased into her garage without having to touch her brakes. At least something still worked, she thought as she walked into her kitchen. Of course Logan wasn't home. He was with his girlfriend. Yes, she'd finally admitted to herself that he had to be having an affair. His excuses for not coming home had been getting lamer and lamer and he certainly wasn't working tonight. It was Sunday.

She pulled out her phone and dialed Logan's cell. "Yes, Cait," Logan answered, sounding totally exasperated. "What do you want? I'm busy."

"I can hear how busy," she said, listening to the chatter of voices in the background. He was somewhere in public. Probably out at some bar with his bimbo. Maybe Monica was right. All men were shits. "Just wondering whether you're planning on coming home at all."

"I'll be home later."

"Logan, I think I've had enough." Eve's talk about cancer had frightened her enough to make her realize that she had nothing in her life, no children, no marriage, no nothing. Actually, Logan made it less than nothing. Money or no money, prestige or none, she'd had enough. "If you come home at all, sleep in the guest room. I'm done."

"Cait, calm down. I can hear that you're upset. We'll talk about this." He was using that infuriatingly cajoling tone he used when he wanted something. This time he wasn't getting it.

"I am upset, but I'm also calm. I'm done with this sham of a marriage."

"Honey, relax. We'll talk in the morning."

"Damn him," she hissed as she pressed the END button, then flipped the phone closed and dropped it into her jacket pocket. No use fooling herself, she thought. Her life was falling apart. Except for Angie, Monica, and Cait, she had nothing. She let out a long sigh. Monica had Dan, Angie had Tony, and Eve had her daughter. She walked slowly up the stairs and dropped her purse on her dresser. She didn't immediately flip on the light, preferring the darkness. Moonlight shone through her bedroom window, giving her enough light to make out the door to the bathroom. A hot shower would clear some of the fog that had invaded her brain. She started to slip her arm out of her jacket.

"Hi, Cait, or should I say Loverlady." The voice came from a darkened corner of the room. "I've been looking forward to this for weeks."

Hotguy! She recognized his voice. This was no nightmare. Everything she'd dreaded was right here in this room with her. Her brain seized up like a motor running without any oil. *No,* she thought. *I can't let him terrify me. I have to keep my wits about me.* She tried to calm herself with her yoga breathing, then slipped her arm back into her sleeve. "What are you doing here?" she asked, feeling a bit calmer but making sure fear showed in her voice. *Go ahead. Underestimate me, you bastard.*

"I'm here to be with you, of course," he said.

Brett. That was the name he'd told her. She'd been calling him Hotguy so long she'd almost forgotten. She schooled her voice to show fear, and the attempt to cover it up. Most of that was true, of course, but she wasn't going to be the wimp he expected. "Brett, I think I told you I wasn't interested. I'm not, so go away."

"You're such a liar. You know you're interested. Rape fantasies. That's what turns you on, and I'm about to make your fantasies real. Isn't that wonderful?"

He sounded so calm, so reasonable, as if he believed that she wanted it. She didn't. "This isn't what I want at all, Brett, and I think you know that."

"It's not Brett. That's just one of my identities. I'd like you to call me by my real name. It's Nick. Say it, Cait. Nick."

My God, she really knew nothing at all about him. Even the name he'd given her was a phony. She really was a fool, one who could get badly hurt if she wasn't careful and very, very clever. She took a slow, deep breath. Whether for his own gratification or because he really thought she wanted it, she was going to be raped unless she could think of something to stop it. Under the cover of the shadows she reached into her pocket, slowly flipped her phone open, felt around the keypad, and pushed the SEND button twice to redial. Then she pressed her thumb over the speaker opening so any sound Logan might make would be at least partially muffled.

Hoping that Logan could hear what was going on, and that he cared, she said, "Nick. Don't hurt me. What are you doing in my bedroom?"

"I thought I made that clear," he said, his voice totally matter-of-fact. "I'm here because you want me here."

"I do not want you here so get out." Could Logan hear anything? She palmed the phone and pulled it slightly out of her pocket so the sound would be louder. "Get out. My husband will be home any minute."

"That pussy-whipped idiot? He's not good enough for you. I'll admit you've got a nice house, but any guy who'd let his wife play with me on the 'Net isn't man enough for you.

Anyway, he hasn't been home before midnight any night this week, including last Sunday night."

"I'm sure someone saw you sneaking around the neighborhood and into my house. They'll call the cops." She prayed Logan was getting the hint and had already called the police.

Nick stepped from the shadows, dressed in black jeans, a black, long-sleeved polo shirt and black leather jacket. He held out the rubber head and face mask he had in his hand. "That's why I chose tonight," he said, as if explaining himself to a small child. "Anyone who saw me thought I was your run of the mill trick-or-treater." His laugh was deep and menacing. "Trick being the operative word. And you're going to be my treat."

Her glance flicked to the control panel for the alarm system but Brett—no, his name was Nick—followed her eyes. "Don't think about tripping the panic button. I can be on you before you move. I might hurt you that way and I really don't want to." He took a step forward. "I love this game you're playing with me. I can see how much you want this, and how good a job you're doing covering it up. You're doing it all so well. Have you practiced this with many other men?"

Maybe he really was deluded. "I don't want this! Not even a little bit! Playing out a rape fantasy is very different from wanting it in reality. Why don't you just leave and we'll forget this entire mix-up?"

He laughed as he took another step forward. "Mix-up? That's a good one. Right, a mix-up. Like you didn't all but invite me over to do this."

What would the cops do, assuming Logan had called them? Would they show up with flashing lights and sirens? Probably not, she reasoned with the part of her brain still functioning. They'd consider this a hostage situation since she was in the bedroom with a rapist. They'd probably sneak up to the house, then get on the loud speakers like in the TV cop shows. She had to stall him until that happened. What if Logan didn't hear her and had just hung up? No, she had to think positively. The cops were on the way. She used her thumb to stroke the back of the phone, warm in her hand. "I didn't invite you. I can see how you'd think that way, but it's all a misunderstanding. If you leave now then there's been no harm done."

Suddenly he was on her, his hand twisting her hair behind her head. "No harm done? You bitch. Of course there's no harm done. I haven't done anything yet." The phone dropped to the bottom of her pocket and she stumbled backwards until the backs of her thighs hit the bed. "There's lots of time. We've got all night." He grabbed the front of her blouse and pulled, sending buttons flying everywhere. "That's better. Let's get some harm done."

He pushed and overbalanced, Cait fell backwards onto the king-sized bed. *Logan, hear me!* She felt the phone trapped in her jacket pocket beneath her, pressing into her hip. *Call the cops, Logan. Please.* In case he wasn't there, she knew she couldn't let this happen. She scrabbled until her knees were beneath her then skittered across the bed.

"You're doing this just right." His voice was low and she could make out the wide smile on his face. "I love it when women fight me." He reached out and snagged her ankle with one hand. "Keep it up, Loverlady." He rubbed the front of his jeans with his free hand. "You're making it better and better. My cock loves this."

She twisted and kicked out with her imprisoned ankle and was almost free when he suddenly backhanded her across the face. She saw stars and the pain made her crumple. When he hit her again, this time with his fist, she felt her teeth snick together. She tasted blood from the spot where she had bitten her cheek and her entire face began to throb. "Lie still or I'm going to have to hurt you more."

Although her urge was to run, she quieted. She'd get her chance. "That's a good girl." He grabbed one wrist and pulled a strip of cloth from his pocket. "See? I've come prepared." As he bent over to tie the cloth to one wrist, she measured her leg's reach, and in one quick motion, backed by all of her body's yoga training, she lashed out and caught him in the groin with her heel. It had the desired effect. He let out a huge burst of air, then crumpled to the floor, hands cupping his crotch. "Bitch," he hissed. "Bitch." He pulled in a large breath. "You'll pay for that and it won't help!"

She ran for the bedroom door, then down the stairs. Bursting out the front door, she was met with a bright light in her face. "Stand still!" an authoritative voice commanded. "Police. Don't move." She took a deep breath. Logan had heard her after all.

"He's upstairs in the bedroom," she said, suddenly seeing stars.

"Keep your hands out where we can see them," the voice said, "until we sort this all out."

It was as though every bit of strength she had abruptly drained out of her body. Barely able to stand, she extended her hands at shoulder level. Her entire head was throbbing, her jaw ached, and her nose and mouth were bleeding. "Name?" the voice asked.

"Cait Johnson. That's Caitlin. I live here. The guy was . . ." That's when it all fell apart. She crumpled to the ground, started to weep, and couldn't stop.

Several minutes later she came around, lying on the ambulance stretcher, waiting to be loaded inside. She saw three women run across the lawn, looking almost as stricken as Cait felt. "My God," Angie said. "Are you okay?"

"What happened?" Eve asked, while Monica just wrapped her arms around her friend. "It's okay," she said. "We're here for you, whatever you need."

The medic handed her an ice pack, and as she placed it against her cheek, Cait sniffled. "Right now I need a tissue." Angie handed her a pocket pack while Eve held the ice lightly against her face. She gently blew her bleeding nose several times, then took the ice pack back. "I must look a fright," she said, trying to smile through the excruciating pain in her face.

"Well," Monica said, "the Miss America judges rated you very low."

She started to chuckle but the pain stopped her. "God, don't make me laugh."

"I'm amazed that you can," Eve said. "We got a sketchy description of what happened from the cops. Kneed him in the balls, I gather."

"Kicked him right where he deserved it," Cait said.

The medic arranged the back of the stretcher so she could sit up. "Ma'am, I think the cops are pretty much done with this for now, but someone will follow the ambulance. We really need to get you to the hospital. One of your friends can ride along, the others can follow by car."

"I'll go," Angie said, "then Monica can drive me back later." She told Cait that Monica had picked Eve and her up so they had only one car.

In the back of the ambulance, the paramedic started an IV, "Just in case," he told her, and she told Angie the details of what had happened. "You're amazing," Angie said. "You had the presence of mind to call Logan."

"I just did what I had to. How did you find out I was in trouble?"

"Logan called me, frantic, after he'd called the police and I called Monica and Eve. Logan's in the city, and he said it would be at least an hour before he could get here."

Logan. Before Hotguy had showed up she was ready to end her marriage. Now she wasn't so sure. She felt needy and small, and wanted Logan beside her. "God, I was such an idiot. I didn't pay serious attention to any of the warning bells in my head. I should have made sure Brett—no, Nick—didn't know things about me. I should have been sure to set the alarm system when I got home. I should have . . ."

"Stop right now," Angie said, sternly. "You could have and should have but what happened, happened, and that's that. Move on."

"That's very good advice," the medic said.

As she was wheeled into the emergency department, still holding Angie's hand, she saw the other two women giving her the thumbs up sign. It was okay. She didn't think she was seriously hurt and Nick would be put away. But what could they charge him with? Could he convince the judge that she had invited him? What if he wasn't sent to jail and came after her again?

In the trauma bay, a doctor poked and prodded, then X-rayed and scanned with their CAT scan machine. An hour later she was bandaged and the ER doctor told her that they wanted to keep her overnight for observation. "There's a hairline fracture of the right orbit and your jaw is badly bruised. It should all heal without treatment, but you'll also need to see your dentist to be sure the teeth he loosened will stay put. I'll give you a prescription for some pain medication." He patted her arm. "You're pretty lucky. The police will want your statement but they've already linked this guy to another assault in Ossining."

"Another assault?" She might have guessed. "I want to go home," she said. "Is there any real reason you want to keep me here?"

"You shouldn't be alone, and sleeping more than a few hours at a time isn't a good idea for tonight. You need to be awakened periodically to be sure there's no serious concussion."

"I won't be alone. I'll have my husband and/or one of my friends stay with me. Can't they do whatever needs to be done?"

He let out a long breath. "I can't keep you here against your will, of course, and I won't insist if you're sure someone will stay with you. You might be better off not going back to your house until you're feeling a little stronger. It might not feel too comfortable yet and the cops are probably still there, making a mess."

She smiled weakly. "You're right about the house and I'm sure I can find somewhere else to stay. I really am okay and I want to get out of here." Eventually he agreed and gave her some written instructions and information about crisis centers if she needed counseling. Then he wrote out a prescription to take to a pharmacy, and told her she could leave when she was ready.

She told yet another police officer everything she could remember, including her meetings with Hotguy344. He assured her that Nick Montrose, which was his real name, wouldn't be bothering her again. He'd been linked by his fingerprints, not only with the assault in Ossining, but at least one more down county. "We're still gathering evidence and we'll be taking his DNA. It's Sunday night, but we've already got calls to two other jurisdictions on two other Internet-related assaults. We'll want to talk to you again but it can wait until you're feeling better. You were a lucky woman, with great instincts. That cell phone trick was a wonderful idea."

His praise was warming. "Thanks, officer. I'm grateful."

"Be grateful to your husband. He's the one who called us, very confused but very worried. He's outside, by the way, when you feel up to seeing him."

"He's here?"

"It's been more than two hours. He's in the reception area with your three friends. Shall I let him come in?"

"Of course. And tell my friends I'll be out in a few minutes."

While she waited for Logan, Cait changed back into the clothing she'd been wearing when Hotguy attacked her. As she slipped her jacket on and felt the phone in her pocket, she smiled. The officer was right, even if she did say so herself. She'd had the presence of mind to call Logan. As she pushed her feet into her shoes she saw the curtains around her cubicle part and Logan entered. He quickly enveloped her in a huge bear hug. "Oh God, Cait, I was so terrified. I'm so glad you're okay." He stroked her cheek, now turning a deep shade of purple. "Your poor face."

Cait returned the hug. "Thanks for understanding what I wanted."

"I heard you say that someone was in your room and then you said call the cops, so I did. God, don't ever scare me like that again."

Cait wanted to clear the air about a lot of things, but this wasn't the moment. "Let's get out of here. I want to see my friends before we go, then we can stop at the drugstore and pick up a few things. I don't want to go home tonight."

"Of course. We'll go to the East Hudson Inn for the moment and go back home only when you're ready." The East Hudson Inn was the nicest hotel in the area. Many of Logan's out-of-town clients stayed there and they'd had dinner in their fine restaurant many times. This would be the first time they'd ever stayed there. Or had Logan taken a room there with his mistress?

Eve, Monica, and Angie had waited patiently in the outer reception room and all but mobbed her when she walked out of the treatment area. "We've spent too much time in emergency rooms in the past month," Monica said, almost in tears. "No more."

Cait's eyes filled. Her friends. Her best, best friends. She'd often made fun of the "group hugs" she sometimes saw in chick flicks, but without reservation she joined the other three as they all hugged and blubbered. As she thought back on the past few hours Cait laughed inwardly with the joy of having not only survived but gotten the best of a total bastard.

Angie had obviously filled them in on the details of what had happened, so after each of the three stepped back to look her over carefully, satisfying themselves she was indeed all right, they all left. Logan escorted Cait to his little car and together got her prescription filled at an all-night CVS, then drove to the inn.

It was more than three hours after her encounter with Hotguy that they were finally settled in a luxurious hotel room. She sank onto the king-sized bed, spread some salve on her face, then slowly told Logan all about her adventures on the 'Net, about Hotguy, and then about the evening. "That's about it. I know it was about the dumbest thing I've ever done, but I was so lonely." She paused, then said, "Logan, tell me about her."

"Her?"

"There must be another woman and I think I'm ready to hear everything."

Logan unfolded himself from the small side chair he had been sitting on and opened the small minibar. At her request, he handed her a bottle of water then took out a bottle of scotch for himself. "I don't know where to begin. Or better still, when."

He poured the contents of the tiny bottle into a glass. "Back when we were trying to have a baby I slowly became aware that I didn't want to have sex with you."

To have something to do with her hands, Cait twisted the cap off the water bottle and poured a little into a glass. She tightened her stomach muscles, girding herself for whatever he was going to say.

"I figured it was just some midlife thing so I started going to bars after work, trying to find someone who turned me on, but there was no one. I saw lovely, willing women but no one did a thing for me. That's when I began to suspect. No, that's a lie. I think I've suspected for a long time but I didn't want to admit anything to myself."

Suddenly Cait knew what was coming but she let Logan spell it out. "I met a guy through work. He was looking at some property in Mamaroneck and well, one thing led to another and you can guess the rest. It was the best sex I'd had in a very long time. We haven't seen each other since but I couldn't stop thinking about it. I decided I was sick, some kind of a pervert. I agonized. I began hanging out in gay bars, just to prove to myself that it wasn't true, but it was."

Cait slowly let out a long breath, then clasped her hands in front of her. She should have been shocked, sickened, but she found she wasn't. All she felt was a deep sadness. "Have you found someone in particular?"

"I've spent about a dozen evenings with a marvelous man named Gary. He's my age and almost as confused as I am. We talk and seem to understand each other. And we have sex. Cait, it's such a betrayal. I don't know what to say."

"Could you give it up and come back to me?" Somehow Cait hoped he'd say no, and he did.

"I don't think so. I don't know whether Gary's someone for the long term but I know I can't go back to the way things were here. I have to admit to you, and to myself, that I'm gay, and I probably have been for a long time."

Cait stood, crossed the room, and nudged Logan to his feet. Then she put her arms around him and just held him. "It must have been terrible for you. I'm so sorry."

"What are you sorry about? I'm the one who's been cheating on you."

They'd both been cheating, trying to find something to hold on to as their marriage fell apart. "Somehow it feels different than if it had been a woman." It wasn't what she'd feared, another woman, a rival. He wasn't interested in women, any women. That wasn't her fault. It still hurt, of course, but in a different way. "What I'm sorry about is that you couldn't talk to me about it. I love you. As a friend, if that's the way it has to be. I care that you're so unhappy." *Funny*, she thought, *I think I've always liked him better as a friend or a brother. Perhaps I've known about him for longer than he has.*

Logan began to cry and Cait joined him, wincing from the

pain in her face. "I never imagined you'd take it this way. I played the 'Logan tells Cait' scene over and over and in every scenario you cry and yell. I hurt you."

Cait held on, in pain from so many sources. "Yes, you did. Very much, but I did some bad stuff, too. Let's just decide it's a wash and try to figure out how to move forward, together or separately."

Chapter
27

It was after three A.M. when Monica arrived home to find Dan waiting up for her. She'd phoned him from the hospital and told him about Cait's assault and he'd offered to pick her up. She'd declined since she'd brought her car and had to drive Angie and Eve home. "How's Cait?" Dan said, holding her in his arms as she shook. Now that the adrenalin was wearing off, she was a wreck.

When she could function again, she answered, "She's doing a lot better than I would be under those circumstances."

"I don't believe that. You're a lot stronger than you think you are." Eventually, after lots of talk and two glasses of brandy, they climbed into bed, still wrapped tightly together, and he didn't let her go until he fell asleep.

The following morning she sat at her desk in her office, still wondering what she was going to do about Mr. Conroy. She loved Dan. That was the basis of all her decisions. The tiny voice that frequently whispered in her ear was still murmuring, more softly now, but still audible. *Men can't be trusted. Power is everything. Take the partnership any way you can get it.*

When the phone rang she answered.

"Hi, sis, it's Bonnie. I saw what happened last evening on

Channel 12 and I recognized Cait's name. I just wanted to make sure everything was all right with you and with her."

"She's doing surprisingly well and I'm pretty good, too. Luckily it wasn't nearly as bad as it might have been, thanks to Cait's quick thinking and yoga-trained foot."

Bonnie's chuckle echoed through the phone line. "That's so wonderful. What doesn't kill you makes you stronger. That probably goes for all four of you." There was a pause, then Bonnie continued, "And me, too. Monica, I have a bit of news of my own and I wanted you to hear it directly from me." She could hear her sister draw in a long breath. "Jake's moving back home."

Monica was speechless. She wanted to rail about his faithlessness, his corruption of their wedding vows, but she quickly stopped herself. This was Bonnie's decision and Bonnie's life. "Tell me about it."

"He came over last evening and we talked for a long time. Monica, I love him. With all his faults, he's the only man I've ever loved and I want him back."

Resigned, Monica said, "I guess I can understand that." Could she understand love so powerful that her sister would risk everything?

"He swears to me that this was the only time he ever strayed and I believe him, or at least I want to. Trust will take a bit longer but I want to try. We made an agreement. He'll be home on time and spend lots of time with me and the kids. If there's ever a hint of any more nonsense he's out of here for good. No arguments, no nothing. I think he's really ashamed of what he did."

Monica swiveled her chair, leaned back, and stared out her wide office windows. This certainly had been quite a couple of weeks. "If that's what you want, then you should go for it." As she said the words, she thought about Dan. Maybe that was her answer. She had to go for him, too, whatever the risk.

"He'll be sleeping in the guest room for a while, until I'm

willing to have him in my bed again, but we both want to make this work."

"What about the kids?"

"They're delighted, of course, but a bit leery, as I am. I'm not sure they'll ever completely trust our relationship again, and so be it. We'll all have some adjusting to do. Sis, will you and Dan come over this Sunday and be family with us? Please? Janet and Walt and the kids are coming, too."

You and Dan. It sounded so natural, so good. It would be difficult for her to forgive Jake for all the pain he'd caused her sister, but this was Bonnie's life and she had a right to live it whatever way she wanted. Monica would be there in case things went bad again but she'd say a prayer every night that everything go smoothly from here on out. "Sure. We'll be there. About three?"

"Sounds great." She could hear the relief in her sister's voice. She'd probably been expecting a lecture from her "don't trust men" sister. *Never tell people things they already know*, Monica thought. Maybe it wasn't altogether true, either. Maybe you could really trust some men. "Bring pie, and maybe ice cream from that great place of yours?"

"Will do." She replaced the phone in the cradle and leaned back, watching tugboats and barges make their way up and down a white-capped Hudson River. For better or worse, Bonnie was taking Jake back. He might be a louse who had treated her really badly, but she wanted him, and she was willing to take the risk that it might go wrong again. Eve was attempting to reunite with her daughter, for better or worse. Logan and Cait? Who knew whether they could work things out, but they'd find something. Angie had said that she would support Tony's decision if he wanted to go back to teach in the South Bronx. Monica wanted Dan and she'd risk the pain of his leaving to take what she could from the present. She turned back to her desk and picked up the phone, only to remember that Dan would be in a meeting all morning.

As she replaced the phone in its cradle, her door opened and Harrison Conroy walked in. "Good morning, Monica. Ready for a brand-new week?"

"Yes, sir." She was ready to take on the world, for better or worse.

"The partnership meeting is this Friday. Have you thought over what we discussed last week?"

The moment of decision. But it wasn't. She'd made the decision the previous evening and again a few minutes ago. The partnership wasn't that important. "I'm sorry, Mr. Conroy, but I'm afraid I'm busy this week. I'm going to take a friend to the doctor tomorrow so I won't be in the office at all, and then I'm going to take another day to be with my fiancé." Fiancé. She almost grinned at the sound of that wonderful word. Granted, it was an overstatement. They hadn't discussed marriage yet, but she knew Dan felt as strongly as she did. He'd be in town all week, and she hoped he could take a day off to play, and talk about their future. They needed it. And she needed to tell him everything.

Obviously disappointed, Mr. Conroy said, "Taking time off might not be the best impression to make on the other partners. They like to think you'll give your all for Conroy & Bates. I thought that, too."

"I will give you the best job I can do within limits, and if that doesn't make me partnership material then that's that. My dearest friends and family come first." She felt a weight lifting from her shoulders. These people at C & B weren't family like Dan, or Bonnie and Janet, or her three best friends. It was just a job.

"Women always think about their love life first. Typical." He looked totally disgusted with her.

"And you, Mr. Conroy, were thinking with your . . ." She didn't finish but as she stared at his crotch, her meaning was perfectly clear. "Thank you for the lovely offer, but no thanks."

In a huff, Mr. Conroy silently turned on his heel and left.

Monica giggled and swung her chair around three times, her arms in the air. Life was wonderful. But she still had things to settle with Dan.

That evening, she sat with him in her living room and told him everything: from the way she solicited clients to Mr. Conroy's proposition. She'd even called herself a whore.

While she talked, Dan had sat quietly beside her, listening. She watched his face and his body language to try to judge how he was taking everything she said, but he didn't move. "I know there are lots of people who think that I shouldn't tell you all this since it has no real bearing on our future, but I couldn't move on until you knew." She deflated like a balloon. Telling him had seemed important earlier but what if he decided he couldn't deal with what she'd been?

"I knew that yours was a cutthroat business but I never thought it was that competitive." His tone was matter-of-fact so she still couldn't gauge his mood. "That's quite a story. Have you done any 'entertaining' recently?" His voice steady, he made quoting marks in the air around the word.

"Not since that day at the zoo, actually."

"Why not?"

"It didn't seem right. I felt something, a kind of connection, after that day, and I didn't want to confuse everything in my mind."

His sudden smile warmed her. "I'm glad. I guess that says that you felt what I felt from the start."

Her grin was rueful as she said softly, "I guess so. You're not too jealous or angry with me for what I've been?"

"Neither of us came into this relationship without a past," he said, his eyes locking with hers. "I've had several intense relationships and I've done things I'm not totally proud of, as well. That's over now. It's just you and me in this relationship. No past, no lies, nothing but lots of love."

Everything she felt whirled inside of her, blending into swirls of guilt and love. She could trust him.

"You told your Mr. Conroy no?"

"This morning, and he got the message loud and clear."

"Will that mean the end of the partnership?"

"He says he controls the other partners, so I guess so."

"Are you very disappointed?"

"Strangely enough, no. I feel a lot lighter."

Their embrace was long and passionate. When they parted, Dan asked, "How's your business been? Since you stopped putting out, I mean."

"Putting out? That's a very nice way of putting it." She thought about it. "Actually I've been doing great. I landed a big new account just last week. Amid all the turmoil, the proposal I put together worked."

"Without any beds in sight?"

She hadn't focused on it until that moment and he was right. "None. Maybe I am pretty good at my job after all."

"The partnership would have meant lots of extra hours. I'm sort of glad it won't happen."

"I'm a bit disappointed, but for the most part I find I don't care anymore." She paused. "Much." She planted a quick kiss on his lips. "From now on I'll put in maximum hours during the weeks you're out of town, but for the rest, I come first. We come first."

"I love you, you know."

Monica felt herself blossom. "I know."

After everything that had happened in the past few weeks, Eve knew that she had to confront her daughter. Life was too short, for her and for everyone else. She hoped her cancer scare would turn out to be just that when she had the tests, but she knew she needed to see Brittany. She called the Liggetts from work the morning following Cait's attack, and she explained what she wanted and asked whether she could talk to their daughter. Not her daughter, but theirs.

"Of course you can, Eve. I've been hoping for a long time

that you'd call. Two of Brittany's friends' parents are divorcing and she's been asking questions about us and about you. We've told her just what you wanted us to, that we didn't know anything about you but we know that you loved her. Your past is the only thing we've ever lied to her about."

"What's she like?" Eve asked in almost a whisper.

"You'll see for yourself, but in general she's a good kid. Oh, she's a little rebellious like all teenagers, she dyed her hair ink-black and had her ears pierced four times, but all in all, she's everything any of us could have wanted. When would you like to come over?"

Oh, God, face to face? Could she carry this off? Suddenly terrified, Eve said, "I don't know whether I could face her. Would you tell her about me? I'd like her to know why I gave her up."

"I don't think it's my place. It's your story and it's for you to do," Michelle Liggett said. "I'll just tell her that you're a relative and want to see her. You can decide how much you want to say when you see her."

She wanted to do this, but it frightened her more than she had imagined. They agreed that Eve would come over the following evening. Eve wanted to see her daughter before her tests.

She left work early and drove from the train station to the Liggetts' neighborhood, arriving half an hour before the meeting. Nice, neat house, she thought, with rose bushes across the back of the driveway and evergreens along the property line. There was a Toyota in front of the garage and she could hear a dog barking next door. She sat in her car in front of the house debating. Was she being selfish? What was best for her now sixteen-year-old daughter? She had no idea but this seemed right.

Finally, at the appointed time, she walked up the well-maintained front walk, hugging her coat around her, and rang the bell. Someone called, "It's open," and she walked in.

She recognized Brittany from the pictures she'd seen of her. She sat in the neat little living room, and after a quick look, she snapped her head around so she was turned away from the door. She was a slender girl with long blue-black hair the color of coal and chandelier earrings that sparkled between the strands as she turned quickly away. Eve had rehearsed her speech several times in her mind but now that she was here, she found herself tongue-tied. She looked around the comfortable living room. Pictures covered part of one wall, photos of a small girl as she grew toward womanhood—posed school photos, ones she had copies of, and casual ones with her parents and a large shaggy German shepherd. There were trophies on the mantel, and she walked over slowly and saw that they were for baton twirling.

She pulled off her gloves, stuffed them in her coat pocket, and turned. "Brittany, I don't ask that you look at me or speak to me, I just want you to listen. When I'm done, you can do what you want with the information."

Eve watched her daughter sit stonily, arms and legs crossed, face turned away. She took a deep breath. She knew she had to do this, wanted to do this. "As you've probably guessed, or maybe your mom told you, I'm your birth mother. You've always known you were adopted and I know that your mother told you nothing about me, as I requested when I gave you to her."

She could see resentment in every line of Brittany's body. Her shoulders were tight with suppressed anger and she remained totally silent. "Let me tell you how it all happened. I was sixteen, the age you are now. I won't make excuses for anything. I made a lot of mistakes and did a lot of things I'm not proud of. My parents were difficult to get along with, impossible to talk to about anything. They were much older than my friends' parents and I think, decided to have a baby because they were having marital problems and thought I would bring them closer together. I didn't. I kept them together, but drove them emotionally far apart." Eve stood in the center of the room, hands clasped in front of her to keep them from shaking.

"They both worked in the city and resented any time they had to spend with me while I was growing up. I had nannies until I was about ten, then I became a latchkey kid. That's no excuse for anything that came later but I can tell you that I was lonely. Terribly, terribly lonely. I thought I was grown up, and the first boy who made me believe he cared about me and wanted to be with me, well, I let him have sex with me. We didn't use protection. I will regret that to my dying day." She heard the last sentence and quickly corrected any misinterpretation. "I don't regret you, not at all, just the problems that the whole thing created."

Brittany's shoulders had relaxed a bit but she remained facing the kitchen, her back to Eve. Eve pulled off her glasses and polished them on her shirt, then took a deep breath and continued. "When I realized I was pregnant I went to him, but he couldn't have cared less. He taunted me, wondering whether it was indeed his baby. I was probably doing half the guys in school, he told me. I knew it was his, but I couldn't fight him and I guess I didn't want to. None of this was his fault, really, it was my own stupidity. If you're curious, he went off to college and his parents moved away. He never did come back to Westchester. I can give you the little information I have if you want to try to get in touch with him."

Her daughter didn't move. "I loved that first few months. You were mine, a part of me, and with you in my life I'd never be lonely again. I deliberately waited until it was too late to end the pregnancy, and when I was about four months along I finally told my parents."

Eve huffed out a breath, remembering the screaming scene her folks had created. "Needless to say, they were furious. When the rage let up, they insisted that I give you up. I wanted to protest, but they convinced me that I couldn't take care of you and they didn't want to be burdened with yet another unwanted child. Eventually I admitted to myself that I couldn't take care of you alone and they made it plain that I'd never get any help from them."

Not censoring her words, Eve charged on. "My dad knew someone who knew a lawyer who arranged what was called an open adoption. I met Larry and Michelle, your parents, and I liked them a lot. They couldn't have children of their own and they wanted you very much."

Brittany whirled around on the sofa and spat out, "How could you do that? You gave me away. I couldn't give my baby away." She folded her legs up in front of her and dropped her head on her knees. "I couldn't."

When her daughter started to cry, Eve wanted to go to her, but it was too soon. She had to finish what she needed to say. "I would hope that your parents would be more supportive than mine were. I did what I felt I had to do and I don't regret it. I would have liked to watch you grow up, but I wouldn't have been a good mother, not the little girl I was then. My folks would have abandoned me, so I'd have had to work and leave you with strangers. I wouldn't do that to you. Was I wrong? I don't know, but it's done now." Tears were flowing freely down Eve's face and she waited a moment until she could continue.

"When we met in the lawyer's office I asked your parents for two things. First, I wanted you to know you were adopted from the beginning, and I didn't want them to tell you who I was. I reasoned that it would have been too confusing for you and I was really just a child myself. And I wanted you to be named Brittany. I always loved that name and that's what I'd been calling you while you grew inside of me."

"Why didn't you ever want to see me?" Eve could tell that Brittany was still weeping, too.

Eve heaved a shaky sigh. "I was afraid. When you were a baby I didn't want to be tempted.to change my mind, and as you grew I didn't know how you'd react, or how I would. Your folks sent me pictures of you once or twice a year so I'd know how you were doing, with letters about your schooling. I assume they were good parents."

Her face still lowered, shoulders shaking, Brittany said, "They were. They were my mom and dad."

"They still are. Nothing I've said will change that. The fact that you happen to have my blood means nothing. They were and are your parents. They held your head when you were sick, celebrated your wonderful grades, and worried when you had your tonsils out. Yes, I know about that. I sat in the waiting room until your mom told me you were doing fine."

"You were there?"

"Yes," she said softly.

"What do you want from me?"

"Nothing that you don't want to give."

"You're not my mother. Not really."

"I know, and I regret that more than you will ever imagine. I missed so much." She couldn't smother her weeping. "I'd like to spend some time with you but if you don't want to, that's your choice. I can only offer."

"Why would I want to do that? Why would you want to spend time with me? Why now, all of a sudden?"

"I had a health scare recently. It really shook me up." She didn't want to use her illness as a lever to push them together so she'd decided to say very little about it. Brittany raised her head and looked genuinely concerned. "I'm sure I'm going to be fine, but while I was answering all the health questions about my family history, I realized you would never have that history if I didn't contact you."

Brittany continued to stare at her. "Is that the only reason?"

"Okay, I was scared, too. It really shook me up and I wanted to touch someone who was my blood. My folks died several years ago, and I've got no other family. So here I am.

"I've made plenty of mistakes over the years, but not trying to see you was a biggie. I'd like an opportunity to make up for that. The things I've told you aren't excuses, just explanations. I hope you'll talk this over with your folks and maybe your best girlfriends and decide that we might have pizza together someday. But if you don't want to, I'll understand and I won't contact you again."

"I can't call you Mother. What's your name?" Brittany asked and Eve laughed, the first real laugh she'd had since the doctor told her about the lump. "It's Eve. Eve DeMilo, like the statue."

When Brittany remained silent, Eve took a card from her purse. She'd written her home, work, and cell phone numbers on it. She handed it to her daughter, then walked to the door. She'd never even taken her coat off. "I hope you'll decide to call me sometime. I care about you." She felt herself starting to break down so she pulled out her gloves and slowly put one on. "I love you."

Brittany remained on the sofa, staring at her. "I'll think about it."

"Good."

"Eve?" Brittany said as Eve opened the front door. "I really will think about it."

Epilogue

H uckleberry's was festively decorated for Christmas and although it was a week away, everyone was in a particularly joyous holiday mood. The four women sat in their usual booth as the red- and green-clad waitress put a cup of decaf coffee in front of Angie, and one laced with Bailey's in front of each of the other women. "Not like diner coffee, is it?" Monica said.

Angie picked up the steaming cup and inhaled the heavy fragrance. "Not in the least."

"Remember that first lunch, with that awful coffee?" Cait said. "Part of me feels like it was years ago, but another says it was only yesterday."

Monica sipped. "You know, I didn't really hate that coffee. Saying it was just something to break the ice."

"You, too?" Eve said. "I was sort of nervous. I'd never been much for women friends before then." She'd finally unwound after her scare. Fortunately the lump had proved to be benign.

"Are we getting maudlin already?" Cait said, setting her cup down. "This is supposed to be a Christmas party."

"And it will be," Eve replied, reaching beneath the table and pulling out a small red and green gift bag. "I think I've been ladylike and patient long enough. It's time for presents."

"God, I thought no one was getting antsy besides me," Angie said, putting a shiny silver gift bag on the table. Cait followed suit. They had agreed on a Secret Santa format, so they drew names from a hat and were only permitted to buy something for the person whose name they picked.

Monica pulled a shopping bag from beneath the table and pulled out three small gold boxes. "I violated the rules. Well, partly anyway. I got the Secret Santa gift, but I got each of you something, too."

"Not fair," Cait said, grabbing the box. "But I do love presents."

"Me, too," Eve said, untying the white satin bow and pulling the top from the box. Inside each was a small sprig of baby's breath, the small white flowers lying on a bed of ferns. Puzzled, Eve looked at Monica and cocked her head to one side.

"I want each of you to be a bridesmaid, along with Bonnie and Janet."

Eve squealed. "You and Dan? Truly?"

"No," Monica said with deep sarcasm, "me and Mick Jagger. Yes, me and Dan. In March, we think, but don't get your hopes up. No matching dresses. It will be a small wedding, his family and mine, and a few friends. You do get matching flowers, however."

The women spent the next few minutes making a large fuss about the impending wedding. The issue of trust was never mentioned.

Eventually the women put their gifts in their laps, and in an attempt to keep the giver a secret, wrapped each in a Huckleberry's napkin and dropped them into Monica's shopping bag. "Okay, since Monica gave us these first, she gets hers first." Cait dumped the contents of the shopping bag on the table and found the package with Monica's name on it.

Monica opened the small box and withdrew a small gold key with a ring and tag attached. "For the executive washroom," the tag said, and they all laughed. Her partnership would be made official after the first of the year. The partners had told her informally that she had always been an asset to Conroy & Bates and now she'd have her name on the letterhead. She'd managed to balance her work schedule with her life with Dan and it was working out perfectly. She assumed that Harrison Conroy didn't have as much power as he'd told her he had.

Cait took her package and unwrapped it. "A gift certificate to Match.com and a book," she announced, laughing, "called *Being Newly Single in the Twenty-First Century*. Very appropriate. It will certainly come in handy."

"How's Logan doing?"

"He's having a difficult time dealing with his sexuality, but he's getting counseling."

"Is he still living with you?"

"In another bedroom, of course, but we're the best of friends now and I'm trying to help him adjust. I really care about him and I can't just turn that off."

"Of course not," Angie said. "Okay, me next." She took a box from the table and untied the ribbon. Inside the box was an envelope. Inside that was a folder. "It's a gift certificate for a manicure and pedicure, with baby-sitting thrown in. How wonderful! A present is supposed to be something you'd never buy for yourself, and this is perfect." She was obviously delighted. "I'll have to do it soon, because by spring I won't be able to appreciate it, not seeing my feet around my big belly and all." Her pregnancy was just starting to show and she and Tony were relieved that, according to Angie's obstetrician, it wasn't going to be a multiple birth this time. "Tony's going back to the Bronx," she'd told them a few weeks before. "It's what he wants to do, and although it makes me a bit nervous, I'll support him."

"Have they made another settlement offer?"

"The city's offer is really wonderful, but we're leaving it all up to the union's lawyer. Whatever it turns out to be, it will give us a little cushion and put a good chunk away for the children's education."

Cait sipped her coffee, then said, "Okay, Eve, it's your turn."

Eve's envelope contained a gift certificate, as well. "For a full set of family photos. The note says that it's for Brittany and me. How wonderful," she said, beaming. She and Brittany had met several times and had been spending more and more time together. At first it had been awkward, but soon they were sharing secrets like old friends. They had already spent two afternoons at Eve's watching movies. Eve had almost cried when she found out that Brittany loved train whistles.

Cait lifted her cup in a toast. "To the last six months, and to learning what real friends are for."

The other three clinked their cups against hers and sipped. "The last six months have been quite something," Monica said. "Who'd have thought that four such ordinary women could have such amazing times?"

"Yeah," Eve said. "Mike and Brittany for me, Hotguy and Logan for Cait, Mr. Conroy and Dan for Monica, and Tony and the new baby for Angie, it's been quite a ride. Who'd have thought we'd reveal so many secrets, and discover that, in the telling, we'd all gain so much?"

Angie raised her cup again. "To us. To the women of East Hudson."

Monica lifted her cup. "To the secret lives of the wives and mothers of East Hudson."

Dear Reader,

I hope you've enjoyed reading *The Secret Lives of Housewives* as much as I enjoyed writing it. When I complete a novel, I miss the characters a great deal and I will miss these four ladies more than most. You never know—one or more of them might show up in a future book.

Please drop me a note at Joan@JoanELloyd.com and let me know which of the women you'd most like to meet. You can also reach me at Joan Elizabeth Lloyd, P.O. Box 221, Yorktown Heights, NY 10598, but snail mail takes quite a bit longer for me to answer.

I've written quite a few other books that you might enjoy. Please check my Web site at www.JoanELloyd.com, for excerpts from all of them, in addition to advice about sex and relationships, letters from other visitors, and so much more. I look forward to your visit.

Joan